TIMELESS *Regency* COLLECTION

A Holiday in Bath

TIMELESS *Regency* COLLECTION

A Holiday in Bath

Julie Daines

Caroline Warfield

Jaima Fixsen

Mirror Press

Copyright © 2018 Mirror Press
Print edition
All rights reserved

No part of this book may be reproduced in any form whatsoever without prior written permission of the publisher, except in the case of brief passages embodied in critical reviews and articles. These novels are works of fiction. The characters, names, incidents, places, and dialog are products of the authors' imaginations and are not to be construed as real.

Interior Design by Cora Johnson
Edited by Jennie Stevens and Lisa Shepherd
Cover design by Rachael Anderson
Cover Photo Credit: Richard Jenkins Photography

Published by Mirror Press, LLC

ISBN-13: 978-1-947152-37-3

OTHER TIMELESS REGENCY COLLECTIONS

Autumn Masquerade
A Midwinter Ball
Spring in Hyde Park
Summer House Party
A Country Christmas
A Season in London
Falling for a Duke
A Night in Grosvenor Square
Road to Gretna Green
Wedding Wagers

TABLE OF CONTENTS

Trial of the Heart
by Julie Daines

Lord Edmund's Dilemma
by Caroline Warfield

The Fine Art of Kissing in the Park
by Jaima Fixsen

Trial of the Heart

BY JULIE DAINES

OTHER BOOKS BY JULIE DAINES

A Blind Eye
Unraveled
Eleanor and the Iron King
Willowkeep
Happily Ever After
Road to Gretna Green
Havencross

Summoned

The coach moved at a snail's pace through the crush of carriages and pedestrians making their way through the streets of Bath. Most of them were here for a holiday. A few, like Marianne, were here for the inquest. It wasn't every day they got to witness a man prosecuted for murder. Marianne would rather be anywhere in England besides Bath.

The coach's horn sounded, trying to move people out of the way and leaving a painful ringing in Marianne's ears. It did little good at clearing the streets until a clap of thunder rattled the carriage. Those on foot looked up at the darkening sky and scurried for shelter. The woman she'd been wedged beside for the last twenty miles squashed against her, leaning over Marianne to look out the window.

"Bless me. It looks like rain."

Marianne made a small noise she hoped sounded like agreement instead of her gasp for breath. Her neighbor was not of small stature.

The driver brought the horses to a stop in front of an inn. A man opened the door, and her traveling companions fought their way out. She waited patiently, in no hurry to begin her ordeal.

The coach emptied, rocking to and fro as the passengers clambered down the step and the boys shifted the luggage on top. It seemed Bath was everyone's final destination.

She took a deep breath, clinging to this last moment of quiet and safety. Perhaps she should stay in the coach and ride on to Plymouth. Surely there would be a ship of some sort she could board and sail across the sea to the Americas. He could never reach her there.

For two years, she'd been looking over her shoulder, afraid of seeing his face in the crowd. For he was always in her dreams. Her nightmares.

"Miss Wood?"

She started with a jolt. A man's form filled the coach's doorway.

"You are Miss Marianne Wood, I presume?" he asked again.

She nodded.

He gave her a broad smile. "I'm Mr. Harby Northam. I sent you the letter." He held an umbrella over his head, rain water drizzling off the sides.

She sat unmoving in her corner of the empty coach. He was taller than she'd expected. And younger. Ever since receiving the summons, she'd pictured its sender as a squat old man wearing a fading white wig. Instead, she found Mr. Northam, who looked like he could just as easily take off his coat and split a cord of firewood.

"You there," came a gruff voice from beyond her sight. "This ain't no room for rent. We got passengers waitin' to load."

Mr. Northam turned aside. "Stand down, sir. You will give us a moment."

She could see why he was a barrister. He spoke calmly, but his voice carried a strong air of authority. When he turned his attention back to Marianne, he was smiling again, his deep blue eyes oddly gentle for his brawny size.

He held out a hand. "Come, Miss Wood. I promise you are safe. No one besides myself knows you are here. I assure you, Bartholomew Hayter is locked up and secured behind bars."

Of course he was. That was why she was here in the first place. She glanced down at her attire, feeling as though she'd forgotten to put on an essential piece of clothing by the way he saw right through her.

"Bartholomew Hayter," she said. "That is his name?" It didn't fit him at all. But no name in the world would be suited for such a man.

"Bit of a mouthful, if you ask me. What ever happened to good old John?" This coming from a man named Harby.

She stood, bending low as she moved toward the door. She took his offered hand and carefully climbed down the step.

Mr. Northam held his umbrella over her head as he guided her to the side of the coaching yard. The rain made a steady beating of soft thuds on the black umbrella.

"Welcome to Bath, Miss Wood."

Marianne looked up at the inn. "Will I be staying here?"

"No, no. I wouldn't leave my dog here. I have rented you a set of rooms in Green Street. It is a small and quiet place, but I think you will find it comfortable. Mrs. Strumpshaw will stay with you as help—and for company. She is a widow with a son."

Nice to know she stood on equal footing with his dog. Rented rooms and a servant. Quite a luxurious arrangement. She could little bear such an expense on her governess salary.

"And who is to pay for it?"

"My client," he said.

"You mean Bartholomew Hayter's latest victim." Mr. Northam was very kind to soften his words for her. Despite her sleepless nights and the endless glances over her shoulder, she did not enjoy being coddled. Nor did she appreciate being lied to. "You said only you knew of my being in town."

He smiled again, this time a little sheepishly. "You are absolutely right. Forgive me. I wanted to get you out of the coach before the coachman tried tipping it on its side and shaking you out. My client is Martin Palmer, a doctor who has made quite a name for himself here. He is very determined to see Hayter hanged."

Marianne liked Dr. Palmer already.

Mr. Northam motioned her toward another carriage, a smaller, privately owned chaise waiting in the street beyond. "Let's get out of this rain. I'll explain more on the way."

She walked with him, leaning a little too close to keep herself out of the rain. But there was safety there, next to this tall ox of a man she'd only just met. In those few moments, he'd done more to ease her fears than anyone else had in the two years since the attack.

A stable lad hurried past, carrying her trunk toward Mr. Northam's carriage. Mr. Northam handed her up, then climbed in and sat beside her. He rapped on the roof, and the carriage rolled away, back into the crowded streets of Bath.

"Now, perhaps we could start over," he said. "I believe we missed some important formalities."

She stared at him. Start over with what?

"It is a pleasure to meet you, Miss Wood. I hope your journey was pleasant?"

She looked down at her lap, twisting the strings of her reticule around her finger. "It was fine."

"And the roads were not too wet?"

"The roads were fine."

Trial of the Heart

He angled his body toward her. "And I trust the occupants of the public coach were as colorful an assortment of humanity as one hopes to find?"

Mr. Northam was a strange mixture of a man. Authoritative barrister one moment, kindly gentleman the next. And now, if he had been one of her pupils, she would have called him out for being silly. Oddly enough, this mixture suited him.

"The occupants were also fine."

"I'm glad to hear it." He nodded with satisfaction. "I'm also glad to see you smile. It suits you well. But I fear it will not be there long."

"What do you mean?"

"Miss Wood, I'm afraid our first item of business will be difficult for you."

Mr. Northam the barrister was back. The clouds thickened, darkening the sky. The rain came harder, pelting onto the roof of his carriage. She shrank into her seat to get away from it.

"You are not taking me to my rooms?"

"Before we can continue with any of the proceedings, we must be certain that the Bartholomew Hayter in custody is indeed the same man responsible for the death of your family."

She shook her head. "No."

How could he ask such a thing? She shook her head again, pushing herself into the corner of the carriage, wedged between the papered wall and the blue velvet padding of the seat back. She hadn't yet come to terms with being in the same town as him, let alone meeting face-to-face.

The carriage turned off the crowded streets, down a cobbled lane toward a darker set of buildings. She should have ridden on to Plymouth. If she left the country, she'd never have to see him again. Never have to glance behind or search the crowd for his face. But her family would never get justice.

They came to a stop in front of a low building. Iron bars created dark columns on the windows, like some kind of architecture from the underworld. He was in there. She hadn't been this close to him since the day he killed her family—save in her nightmares.

They'd been driving home from the Moores' house where they'd dined. It was her fault it was so late. She always stayed too late talking with Charlotte. Before any of them knew what was going on, the carriage was in flames.

Marianne reached up and rubbed the scar running from her shoulder across her chest. The present he'd left her as a reminder of his unfinished business. And of what would happen should she open her mouth.

"Miss Wood," Mr. Northam said. The rain beat on the roof, and a small leak in the door left a trickle of damp below the window. A dark stain against the light cloth that lined the wall.

"Miss Wood," he said again. "I know this is hard for you. You are very brave to come here."

"Your letter said I didn't have a choice." She had been summoned, after all.

"You will always have a choice. Neither I nor my client would ever force you into doing something that is too difficult. Not if you truly desire not to." He scooted closer. "But consider. Your testimony could be that last thing we need to slip the noose around his neck. No one else need die because of Bartholomew Hayter."

She twisted the strings of her reticule around and around her fingers.

"He is behind bars," Mr. Northam continued. "He can't hurt you anymore. But you can hurt him. He has no power over you. On the contrary, it is you, now, who holds the power."

She looked up at him. He had chosen his profession well, with his pleasing face and smooth words. He could be very persuasive. Yet, there was truth in what he spoke. If she did not go through with her testimony, Bartholomew Hayter might go free. If he did this to another family, part of the blame would be on her. This was her one chance to stop him. This was why she'd come.

Someday, Bartholomew Hayter would be her end. This she felt in her heart. He'd already taken her entire family; she could not expect less for herself. If this was to be her end, so be it. She owed it to her family to at least try to bring them justice.

She nodded. "I will do it."

"See, there." He smiled. "You are brave. I knew you would be."

"How could you have known anything about me? We've never met before today."

Mr. Northam raised his eyebrows. "Because you have survived. You have picked up the pieces of your life and forged onward. Because you came here, to face the worst of the worst. All acts of bravery."

Marianne's eyes went to the dark building outside the carriage window. If ever there was a word that did not describe her, it was brave. Over the last two years, she'd slunk around, afraid of every stranger. Afraid he would find her and finish his work. Hardly acts of bravery.

"When you are ready," he said. "I'm sorry this must be done today, but the assizes are quickly approaching, and we must know whether we have enough evidence to press forward."

Meaning there was still a chance the man behind the

stone walls may not be him. That they'd taken the wrong man. That he was still roaming free.

She had to know. "I am ready."

Mr. Northam opened the door and stepped down, holding the umbrella while he helped her out.

"You will come in with me, won't you?" she asked Mr. Northam. She couldn't face him alone.

He held out his arm. "Of course."

Marianne looped her hand into the crook of his elbow and accompanied him into the building.

The Game

The moment Marianne ducked through the doorway, the smell hit her. The sting of a cesspit filled her nose and left a noxious taste in her mouth. She took out a handkerchief and covered her face.

"We're here to see Bartholomew Hayter," Mr. Northam told the attendant.

"Wait here, sir," the man said and left through an iron-reinforced door at the rear.

A man stood up from a bench in the shadows, dressed in a pair of gray breeches and a dark coat.

"Mr. Northam," he said, extending a hand.

Mr. Northam maneuvered Marianne until she was partially behind him, shielding her from the man. It was quite a formidable bulwark, and Marianne was glad to have Mr. Northam on her side. Only when she was tucked away did Mr. Northam extend his hand and offer a cold greeting.

"Mr. Shadwell. I wasn't aware that you would be here today." He turned to Marianne. "The defense for Hayter."

No wonder he wanted to keep her hidden. No man in good conscience could defend a monster.

"I have a right to know whether or not there is a case against Mr. Hayter. He may not even be the man in question."

"Well," said Mr. Northam with his most presumptuous air, "we shall see." He turned away from Mr. Shadwell, taking Marianne to the opposite end of the small room.

He leaned in close and whispered, "That man is only here to cause problems. He will try to make you doubt your own name. You are under no obligation to speak to him, do you understand?"

She nodded, peering at Mr. Shadwell around Mr. Northam's shoulder.

"Do not let him rattle you. Just focus on the job at hand. I'll be with you the whole time."

"All right."

Mr. Northam's letter of summons had not given her the full picture of what she was getting herself into. All it said was that she was needed as a witness. It had mentioned nothing about visiting him in jail.

The heavy barred door opened, and a short man with no hair on his head and a beard down to his waistcoat entered the antechamber.

"Mr. Northam," he said. "This way."

Mr. Northam blocked the doorway. "Might I have a word privately, first?"

Whether the jailer was willing to have a private word or not seemed to matter little. Mr. Northam used his great height and ox of a body to give him no choice. They stepped into the corridor beyond the door.

"So," said Mr. Shadwell from his place in the shadows. "Northam seems to have a great deal of confidence in you. His whole case depends on your testimony."

Marianne kept her eyes on the map of Bath hanging on the wall beside her.

"I hope you are certain," Mr. Shadwell continued. "I'd

hate to be the one standing before the final judgment bar having sent an innocent man to his death."

"And I'd hate to be the one standing before the judgment bar having helped a murderer go free," said Mr. Northam, coming back through the door. "How many more people do you want to see in coffins because of him?"

He didn't give Mr. Shadwell a chance to answer. He took Marianne by the arm and led her down the corridor.

Mr. Shadwell started after them, but the jailer stopped him. "Sorry, sir. Can't have all three of you back here. It's against regulations."

Mr. Shadwell swore. "I have every right to accompany them. You can't stop me—"

The jailer swung the door shut, cutting him off. The lock clicked, and that was the end of Mr. Shadwell's protests.

The corridor was dark and wide. If the antechamber smelled bad, this place must be the devil's chamber pot. She'd never set foot in a jail or prison of any sort before now. A row of cells lined either side of the passageway, each crowded with people.

"Who are they all?" Marianne whispered. Some looked absolutely pitiful while others sneered at her with wolfish lips.

"Thieves, debtors, blasphemers."

"I'll show you blasphemy," called a ragged man, his beard laden with filth. He stumbled toward the bars, opening his mouth to speak.

Mr. Northam turned on him. "Not in front of the lady, unless you want a hangman's noose to warm your neck."

The man's mouth snapped shut, and he backed away to the depths of the cell.

Marianne edged closer to Mr. Northam until she was pressed up against his side. It seemed the only safe place in the building.

Mr. Northam pointed to the next cell. "He's in there. Are you ready?"

She closed her eyes. His face came to her, as it always did, bidden or not. If she looked on him again, she would never be able to wipe it from her mind. He would always be a part of her, lurking in the dark corners of her mind, waiting for the perfect moment to rise up and kill her.

Such a mistake to agree to this. She should have stayed hidden in her little room in Shrewsbury.

The answer to Mr. Northam's question was no, she would never be ready. But she would do what she'd come here to do. For her family.

She smoothed the front of her dress and straightened her bonnet as if being properly attired would somehow imbue her with needed strength. "I am ready," she whispered to Mr. Northam.

He offered his arm again and took her the few steps forward until she could see the feet of a man sitting on a three-legged stool.

She gripped Mr. Northam's arm like it was a lifeboat saving her from a hungry sea. When she raised her eyes to the man behind the bars, she knew instantly.

It was him.

Her knees faltered, and Mr. Northam's hand wound swiftly around her waist.

The man's yellow eyes fell on her. She remembered that look, and the pure evil that raised gooseflesh on her arms. Hair blacker than coal. Skin the color of spoiled cream.

He stood and walked forward, almost as tall and broad as Mr. Northam, but not quite. "Well, well. What a pretty thing you brought me. Better than the maggoty bread, ta be sure."

His teeth were small in his mouth, leaving gaps between each where the rot leaked through.

"Is it him?" asked Mr. Northam.

She lifted the handkerchief from her mouth. "It is," she said, turning away so she couldn't see him, but all she met was the broad chest of Mr. Northam.

"Are you sure? We must be sure."

"It is him."

"Yes," said Hayter. "You'd better look again just ta be sure. It's easy ta mistake a face in these dark rooms."

She turned to look again.

Hayter was grinning at her. He didn't say it, but he knew her. He recognized her. She could see it in his eyes that glowed like a flickering candle flame as he watched her.

"It's him."

"All right, then." Mr. Northam steered her away.

"Thanks for the visit," he said. "I hope we meet again sometime. I never forget a pretty face."

She looked back at his unshaven face pressing between the bars. He made a swiping gesture across his throat. "I'll see you in Hell."

Mr. Northam whacked his umbrella against the bars, and Hayter dove out of the way.

He did remember her. Those were the exact words he had spoken to her two and a half years ago—right after he'd threatened to slit her throat should she mention his deeds to anyone.

Her hand went immediately to the scar on her shoulder she kept hidden with a lacy chemisette. He had indeed almost ended her life that night. But the vicar happened upon them and Hayter fled—after leaving her the warning.

"You all right, miss?" asked the jailer.

Marianne shook the memories from her head, bringing herself back to the jail. Mr. Northam had both of his arms around her, and she was leaning into him. Had she fainted? No, she didn't think so.

She straightened herself, righting the bonnet that had been pushed askew by Mr. Northam's shoulder. "I'm fine. I just need some air."

"We all do," said Mr. Northam, urging the jailer to open the locked door.

Mr. Shadwell was waiting for them, pacing the small antechamber. "Well?" he asked as Mr. Northam pushed past him.

"Thank you for your time, sir," Mr. Northam said to the jailer. He pushed open the front door, and a burst of air rushed in. He opened his umbrella. The instant she stepped out under it, he swung the door closed.

He smiled at her. "I knew you were brave."

Then they were up into his carriage and away. She leaned back, looking out through the drops of rain on the window as they crossed the River Avon and at the shops as they drove through the streets of Bath. Most were closed now, the crowds of people gone home to prepare for the evening's entertainments.

Bartholomew Hayter. It was still strange that the man had a name. He'd always been *him* for so long—the man with the yellow eyes.

"Miss Wood?" Mr. Northam said. "You've been awfully quiet."

"I'm sorry. I'm not good company." She could not pull her mind away from the horror of those eyes. They would haunt her forever; she may as well resign herself to that.

"I'm not worried about company," said Mr. Northam. "I'm worried about you. I thought you were going to faint for a moment back there. That man is despicable. He deserves the noose."

If anyone could put him there, it would be Mr. Northam.

From what she'd seen of him in these few short hours, he was not a man to be denied.

"Do you always get what you want?" she asked.

He seemed surprised by her question. "What do you mean?"

"You didn't want that man, Mr. Shadwell, to come with us, and the jailer shut him out." This was only one example.

"A crown goes a long way in a place like that."

"You bribed him?" No wonder the jailer had been so accommodating. "Isn't that wrong?"

He shrugged. "I don't always get what I want, to be sure. But I do know how to play the game."

"The game?" Murder was hardly a game.

"The game of life," he said with a grin. "Know who you're dealing with and what they desire. Then, yes, you can get what you want."

She turned back to the window. It was all clear now. His kindly manner, his steady arms. He had managed the whole thing very well. Summoning her to testify. Coaxing her out of the coach. Encouraging her until she mustered the courage to enter the jail. He'd gotten her to do exactly what he wanted. So much for the friendly stranger.

"Well, I'm glad I could play along," she said, swiveling her whole body away from him. She would take care with this man to keep her guard up. She would do her part to see Hayter hanged, but she would do it for her family. For all the people he had hurt. And to keep him from ever hurting anyone again.

"Miss Wood?"

"I'm very tired, Mr. Northam. Could you please take me to my rooms?" She spoke to the carriage window.

He let out a huff, then said, "Of course."

The carriage turned a few more times before pulling up in front of a row of modest town houses, all in the light honey stone that marked Bath. The footman opened the door, and Marianne climbed out without a word to Mr. Northam.

The front door of the town house opened, and a woman motioned to her. "Come in, come in. It's pouring hogs and dogs out here." She must be Mrs. Strumpshaw.

Marianne hurried across the paving stones and ducked inside the house before the rain could completely soak her through. The footman unloaded her small trunk and placed it inside the front door.

Mr. Northam stood on the doorstep, holding his umbrella about two minutes too late.

Marianne gave a quick curtsy. "Good evening, Mr. Northam."

He bowed to her with a look of uncertainty—something he'd not yet pulled from his wardrobe of masks. He changed his personage to fit whatever part needed playing much faster than she would be able to change out of her traveling clothes.

Mrs. Strumpshaw waited for Mr. Northam to enter, but he only teetered on the threshold. In the end, he turned and climbed back into the carriage. Marianne closed the door before it pulled away.

Bedfellows

"Mrs. Strumpshaw?" Marianne asked as she tugged on the sleeves of her pelisse, pulling it off.

"Yes, miss." Mrs. Strumpshaw dipped her head, taking the pelisse.

"I'm Marianne Wood." Her bonnet came off next.

Mrs. Strumpshaw reached for it. "Yes, dear." She gave Marianne a warm smile. "I've been told. Now, you must be famished for some tea and supper. I've got it all laid out in the dining room for you. This way."

She followed Mrs. Strumpshaw into a room with a small table better sized for card playing than dining. An elegant lace cloth draped over it, set with lovely china for two.

Mrs. Strumpshaw hustled away.

Marianne leaned back, taking in a deep breath—the kind that filled her lungs near to bursting. She let it all out, hoping it would blow her back to her little room in Shrewsbury. Then she'd wake up the next morning with the simple task of teaching Mrs. Lasham's daughters their geometry.

Though she had to admit, these rooms Mr. Northam had arranged for her were perfect. Much better than an inn, with coaches constantly coming and going and rowdy drinkers at the bar until all hours of the night. This street was off the main roads, and the quiet solitude eased the tightness in her head.

Blue songbirds perched in linear patterns on the wallpaper. They matched the birds on the dishes almost perfectly, the only difference being the birds on the plates were caged. She glanced back and forth between the two. Which was she?

The caged bird, no doubt. She had not been free for some time. Before Bartholomew Hayter had murdered her family, she'd been the daughter of a gentleman. Hayter had taken away her freedom and left her penniless. Not only that, but she'd had his threat hanging over her head like an anvil. She'd lived the past two years in terror that he would come back and finish the job.

Mrs. Strumpshaw returned, struggling with a heavily laden tray. She edged it onto a sideboard and set the serving dishes on the table. Roasted woodcock, boiled potatoes, carrot and beet salad, celery root in cream sauce, stewed eels, pâté. It was enough to feed a family of eight.

"This is quite a quantity of food," Marianne said. "More than I can ever eat in a week."

"Mr. Northam said he'd be taking his dinner here tonight. But I s'pose something come up, and he had to be off." Mrs. Strumpshaw set out a loaf of steaming bread. "He's a bachelor, you know, and he has such an appetite."

He should have said something. No wonder he'd been hesitating at the doorstep. He must think her the most ungrateful person in the world.

Marianne had seen the two place settings and assumed she'd be dining with Mrs. Strumpshaw.

"Will you not join me in his stead?" she asked. Now that she'd denied Mr. Northam of his meal, there was no reason for all this food to go to waste. Besides, a distraction would do her good.

Mrs. Strumpshaw stared at her.

"Please," she said. "Let us not stand on ceremony here. I have few enough friends as it is. Sit here and eat with me."

"But . . ." Mrs. Strumpshaw glanced around as if she might get transported for breaching the servant familiarity line. "It would be unseemly."

"Life is unseemly, Mrs. Strumpshaw. Of that I am certain." She'd more than learned her lesson in that regard. "I am a governess, not a duchess."

Mrs. Strumpshaw eased herself onto the seat like a frightened kitten. After a few moments, when she did not spontaneously explode, she let out a soft sigh. "I suppose since my Jamie's not back yet, I may as well."

Oh, yes. Mr. Northam had mentioned she had a boy. "Jamie's your son?"

She beamed. "Aye. He's almost twelve now. Nearly a man."

"I look forward to meeting him." Marianne spooned some celery root and cream sauce onto her plate, then passed the bowl to Mrs. Strumpshaw. Marianne helped herself to a thick slice of woodcock and some salad. Mrs. Strumpshaw stared at the food for a few moments, then seemed to give in and piled up her plate.

"Your cooking is delicious," Marianne said. "This is one of the best meals I've had in ages." The cook at Langford Hall kept everyone thin with her reckless cooking.

"Thank you, miss. Mr. Northam seems to like it. These eels are his favorite."

Marianne passed on the eels. As far as she was concerned, eels did not belong on the dinner table.

She could barely keep her head up as she sopped a wedge of bread in the cream sauce. Yet every time she closed her eyes, his face loomed into her vision, leering with his greedy yellow eyes. It would be a long and sleepless night. Like always.

"Poor thing. You look worn to the bone," Mrs. Strumpshaw said.

"I am. I think I shall retire. Thank you again for the meal."

She made her way up the stairs where two bedrooms opened onto the hall. Her trunk, pelisse, and bonnet had been placed in the front one, which had two large windows overlooking the street. A seafoam green coverlet stretched across a large and comfortable bed. The place was pleasant and clean.

She tiptoed down the hall to check the other room. This one's bed was covered in a whey-colored spread with soft blue walls. Neither the bed nor the room was as big as the front bedroom, and only one small window let the light in from the setting sun.

This was perfect, tucked away at the back of the house. Secluded. Protected. She could never sleep in chambers so open to the street as the other room.

Since this back bedroom had an empty wardrobe and no sign of occupancy, Marianne carried her things here and went about unpacking.

She retrieved a candle from the dining room. She could hear the clanking of cookware as Mrs. Strumpshaw worked in the kitchen below. Marianne could have pulled the bell for her, but her days of being a governess had changed her. If she could do it herself, she certainly would.

She locked her bedroom door and checked the window before setting the candle on her bedside table and slipping under the covers. She always read for a while, hoping to stay awake as long as possible. Mrs. Radcliffe's *The Romance of the Forest* was perhaps not the best choice under the circumstances. The only other book she'd brought was Robert Burns, and poetry was not strong enough to keep her awake this night.

She leaned back into the soft pillows and read. Adeline, like Marianne, had been denied her birthright and thrust into a foreign life by cruel men. There was nothing she could do about it. She, too, had lost everything.

Marianne was with her, riding through the wild heath, fleeing with Monsieur la Motte and his wife—until their carriage was stopped by angry men. The carriage door opened, and a large man with black hair and yellow eyes peered in. A large woman screamed and fainted on top of her. Marianne tried to run, but she couldn't budge under the weight.

Marianne looked down at the woman sprawled across her lap. Her empty eyes stared back at her, her throat slit from ear to ear. Marianne cried out. The carriage rocked and teetered as the men swarmed it, all of them sneering, wielding pistols and knives.

The coach wouldn't stop shaking. It was going to tip, and Marianne would be trapped in it forever with the yellow-eyed man.

"Miss Wood," a man said, shaking her shoulder. A man she could not see. "Miss Wood. Wake up."

She gasped and opened her eyes, sitting up.

Mr. Northam stood on one side of the bed, Mrs. Strumpshaw on the other holding a candle.

The world beyond her bedroom was midnight black. The candle illuminated Mrs. Strumpshaw's thin face, but Mr. Northam's was cast in shadow. Her heart beat like the drums marching along with a piper. Sweat trickled down her back.

She gasped again and fell back into the pillow. "What is it?" she asked with a thick and raspy voice. "Am I late?" Why else would Mr. Northam be hovering in her chambers?

Mr. Northam and Mrs. Strumpshaw looked at each other.

"You were screaming in your sleep," said Mr. Northam.

That was not unusual, but not something that should summon Mr. Northam from wherever he lived.

"Forgive me," she said to Mrs. Strumpshaw. "I should have warned you that I'm a troubled sleeper. I'm sorry it woke you."

"A troubled sleeper?" Mrs. Strumpshaw repeated.

Marianne nodded.

"You've been screaming for over an hour," Mr. Northam said.

"An hour?" No wonder her throat tasted like sand.

"Mrs. Strumpshaw tried to check on you, but your door was locked," he explained.

"You wouldn't stop, and I didn't want to break the door down." Mrs. Strumpshaw's face was creased with worry. "I thought you must be dyin' so I sent my Jamie to fetch Mr. Northam. 'He'll know what to do,' I says."

Marianne glanced at the door. It seemed intact. They must have found a key.

Bad dreams were a nightly occurrence for her. He was always there when she closed her eyes, her constant and loathsome bedfellow. She often woke herself with her cries. But not like this. Not for over an hour. Not that she knew of, anyway.

"It must have been seeing him today," she told Mr. Northam. "I'm very sorry for all the inconvenience." Hopefully, he had not come too far.

"Inconvenience?" he said with a stilted laugh. "Inconvenience is when it rains and I've forgot my umbrella. Or when I am obliged to dine out but I'd prefer to stay in. You had me worried sick. I thought for sure the worst might be happening."

She glanced around the room, searching the shadows. "He's not out of jail, is he?" For that would be the worst that could happen.

Mr. Northam pulled a chair to the edge of her bed. "No. Of course not. I didn't mean that, only that you sounded like perhaps you'd taken very ill."

"You do look pale," Mrs. Strumpshaw added.

"I could use some water," Marianne said.

Mrs. Strumpshaw nodded and hurried out.

Mr. Northam took hold of her hand, the warmth and strength of his touch pulling her out of her dream world and back to the safety of Green Street.

"Miss Wood, you must forgive me. I should not have urged you to see him so soon. I did not fully realize the extent of this man's hold over you. I should never have asked you to see him until you were ready." He gave her hand a little squeeze before releasing, breaking her tether to reality.

His eyes were dark and troubled. She must have made quite a commotion with her nightmares.

"Do you always lock your door?" he asked.

He must know the answer. He knew what Hayter was capable of and why she would put as many barriers as possible between herself and him.

"Always." She shrugged. "Do you really have to ask?"

"No, I suppose not." He gazed down at her coverlet for a few moments, then said, "Perhaps it might help if you tell me what happened the night you lost your family."

These were things she'd not discussed with anyone. Of course the night it happened, she'd told the vicar and the magistrate, leaving out her description of Bartholomew Hayter. And then she'd left her home behind and taken up residence with the Lashams as their governess, never again mentioning her past or why she suffered every night with terrors.

But there was something about the way he leaned forward in his chair, his hands clasped tightly, his eyes studying her, piercing and fierce. It made her want to tell him, to surrender her troubles to someone else, even if only for a moment.

"We were coming home late one evening when we had to stop because a tree had fallen across the road. He appeared out of nowhere and set our carriage on fire." She tried desperately not to see it all over again in her mind. "The whole thing was engulfed in flames in only moments. I alone made it out." She turned her hand palm up, exposing the web of scar left by the burning coach.

He glided his fingers over it lightly. His touch once again sent a thrum of heat through her body. She pulled her hand away. Whatever it was about this man that affected her so, she must not let it cloud her judgment. She would not allow herself to be taken in by him and his beguiling ways.

"Tell me about your family," he said. "I should like to know something about them."

Her family. No one ever asked about them. Or if someone did, she'd mention they were all dead, and that would be the end of the questions. But Mr. Northam wanted to know.

"My father." She closed her eyes, trying to recall his face without flames and fear stricken across it, then she opened her eyes because she could not. "He laughed at anything. He loved a good joke and found humor in the most ordinary things. My mother always complained about his frivolity, but we all knew she loved him for it. She was so elegant and graceful. Always sought after on the dance floor.

"My brother, Frank, was older than me by exactly one

year and a day. We both inherited my mother's light hair and my father's hazel eyes." She looked up at Mr. Northam as he watched her talk about her family, a gentle smile on his lips. "Frank was all about the sport—riding, shooting, boxing, though my parents never knew about that last one."

"I'm sorry you lost such wonderful people."

"Thank you," she whispered, partly because her throat was so dry and partly because of the way Mr. Northam's hand had skimmed over her burn marks.

Mrs. Strumpshaw returned with a glass of cold water. Marianne drank deeply, the coolness soothing her weary voice.

"Perhaps what she really needs is something stronger—to help her sleep," Mr. Northam said.

"I could make her a cup of chamomile tea," Mrs. Strumpshaw suggested.

"Perfect," he said. "Be sure to add a splash of brandy."

Mrs. Strumpshaw hustled away again.

"So then, after Hayter set your coach on fire, what happened next?" he asked. But he had changed once again. His voice was more distant, more official. She wasn't sure now whether he was asking because he cared about her or to get information for the trial. A moment ago, it seemed he'd left the barrister behind and showed genuine concern, but now the lawman had returned.

"Why?" she asked. "Why do you want to know? Is this important to the inquest? Will I be asked to tell it there?"

His eyebrows rose, a moment of surprise flitted across his face. "I cannot deny that certain details might help our case. The more Hayter is made out to be the worst of villains, the greater the influence we will have over the jurors." He leaned closer. "But, Miss Wood, if you think I do not feel keenly the loss of your family and all that you have suffered, you misunderstand me. I cannot begin to imagine all you have endured. It is worse than I believed."

He was playing his game again. And she was nothing but a governess caught up in the deep blue eyes and dark brown hair of Mr. Northam. Surely she wasn't the first woman to find herself weakened by such a man.

Marianne had come to Bath for one purpose: ending Bartholomew Hayter's reign of murder and terror. If telling Mr. Northam her darkest moment was necessary to achieve that end, so be it.

"After I got out of the carriage, I turned back to help my mother. But he was there, grinning at me with his yellow eyes. I don't know what color they really are, but in the glow of the fire, they were yellow."

They would always be yellow, for that is what she saw every time she closed her eyes. Like two slits of demon fire. She'd not be sleeping any more this night, that was certain. Not with so much of the past being stirred up, creating visions she'd been trying to forget.

He handed her a handkerchief, and she pressed it to her eyes, wishing she could wash it all away with tears.

"He had a knife," she continued. "He... pressed it against me. Told me I had a pretty face. Told me he'd make me very happy." She turned aside. She couldn't look at Mr. Northam—not while she spoke these poisonous words. "His knife was so sharp. He slit my summer muslin like it was naught but gossamer threads. He started on my stays, but another carriage came around the bend. The vicar. He'd been attending a dying parishioner. It must have scared him—Hayter, I mean. He said, 'I'll see you in Hell.' Then he was gone. It wasn't until the vicar found me still alive that I realized he'd given me this."

She unbuttoned the high neck of her chemise, exposing

to Mr. Northam the top few inches of an eight-inch scar that missed her vitals by the smallest of margins.

His face turned the color of putty.

"The vicar carried me to his carriage and went back to check on the rest of my family. Hayter came back, standing at the edge of the trees where I could see him from the open curricle. He pressed a finger to his lips, then dragged it across his throat. His message was clear. If I said a word, he would kill me."

Mr. Northam had asked if she always locked her door. Now he knew.

He sat in silence, his jaw muscles tightening until at last he stood and walked to the window. "I will see him hanged."

However terrifying it had been to stand in front of the iron bars and come face-to-face with him, it would have been ten times worse had the man in the jail not been him. At least now, even if her sleeping mind could not accept it, he was caged. The threat was over.

It would take a long time before he quit her dreams. Perhaps it would take forever.

Mrs. Strumpshaw's footsteps sounded on the wooden stairs. Marianne quickly buttoned her chemise. Mr. Northam smoothed the front of his coat and turned to face the room.

Mrs. Strumpshaw carried a tray with a teapot, a teacup, and a decanter on it. "Here you are, dear. This'll calm your nerves."

Mr. Northam removed the stopper and added a generous splash of brandy to her tea, then Mrs. Strumpshaw handed it to her.

She took a sip. She'd never been fond of chamomile, but this one was not so bad. It must be all the additives Mr. Northam insisted upon.

"Thank you, Mrs. Strumpshaw," Mr. Northam said.

"You may go back to bed. I'll sit here with Miss Wood until she falls asleep."

Mrs. Strumpshaw narrowed her eyes at him. "Is that seemly?"

"Life is not always seemly, Mrs. Strumpshaw." He spoke as if he knew something about this. "And sometimes we do what must be done without regard to seemliness."

Mrs. Strumpshaw nodded and shrugged her shoulders. "That's what she said too." She gave Mr. Northam a curtsy, leaving the door half open as she left.

"Drink up," he said. "I'll sit here till you are resting." He took the chair he'd been sitting in and moved it to the window.

"I can't sleep with you staring at me." What kind of nonsense was this?

He picked up the chair and turned it so he faced looking out the window. "There. Now your privacy is assured." He leaned back and put his booted feet on the windowsill, arms folded.

Marianne finished the last of the tea and set it on her bedside table by her book. She rolled over, her back toward Mr. Northam. She couldn't possibly relax with him sitting there. She tried to lift her head to tell him to leave, but the heaviness of the brandy was upon her, and her head would not move.

Business Friends

Mrs. Strumpshaw handed Marianne her pelisse, a lighter, softer gray than the dark blue of the dress she wore underneath. She wished now that she had thought to bring some of her nicer dresses, even if they were several years old. It would have been good to have something to wear around Bath besides the dark frocks she'd become accustomed to as a governess.

In the days she'd been in Bath, Mr. Northam had taken her to church at St. Michael's, the large structure at the end of Green Street. The next few days were dampened by heavy rain, and she was forced to stay indoors and play backgammon with Mrs. Strumpshaw's Jamie. Mr. Northam had come by several times, dripping wet but always with a warm smile for Marianne and a handful of pastilles for Jamie.

He never stayed for dinner, even though Marianne tried to convince him he was welcome.

At last, today the sun shone. Carriages clattered up and down the cobbled roads, but the clatter of pattens had ceased. Mr. Northam had promised her a tour of Bath.

A knock came from the front door.

"That must be Mr. Northam," Marianne said.

Mrs. Strumpshaw hurried to answer it. Marianne picked up her reticule, stuffing in a clean handkerchief, then started down the stairs.

Mr. Northam waited for her in the small parlor.

She stepped in, ready to go.

He watched her for a moment, then smiled. "We're off, then."

They stepped out into the glowing sunlight, and he handed her into the carriage. She settled in, keeping well to her side of the seat. She'd not forgotten the way his touch affected her.

He climbed in, giving her another easy smile. He tapped the carriage top, and it rolled forward, clacking on the paving stones.

The streets this morning were crowded again with carriages and people. They'd all come out to enjoy the sun. It took them some time to only travel a short distance as the going was so slow.

They drove through row upon row of honey-colored stone houses and shops. He pointed out places of interest. The Circus. The Royal Crescent where the curved row of elegant apartments overlooked a vast green. From here, the prospect took in the River Avon and miles and miles of countryside.

They went downhill, taking the lower road and following the Avon until they came up again on the opposite side. The driver brought the coach to a stop in front of a building with several columns along the facade.

"What is this?" she asked.

"This is the Pump Room. One cannot come to Bath and not partake of the waters." He climbed out, took her hand, and helped her down. "One glass of Bath water and you will be cured of all your ills."

"*All* my ills?" Had he forgotten already the extent of her

ills? He had been there several nights past and witnessed her nightmares firsthand.

"Perhaps not in your case," he said with a wink. "We do not profess to be gods. But it was good enough for Bladud."

"Who on earth is Bladud?"

He offered her his arm as they reached the few stone steps leading into the Pump Room. "Come along, I'll tell you while we take a turn. One cannot be a true Bath-goer until one takes a turn in the Pump Room."

Soft but lively music floated down the stairs and out the door. She followed Mr. Northam inside. The large, lofty room had a gallery where musicians played. The place was crowded with all manner of finely dressed people. Rather than help her blend quietly into the background, her plain governess dress made her stand out—a dark pebble in a sea of elegant pearls.

"I should have brought better clothes," she said. "I did not think I would need them."

"Nonsense. You look lovely." He placed a few coins on the counter and took two glasses of murky water. "And if anyone is looking for a governess, you are advertising yourself much to your advantage."

"Does that make you my charge?"

He laughed and leaned close. "I believe there is much I can learn from you, Miss Marianne Wood." He straightened up. "But I'm a very slow learner. I fear I may try your patience."

On the contrary, he was perhaps one of the cleverest men she'd ever met.

"Here." He offered her one of the glasses. "Water from the ancient springs of Bath."

She brought the cup to her nose. "It smells like someone's been boiling eggs in it. Are you sure it's safe to drink?"

"Quite sure. Look around you." He gestured at the crowd of people. "Everyone is drinking it."

Marianne glanced around the room. A fair number of both men and women held glasses of the stuff. Some were on crutches, two in wheeled bath chairs. Many of them had no discernible ailment and were simply elegant-looking folk, though none of them looked as if they particularly enjoyed the water.

"You first," she said to Mr. Northam.

He lifted his glass and drained it. "*Voilà.*" He smacked his lips. "Delicious. I feel very much improved."

She took a sip. It was much warmer that she'd expected. And though the taste was not quite as bad as the smell, it was not anything close to delicious.

"Well?" he asked.

She took another sip. "It's not the worst thing I've ever tasted. But close."

He set his empty glass on the tray of a passing attendant.

"It's better than stewed eels," she said.

"How can you say such things? Stewed eels are my favorite."

"So Mrs. Strumpshaw was telling me." Marianne took one more sip and decided it would be her last.

"You obviously haven't tasted Mrs. Strumpshaw's eels. Not all eels are created equal. It says as much right in the Bible."

What a ridiculous man.

"Aha! So you do have a smile locked away in there."

She hadn't realized she'd been smiling. Or rather, she hadn't realized she had been *not* smiling. One more item to add to the list of things Bartholomew Hayter had taken from her.

"Oh, dear," Mr. Northam said quietly. "Gone so soon."

He took her glass of spa water, his fingers grazing hers, lingering half a moment longer than necessary. "You are a beautiful woman, Miss Wood. And when you smile, it is something quite exquisite."

She stared at him. Undoubtedly, her mouth hung open and her cheeks burned hotter than the spa water. Mr. Northam had combed through his wardrobe again, coming out this morning dressed in an entirely new personage—one that Marianne had a hard time resisting.

A tall, thin man came striding up. "Mr. Northam. How good to see you this morning."

"Mr. Warren." He shook the man's hand heartily. "Pleasure to see you." He turned toward Marianne. "And may I introduce you to Miss Wood, a business friend."

Mr. Warren bowed graciously. "At your service."

Marianne returned his greeting with a curtsy, praying her cheeks had resumed a more placid hue. And how kind of Mr. Northam to remind her that, even after his extravagant praise, she qualified as his *business* friend. Heaven forbid they should be simply friends.

She was a foolish girl. She'd been having a lovely morning touring the town with Mr. Northam. He had a magical way of making her feel safe but not pitiful. Thank goodness Mr. Warren had come along or she might have gotten carried away with the wrong idea. It was just the grounding she needed to keep her silly head out of the clouds.

"How is your family?" he asked Mr. Warren.

"Very well, thanks to you." Mr. Warren turned to Marianne. "When my wife had a run-in with a local cutpurse, Northam here had him swinging from Taunton Stone Gallows in no time."

"How awful for her," said Marianne. "How much did he steal?" Hopefully not as much as Hayter stole from her.

"Nothing." He laughed merrily. "That's the beauty of it. This man could make a saint look guilty. He's brilliant at it."

She'd almost forgotten about this side of Mr. Northam. The man playing the game—this time with other men's lives.

"That didn't stop my wife from playing up the worst of it. She took off to her cousin's in Scotland and stayed there the whole of the summer. Took her that long to calm her nerves."

"I'm glad she's feeling better," said Mr. Northam. He gave Mr. Warren a genial pat on the shoulder before the man bowed and moved on to the next person of his acquaintance.

Mr. Northam seemed pleased with himself as he ushered Marianne onward in their obligatory turn about the Pump Room.

Business friend. The words continued to tumble in her thoughts. In truth, they hadn't known each other so very long. Somehow, the episode during that first night made her attachment feel greater than it should after so short a time. He'd been very kind to come to the house these last few days and show her about town, but she must not take his civilities for more than simply good breeding.

For all she'd confessed to him about her past, and for what he seemed to already know, Marianne knew very little about Mr. Northam beyond his business with her and Bartholomew Hayter. And his ability to play people like a game of whist.

"What about your family?" she asked him.

His eyebrows went up. "What do you mean?"

"I was just considering how you know all the details of my life and I know nothing about you. Where do you come from? What is your story?"

He laughed. "My story?"

"Yes," she said. "I should like to know what kind of family

you come from—something about your history so that we might be on equal footing."

"Equal footing." He laughed again.

"Yes." It seemed only fair that he might at least divulge a small portion of his background now that she had opened her soul to him. "What about your father, for instance? He must be a man of property."

The smile faded from his face as he looked away, his eyes going to the windows overlooking the street.

She assumed he came from a wealthy family, as most barristers did. Perhaps even a baronet. That he was a younger son who found himself without means and so went into law to earn a living.

"So this is what you meant by equal footing. I am a gentleman's son and you are a gentleman's daughter?"

"No." That wasn't at all what she meant. He had it wrong, anyway. "I used to be a gentleman's daughter. Now I'm a governess. As you already know."

"Well, yes. Don't forget you are advertising." He gestured at her plain clothes. "Tell me again how this came to be."

She did not need his reminder of how she stood out among these elegant and softly dressed people. There was a time she had clothes to hold her own in such company. Too bad Mr. Northam didn't know her back then, before Bartholomew Hayter.

"When he killed my father, mother, and brother, I lost everything. The estate should have been my brother's, but now that he was gone, the entail placed it in the hands of a man I'd never met before. He took it all and went upon his merry way. I received barely enough to live on until I took work as a governess. I didn't know what else to do."

"With the Lashams in Shrewsbury."

"Yes."

"And is Mr. Lasham good to you?"

"Mr. Lasham is dead. Mrs. Lasham is a widow, and she is good enough. I have work and I'm left alone. That is all I want."

They had crossed the length of the Pump Room now and were directly underneath the gallery where the musicians played. He leaned close so they could hear each other without shouting. "Is that really all you want?"

She did not answer immediately. Other than to be free of Bartholomew Hayter and his hold over her, she'd thought very little of wants. Besides, it had never been about what she wanted. "My governess life is all I deserve. I was meant to be among the dead that night. It is not right, I don't think, that they are gone and I, alone, left to live."

He shook his head, leaning even closer. "Do not say that. You were meant to be here, now. In Bath."

She glanced up at him, but his face was turned away. He meant only to testify against Hayter, of course.

"Mr. Northam, what a pleasant surprise." It was a woman with her hair wrapped in the style of a Grecian turban. She wore a shimmering satin dress thinner than crepe and more suited to an evening ball than a morning out. The soft fabric did much to accentuate her figure—and she was well aware of that fact.

"Mrs. Cricklade. You look well today." He bowed, and the woman gave a deep curtsy, which only presented more of her figure. "May I introduce you to Miss Wood, here for an upcoming inquest."

Now Marianne was no longer even his business friend, but only a participant in an inquest—which was as it should be. She must not lose sight of her purpose.

"Mrs. Cricklade's husband was killed in a carriage

accident," Mr. Northam explained. "I helped her with some legal matters."

Mrs. Cricklade's soft laughter was perfectly executed, like the tinkling of Christmas bells. "Oh, you're too modest. Mr. Northam was able to fault the gentleman who caused the accident for nearly his whole inheritance."

"Mr. Northam must be very proud of himself," said Marianne. How many more people in this town owed their good fortune to the skills of Mr. Northam? Soon enough, she would be one of them. *Oh, Mr. Northam. Thank you so much for putting my family's murderer in the noose.*

As ridiculous at it sounded, she had no doubt she would be another admirer left in the wake of his prowess with the law. He played his game very well.

"Nonsense," said Mr. Northam, and he had the grace to look just the right amount of sheepish and grateful to make Mrs. Cricklade set off her chimes again.

"I do hope you're still planning on coming to the assembly on Friday. We always make such a fine couple when we stand up together, don't you think?"

In fact, they would make a very handsome couple. Mr. Northam's brawny physique, Mrs. Cricklade's elegant figure. Both with faces carved from marble.

"I should be happy to enjoy a dance with you," he said. "But I'm afraid all the beauty will be on your part. You are a lovely dancer." His words came out sincere, more sincere than Marianne expected for as much as she considered Mr. Northam still playing his game.

Mrs. Cricklade slapped his arm playfully with her fan—another important accoutrement Marianne had neglected to bring on her sojourn to Bath. But then, since she was only advertising herself as a governess, what use did she have of a lace fan?

He bowed to Mrs. Cricklade, and they set off again on their promenade.

Marianne was done with the Pump Room, especially now that she realized so many eyes were upon them.

He must have sensed her weariness. "Come. There is one more place I would like to show you before our day together ends."

They were stopped three more times by friends, admirers, and people he had saved by the time they made it outside and to the carriage.

They plowed through the crowded streets and crossed over the River Avon. For a moment, it seemed they were headed back to the jail, but they followed a wide street and stopped in front of a hotel.

"Sydney Gardens," he said. "I saved the best for last."

Chapter Five

Crusader

They climbed out of the carriage and walked through the grand hotel, exiting out the back and into the gardens.

Mr. Northam paid a man a fee, and they ducked under the bower into a beautifully laid out garden. Groomed hedgerows created the perfect background to all manner of blooming flowers and trees. It was not nearly as crowded as the Pump Room, but there was still a good number of people. He directed her down a graveled walk.

"You never did tell me about Bladud," she said as they veered off to the left on a path that looked like it would circle the outer perimeter of the gardens.

"Ah, yes," he said. "King Bladud. He was the son of the king, actually. He went abroad and contracted leprosy in some awful place. When he returned, he was so ashamed of his condition he hid himself away. But hiding away—as you've already pointed out—does not pay for living expenses. He took work herding pigs."

Herding pigs, herding children—not that the Lasham children were pigs by any means—but she had the distinct impression she was part of another one of his games just now, though she could not figure out what exactly it was.

"One day, as he followed his charge of pigs, they all ran down a hill and returned covered in mud." He smiled as he told his story, meandering the walkway. The deeper they went into the gardens, the more solitary they found themselves. "Pigs and mud is not so uncommon, of course. But this was a wintry day, and pigs use the mud to cool off. In any case, his curiosity was roused, and he followed the pigs for a few days watching them roll in the mire—all the while their skin growing smoother by the day, their scars disappearing. Bladud was no fool. He began dipping himself in that bubbling mire, finding it to be warm and soothing. Soon enough, his leprosy was cured."

"That is quite a story." A legend she'd never heard of before.

"Oh, I'm not finished. The best part is still to come."

"What could be better than being cured of a gruesome disease?"

"Well, Bladud returned immediately to court where his father recognized him as his long-lost son. Soon thereafter, his father died, and he was now king of Britain. It was he who first built up the city of Bath."

"And that is the best part of the story?"

Mr. Northam shook his head. "This is: he lived happily ever after."

She snorted. "Sentimental nonsense."

"Yes, but it was worth it for a glimpse of that smile again."

She looked away, at a willow tree dangling its limbs over the canal. It was all nonsense. And she could not let Mr. Northam's charm distract her from the real reason she was here: the trial of her family's murderer.

They crossed the canal on a bridge with iron rails. Marianne paused, leaning against the rail to watch the water slipping by underneath. She picked up a leaf and dropped it into the water, then went to the opposite rail, waiting for it to emerge. It took longer than she thought, but at last it floated by, drifting downstream with the current.

Her life was not unlike the leaf. She drifted downstream because that was where the current took her. She could not turn back or choose a different course. It was set for her, and naught could be done to turn it differently. Nor could she get off, just as this leaf must follow the canal to its end.

Mr. Northam leaned against the railing beside her. When she glanced up, his eyes were on her, not the water.

"Where does this canal go?" she asked.

"It feeds into a collection basin, then into the Avon."

And then perhaps it was free. She needed only to stay on this course until all with Bartholomew Hayter was complete. Then perhaps she might be free as well.

The sooner to get it over with, the better.

"What happens next?" she asked.

"Well, it goes on through Bristol and empties in the Severn Estuary."

She had turned the conversation rather quickly without bringing Mr. Northam along. She knew the geography of the River Avon.

"I meant with him. Hayter. Will I have to testify in front of a magistrate or something?"

"Ah." He started walking again, Marianne falling in beside him. "Yes. We go before the magistrate tomorrow, now that we know for certain he is the man. If the magistrate finds enough cause—which I have no doubt he will—Mr. Hayter will be transferred to Taunton for the assizes. Once he is proven guilty there, he will be hanged."

Then he would be out of her life forever. She'd never thought the death of a person would be something to wish for.

"Is it wrong for me to want that?" she asked Mr.

Northam. "Shouldn't I be trying to forgive him, as we are taught? Seventy times seven, I believe is what it really says in the Bible."

Mr. Northam stopped. He turned to face her straight on. "Miss Wood. In order for a man to receive forgiveness, he must be repentant. Did Mr. Hayter seem repentant to you?"

She shook her head. He seemed capable—eager, even—to do it all over again given half the chance.

"He has committed unspeakable crimes, and he must pay for them. When he chose to commit those crimes, he also chose the consequences. You cannot have one without the other. Whether you forgive him or not is up to you. The consequences of his actions are his alone, and he must bear them."

Perhaps. Certainly, he had done awful, evil things—things the world would easily label unforgivable—and death did seem his fair due.

"You seem to have thought much about this."

He started walking again. "I have had some experience with the subject of forgiveness."

He offered her his arm, and she took it. Not so much because she needed it, but because the look on his face was once again a new one. A shadowy cloud darkened his visage, and his stride was not as sure as it had been before.

"What happened?" she asked.

He gazed into the box hedge before saying, "Let me tell you this, you cannot let the choices of others be the darkness in your life. If you choose to forgive Hayter, that is between you and God. It will not change Hayter's life. Or, you can put him behind you and live better because of it."

Live better. To be free from his shadow. "How can I live? How can I while the rest of my family is gone?" They had just as much right to live as she did, but he had taken it from them.

"Because it is what they would want you to do." Mr. Northam straightened up and gave her an easy smile. "Look here." He pointed to a low-growing plant with dark green leaves and a few pale violet flowers just beginning to open. He reached down and plucked one of the small clusters, then held it to her nose.

"Smell this."

Marianne inhaled deeply, filling her senses with the warm, sweet fragrance. "It's lovely."

He nodded. "It's called heliotrope and comes all the way from South America. Helio means sun. This flower follows the sun, bending its short stem from east to west as the day progresses. Then, during the long night, it points its little flowers facing east again, ready to greet the dawn."

Just like his story of Bladud and the waters of Bath, she felt he wanted her to learn something from this. To weather the darkness in hopes of light. But it was not so easy as the little flower made it look.

"How does the heliotrope know the sun will come up again, after the long night?"

He shrugged. "Perhaps it doesn't know. Perhaps it just hopes. Here." He gave it to her. "It is good to have reminders that amid the worst of this world, there is also beauty and goodness."

"And hope?"

"Of course."

She smelled it again, taking in the sweet, mild scent. There was good in the world. The children she spent her days with as a governess. This beautiful garden. Mr. Northam—still a mystery, but quickly becoming more of a friend than she'd had in a long time.

Whatever had happened in his past, it was clear he did not want to talk about it. Perhaps another time she would try again to unmask him. He'd brought her here to brighten her day, not darken it. The least she could do was pretend he was succeeding.

They were alone in this small and secluded part of the garden. She turned her face to the sky. To the sun and the warmth and the light. "This is a wonderful place. You were right. This is just what I needed."

"Good. I'm very glad." He watched her for a few moments. "You are not what I expected, Miss Wood, when I sent you that letter of summons."

"How so?" Though he was not alone in his surprise, she thought as she recollected what she'd expected the barrister prosecuting a murderer to be like.

He shrugged. "I expected, perhaps, a little more tightly bound hair. Pursed lips. A disposition for severity, I suppose. I was not prepared for a woman of such beauty. Such gentle goodness, but also such strength."

"You are confusing me with someone else." For none of those things described her. "You flatter me, I think."

"On the contrary, I could not be more sincere."

Goodness. What game was he playing at now? She looked up at him, at his gaze that seemed to go beyond her dress, past her skin and blood and bones, until he saw completely through her.

Take heed, her heart cautioned. But his eyes were so soft upon her, and he stood so near that she could smell the scent of his shaving soap. Like lavender. Or perhaps it was merely the bank of lavender they walked beside.

It was as though he had a kind of power that drew her to him, no matter how much her practical self warned her. Like a net, and she knew she should swim away, but it kept tugging her in.

"You are not what I expected either," she said, ignoring the warnings in her heart.

"How so?" he asked, turning her own words back upon her.

"You're not wearing a wig, for one thing."

He laughed out loud. "You haven't seen me in court."

"You are not older than the Magna Carta."

"How can you be sure? Perhaps I am immortal."

She raised her eyebrow at him. "Are you calling yourself a god?"

He laughed again. "No, indeed. Quite the opposite, I assure you."

She shook her head. "You forget. I've met the opposite, and he is nothing like you."

He replied with sudden candor, "Coming from you, that is the kindest thing anyone has ever said to me."

She didn't know what to say, so she kept walking.

A mother—or more likely a governess—with a flock of children rounded the corner. Two girls laughed as they skipped along, holding hands and chanting a familiar rhyme. "The moon shines bright, the stars give a light—"

One of the girls tripped and spilled into the bank of lavender. The other burst into laughter.

Mr. Northam chuckled quietly. He turned his gaze back to Marianne, and his hand came up, landing softly on her cheek. His eyes drifted to her lips as he finished the rhyme, "And I may kiss a pretty girl, at ten o'clock at night."

Marianne looked back at the children, then down at her feet, then over her shoulder toward the garden path. Anywhere to keep her burning cheeks hidden by her bonnet. He had finished the rhyme properly, but the way he spoke the words . . . so softly. Intimately.

Of course he meant nothing by it. Her association with

him was purely business. The business of seeing that Bartholomew Hayter pay for his sins. Still, had it actually been ten o'clock at night, who knows what she might have done. Fallen into his arms, most likely. She already felt herself leaning toward him.

Mr. Northam cleared his throat. When Marianne turned back, he had moved a few paces away. He was watching the children as the governess dried the tears of the fallen child. They turned and headed off down another path, and she and Mr. Northam were alone again.

"It's getting late," he said in a voice entirely different from the one he'd been using only moments ago. His barrister voice. His business voice. "I'd best get you back before Mrs. Strumpshaw begins to worry."

"Yes." Of course he had meant nothing by it. What a fool she'd been to even suppose for a moment he thought any more of her than what he'd proclaimed all along. She was here for the trial. To help Mr. Northam put another feather in his cap. Another victory. Another man swinging from the gallows.

The ride back to her rooms on Green Street was a quiet one. Mr. Northam helped her out of the carriage and bowed formally.

"Good day, Miss Wood."

"Will you not come and take supper with us?"

"You are very kind, but I'm afraid I'm engaged elsewhere this evening." He climbed back into the carriage without another word. A moment later, it rattled away.

Mrs. Strumpshaw waited for her just inside the door. She helped Marianne strip off her pelisse and bonnet.

"Did you have a nice outing with Mr. Northam?"

"Yes, I did. Bath is very lovely."

"Supper'll be ready in about half an hour, dear." Mrs. Strumpshaw hung Marianne's bonnet on a small rack near the back of the entry hall. "Will you be needin' anythin' before then?"

"No, thank you."

Mrs. Strumpshaw ducked away to the back stairway leading to the kitchen.

Marianne stood in the entry hall. Now what? She had another long and lonely evening of solitude to look forward to. Dine with Mrs. Strumpshaw. Sit in the drawing room alone. She may as well be back at the Lashams'.

She climbed the stairs to her room, taking each step slowly. Each blink conjuring up images of flickering yellow eyes. It was easier to keep them at bay when Mr. Northam was around.

She would appear tomorrow before the magistrate, then her work here would be done. Back to Shropshire and life as a governess.

She'd be back in a few weeks for the assizes—assuming the magistrate ruled in Mr. Northam's favor—and when Bartholomew Hayter died, then what? Her life would be no different, save for the looking over her shoulder. She might gain peace of mind knowing he was gone, that her family was justified, but she would still have to make her own way.

She opened *The Romance of the Forest* and placed the flower Mr. Northam had given her inside, closing the pages carefully so that it would press just right. She sat on the edge of her bed and stared out the small window overlooking the tiny garden and mews at the back of the house. Then she lay back onto her pillow, tucking her legs up, and closed her eyes.

For the first time in two years, the yellow eyes were not the first to appear. Rather, she saw Mr. Northam's deep blue.

Twenty minutes later, she sat at the cozy table while Mrs. Strumpshaw brought out several serving dishes and a platter of sliced ham. She'd not seen the stewed eels again, thank heaven.

"Won't you please join me again? I could use the company."

Mrs. Strumpshaw always waited to be invited, but by now she seemed to expect it and did not hesitate. She grinned and scuttled off, returning a moment later with another place setting. She plopped herself down.

"I hope Mr. Northam doesn't find out about this. I'm not certain he'd approve."

"I'm sure he wouldn't care one way or the other how we take our meals." Marianne took a sip from her goblet. "How long have you worked for Mr. Northam?"

"Not long, dear." She paused to spread some preserves onto her bread. "Mr. Strumpshaw died last fall of the fever. My Jamie works when he can get it, but these are hard times. All the folks from the country comin' to the towns lookin' for work, but there's not enough to go round."

So Mr. Northam took pity on her. "How did he meet you?" He didn't seem the type to be milling about with the widows of tradesmen.

Mrs. Strumpshaw settled into her meal and seemed to be dining at ease. Perhaps the knowledge that she only broke bread with a governess helped.

"It was an odd thing, to be sure," Mrs. Strumpshaw continued, leaning closer and lowering her voice. "Mr. Northam caught my Jamie tryin' to pinch his purse. 'Stead of lockin' him up, he got him a job runnin' errands and doin' odds and ends and the like. But with the parish school in session, he says if my Jamie wants a job, he has to go to school too."

Marianne stared at her, then down at her half-eaten plate. Mr. Northam had not come across as a crusader. He'd openly admitted that he got what he wanted by playing people right. Marianne would like to know what Mr. Northam got out of schooling a street boy. There must be more in it for him than a pot of stewed eels now and then.

Mrs. Strumpshaw painted a different picture of Mr. Northam than the gentleman and lady she'd met in the Pump Room had. Marianne quite liked this new idea forming in her mind of Mr. Northam, charging out with his sword drawn, defending those who could not defend themselves. It was a much better use of his skills than helping the wealthy get what they wanted.

"Does Mr. Northam frequently offer aid like that?"

Mrs. Strumpshaw's shoulders rose and fell. "I can't say. I did hear somethin' about a woman whose husband got run over by a fancy carriage."

"Mrs. Cricklade?"

"Yes, I believe so." Mrs. Strumpshaw cut herself a slice of ham. "My friend, Mrs. Lovell, used to work for them. A real tyrant, that man was. Out drinkin' all night, then comin' home layin' fists on his poor wife. She must have felt heaven blessed when the coach run him down—until she found out he left her with nothin'."

So Mr. Northam secured her some funds from the driver. Marianne could hardly imagine the man she'd just spent the last few days with as a benefactor.

Or could she?

However shrewd he appeared to be, he had also come over in the middle of the night to wake her from her nightmares, then he'd stayed to make sure she was well. He'd taken an entire day to show her around Bath.

He'd been more than kind to her. How ungenerous of her to assume he was not capable of kindness to others—even the

Mrs. Strumpshaws of the world. Underneath all his many masks, it seemed there lurked a noble heart.

Tomorrow, she must appear before the magistrate. More than likely it would be a busy day for Mr. Northam, but if she had time, she vowed she was going to try again to find out about his life.

"And how does your Jamie like school?" she asked, bringing her mind back to the dinner table.

"Oh, he loves it. He's quite the clever one, readin' and cipherin' and comin' home with all kinds of facts. Did you know," she said, pointing her fork at Marianne, "that Henry III kept a pet polar bear?"

"I did not."

"He did. As a gift from a king of one of them northern countries. Henry let it swim and hunt in the Thames."

"That is fascinating." Whoever was teaching the parish school might want to focus more on preparing the young boys to make their way in a world of labor and craftsmen rather than miscellaneous trivialities. Still, any education was better than none. "I'm glad he is able to increase his learning."

"Yes, dear. I only hope he doesn't turn into another King Bladud, poor man."

"He was cured of leprosy and became king." Hardly a cause for sympathy.

"Oh, that was all fine and good, but after he were made king, he took up studyin' too much. Built himself a pair of wings and tried to fly. Fell right down on Salisbury Church. Broke his neck." She made a snapping sound while wringing her hands. "Killed him just like that."

Happily ever after. Those were Mr. Northam's words. Deceitful man. He did not tell her the final ending.

Marianne pushed away from the table, exhausted and

ready for bed. With the inquest tomorrow, she wanted as much sleep as she could get—which would probably be very little.

"I'll bring your tea up directly," said Mrs. Strumpshaw.

The Inquest

Mr. Northam knocked on her door at precisely nine in the morning. Marianne had worn her best dress, a dark blue linen that Mrs. Strumpshaw had pressed to perfect creaselessness.

"You are very governess this morning," he said.

"Where is your wig?"

He laughed. "I'm afraid you'll have to wait till the Taunton assizes to see that." He opened the carriage door and climbed in beside her, then gave a quick thump on the roof. "I have Mrs. Strumpshaw looking for something a little softer for Friday evening."

"What's Friday evening?"

"I'm bringing you to the ball at the assembly rooms. There's no reason you need to hurry back without at least enjoying one of our famous dances."

The crush of people. The hordes of faces. How would she know if he was there, stalking her? But he was locked up. He couldn't be there. Still, it did not seem safe. Nothing was certain until he was well and truly dead.

"Miss Wood?"

She looked up at him. "I cannot go. Thank you for the invitation."

He watched her as the carriage rocked along the busy street. "Because of Mr. Hayter?"

She glanced down at the strings of her reticule twisting in and out of her hands.

"We don't need to worry about the ball today. Let us focus on the task at hand."

A task that did not seem much better. "Will he be there? At the inquest?"

"I'm afraid so. It's normal for the man accused to be there. He will be given a chance to defend himself."

"What am I to say?" She'd never been before a magistrate—at least not for a formal inquest. She never even went to the occasional hangings. It seemed gruesome to her, to want to watch a person die like that.

"The magistrate will ask you questions, and you must answer them. Be straightforward about it. The truth is on your side, and you have nothing to hide." He sounded confident.

Bartholomew Hayter had done horrible things. "What if I say the wrong thing and he is released? I will never be safe." She looked up at Mr. Northam. "He will hunt me down and kill me. I know it."

"Miss Wood." He reached out as if to take her hand but then did not. His hand instead came down on his knee. "I don't see how that could possibly happen. Mr. Cranmore is an intelligent and fair man. The jury will see that you are telling the truth."

They arrived at the guild hall after only a few short blocks. It would have been almost as fast to walk, but Marianne was glad for the privacy the carriage offered.

They entered a grand building with a statue of Justice above the door. Mr. Northam led Marianne to a large room painted dull gray. At the front, a raised platform held a sturdy oak table behind which sat two men, one with long hair pulled back and tied behind his head. The magistrate, Mr. Cranmore. His hair perfectly matched the color of the walls, and upon first glance, Marianne had thought there was something missing from the top of his head. The other man had a stack of parchments in front of him and was working on a quill with a penknife.

The room opposite the platform was packed with onlookers seated in an assortment of benches and chairs. A fair number more stood around the edges, packed in to see the spectacle. They were talking and laughing and creating quite a din. A great hush came upon the crowd as Marianne entered, followed by a sea of whispers. Bartholomew Hayter was nowhere to be seen. Perhaps he wouldn't be coming after all.

Lined against the side wall sat the jury. Men of business and trade, some old, some young. One with a powdered wig. One with a patch covering one eye. Though she was not the person on trial, these men still held her fate in their hands.

"Sit here," Mr. Northam said, motioning to the two nearest chairs.

The gray-haired man at the table rose. "Mr. Northam, this is your witness, I presume?"

"It is, sir."

"Then let us begin." He poured himself a flagon of ale and took a drink before sitting down.

A door at the far end of the room opened, and Hayter came through. The men sitting behind Marianne jeered and hissed. A few called him unsavory names. She liked them better for it.

Bartholomew Hayter shuffled slowly with both his hands and feet in iron shackles. A man with a rifle perched on his shoulders accompanied him. At least they were taking care to keep him contained.

He had cleaned up. His face was shaven, and he wore a suit of fine wool and a clean shirt and cravat. If it were not for his yellow eyes and wolfish grin, he might have passed as a regular gentleman.

Mr. Northam leaned close. "You are safe. He cannot hurt you again, I assure you."

She hadn't realized she'd been squeezing the life out of Mr. Northam's arm. "Sorry."

"There is no need to be sorry." He leaned even closer, but still careful to remain at a proper distance. "You do not have to apologize to me for feeling scared. Not ever."

Marianne could not decide if he meant only to be kind or if perhaps he, too, had suffered at the hands of an evil man.

She didn't have a chance to ask him.

"Blast," said Mr. Northam.

"What?" She followed his gaze to a man slipping in late and sliding into a seat just down the row from her. The man from the jail—Mr. Shadwell. He smirked at Mr. Northam.

Mr. Northam swung back around. "Ignore him," he said.

Marianne immediately assumed the worst. "Will he ask me questions? Is he here to try to disclaim what happened?" Hayter must not be set free.

Mr. Northam's jaw tightened. "The only thing I know for certain is that he is here to make trouble for me. I don't want you speaking to him, do you understand?"

Mr. Cranmore stood and waited for silence. Then he spoke out in a loud voice. "We are here to uncover the facts of the events that occurred on the night of March the fourteenth."

The clerk perched a pair of spectacles on the tip of his

nose and leaned close over a ledger, dipping his pen rapidly in the ink as he took notes.

"Jury." Mr. Cranmore turned to face the two rows of men. "It is your duty to decide whether the commission of said events involved the presentment, Mr. Bartholomew Hayter, and if this case should go to trial."

Someone from the back of the room called, "Hang him," and a roar of approval filled the chamber.

"Let us hear from the first witness," said Mr. Cranmore once the commotion had died down. "Dr. Palmer, please come forward."

Marianne hadn't noticed him mixed in with the crowd. He leaned heavily on his crutch while he made his way to the wooden chair set out for the witnesses.

"Go on," said Mr. Cranmore.

Dr. Palmer laid his crutch down on the floor beside him. "It was on a Tuesday evening. The moon was only quarter full, so the roads were quite dark that night. I was coming home late from attending a young wife who'd just delivered her first child. A healthy boy," he said to the jury as if that might lend to his credibility. "I came to a felled tree blocking the road. I had barely drawn my horse to stop when the whole curricle was engulfed in flames."

The room had gone silent again as it listened to Dr. Palmer relate his story. He told with gravity how he leaped from the carriage, breaking his leg in the fall, only to find Hayter there with a knife at his throat, demanding all of his money and possessions.

Marianne did not want to hear this. She didn't need any more details to haunt her dreams every night. She would have covered her ears, but as she glanced up, she found Hayter glaring at her with his yellow eyes. She maintained as stoic a face as possible, though she did break the string of her reticule with her twisting.

Dr. Palmer went on. "He would have killed me, of that I'm certain, had it not been for the sudden appearance of a dog followed immediately by shots fired. A poacher, out on the hunt."

Same story as hers. Saved by an interruption.

"Who was the poacher?" asked one of the jury, the man with the eye patch. "Why ain't he here to speak for you?"

"He fled. He was breaking the law. He did not wish to be known, I imagine."

Lucky for the good doctor that Hayter had not decided to return and finish the job. Perhaps the poacher hung around just long enough.

"How much did he make off with, then?" asked a young juror.

Here, Dr. Palmer glanced down. "Nothing. The poacher surprised him enough that he ran off without anything."

"Some highwayman," one of the spectators called out. "My dog could do it better."

The whole crowd burst into laughter.

"Quiet, quiet," Mr. Cranmore called. He turned toward Bartholomew Hayter. "What have you got to say in your defense?"

He stood up, his chains jangling. "It weren't me. He can't prove nothin'. The doctor said himself it were dark. I weren't even there that night. I was down at Bridgewater in March, diggin' lines for their new sewers."

This only started a new round of vulgarities flung at him. It took the magistrate a full minute to put an end to it.

"I didn't realize the crowd would be so hard on him," she whispered to Mr. Northam.

"Don't tell me you feel sorry for him."

"No. Of course not." How could she, when every time she closed her eyes he was there, sneering at her while cutting away her frock, all whilst her father's sightless eyes looked on?

Mr. Cranmore asked him if Hayter had any proof of his whereabouts on the night in question. He did not.

"Thank you, Dr. Palmer. Mr. Northam," the magistrate called out. "Please bring your witness forward."

Mr. Northam ushered Marianne to the wooden chair Dr. Palmer had just vacated. He then proceeded to explain to Mr. Cranmore the nature of the crime Bartholomew Hayter was accused of—highway robbery and attempted murder. He did not go into any details, but merely stated that, "Miss Wood has important testimony about the nature of Mr. Hayter and how he is the worst of men and how, if given the chance, he will steal and murder again."

Marianne dared not look at Hayter sitting in chains directly across from her. Even under guard, it seemed he might be able to reach out and finish what he started two years ago. He was very quick with a knife.

"Miss Wood." The magistrate leaned back in his chair as he addressed her. "Please proceed."

She glanced over at Mr. Northam. He gave her a nod.

"Two years ago—"

"Speak up, Miss Wood. If you please."

She cleared her throat and started again. "Two years ago, this man killed my family."

A murmur drifted across the crowd like a breeze through the treetops. She explained how he had set fire to her family's carriage. How she'd also jumped to freedom only to find herself in the clutches of Bartholomew Hayter. She carefully kept her eyes either on Mr. Cranmore or Mr. Northam. This was the reason she'd come here, and she'd not let Hayter's glare deter her.

"He slit my dress." She looked down at her hands clenched in her lap. "And then . . . before he was fully upon me, another carriage came along and scared him away."

Dead silence filled the room, as if not a single soul dared breathe. Marianne gave Mr. Northam a quick glance, but his eyes were fixed on Hayter with a burning malice she'd never seen from him before.

"Hang him!" someone called from the crowd, this time with even more fervor. A chorus of agreement erupted, sending the room into chaos.

The magistrate stood, waving his hands for order. "Quiet," he said. "Quiet."

The ruckus slowly settled, but before Mr. Cranmore could speak again, Bartholomew Hayter rose to his feet. "It's a lie. What proof does she have for any of this?"

The entire room looked at her, waiting for her proof.

She had no proof. It was her word and Dr. Palmer's against his.

Hayter was going to go free unless she could show something tangible against him. Her family would never have justice. He would hunt her down like a fox, corner her, and kill her.

"I do not need proof," she said to the magistrate, her voice soft but clear. "I was there. I saw his hand on my father's burning coach. I saw it on my brother's clothes, casting flames into the sky. I saw his face in the terror frozen in my mother's empty eyes. He left his proof right here." She pulled her fichu aside, exposing a good portion of the scar. "I will never forget his face. It is branded on my body and in my soul."

Another hush settled in. A few men in the rear stood, craning their necks to see her scar. She fitted her fichu back into place.

"Why did you not go to the authorities with this before?"

Mr. Cranmore asked. "You might have saved Dr. Palmer and perhaps others."

"He made it clear that if I did, he would kill me," she said. Maybe she should have. Certainly waiting and hiding were not the brave things to do—especially if it meant he was free to pursue his life of brutality. What made her so special that her life was worth more than someone else's? Staying quiet had seemed her only option. Now that she was here, at last exposing him for the demon he was, a great veil of darkness lifted from her. Her part in her family's restitution was finally over.

Almost over. If the inquest found him guilty, she'd have to do it all over again in Taunton.

One of the jurors raised his hand and stood. "Sorry about your misfortune, miss." And he seemed like he truly was sorry. "But I was wondering, didn't the magistrate up north make an inquest? Three dead bodies must have caused a stir."

Mr. Northam came to his feet. "Perhaps I can shed some light on this." He waited for the magistrate to nod permission. "Indeed the constable and his people went to great lengths to find the culprit, but, without anything to go on, they could not make progress. I have cuttings from the newspapers describing the event, if you want to see them." He turned to the jurors. "You must imagine how frightening it was for Miss Wood, to see her family slaughtered like that. With the cold sting of his blade still fresh upon her, we cannot blame her for making a quick escape where Mr. Hayter could not find her. Her very life was in danger."

The men nodded in agreement.

"Mr. Cranmore," said Mr. Northam. "This has been difficult for Miss Wood. Surely there is enough now to make a decision. Perhaps Miss Wood could step down?"

"Very well," Mr. Cranmore said.

Mr. Northam was beside her almost immediately, helping her back to her seat while the crowd clapped and cheered for her. Mr. Northam held her as if she might faint.

"I can still walk," she whispered to him.

"I know," he said. "But this looks better for the jury. Though there can be little doubt they will rule in favor of a trial."

"Jury," said the magistrate. "You may retire to confer. Please avoid the bar until after your decision."

The men of the jury shuffled out through the side door.

"How long will it take, do you think?" she asked.

He stared at the door where the jury had disappeared. "I cannot say, though I think not long."

"I hope I did not say the wrong thing."

Mr. Northam turned to her and whispered, "You were excellent. Strong and brave, as I knew you would be. And so powerful. We make a good team." He smiled at her. "I can't imagine how taxing this has been for you, but you've borne it like a soldier."

"Is he still there?" She didn't want to look at him, for she knew he'd be glaring at her, his eyes hungry for more.

"He is. They will take him away after the jury gives their report."

All right, then. She would keep her eyes on the other gray walls. But then, she didn't have to. The side door swung open, and the men filed back in. The crowd hurried back to their seats, many of them steadying fresh mugs of ale.

When they'd all found their seats again, the magistrate asked for the jury's decision.

The man with the wig sitting closest to the magistrate came to his feet. "We have concluded that Mr. Hayter was the man who set upon both Dr. Palmer and Miss Wood."

Trial of the Heart

Marianne could scarcely hear the final words of the statement. The crowd had come to its feet in a roar.

Mr. Cranmore tried to speak above the clamor. "Mr. Bartholomew Hayter, I must now inform you that you will be committed to trial and the next Taunton assize."

The crowd cheered again, stomping their feet, until Marianne could not hear another word from the magistrate.

"Let's go," Mr. Northam said. But before they could get through the throng of people, Dr. Palmer was upon them. He shook Marianne's hand.

"I must thank you, Miss Wood." He released her and placed his hand back on his crutch. "I'm not sure they would have come to the same conclusion without your most powerful testimony. Let's hope that finally the world will have seen the last of Mr. Hayter."

"Indeed," said Marianne.

The magistrate called to Mr. Northam.

"Excuse me," Mr. Northam said, making his way through the field of people thicker than gorse. The crowd only grew louder as the guards dragged Bartholomew Hayter out, all the while shouting his own innocence.

"Again, let me say how sorry I am for your loss," Dr. Palmer said. "I cannot come close to your level of grievance against Mr. Hayter."

"Thank you, sir."

"If there's ever anything I can do to repay you, I do hope you will come to me directly."

"You are very kind," she said, trying to keep her voice low but finding it difficult to be heard over the commotion. "Already I feel better for having at last come forward. I'm thankful to Mr. Northam for his summoning me here, even though I hesitated to respond."

"He is the best."

"Might I inquire," asked Marianne, "why you hired Mr. Northam to be your barrister?"

Dr. Palmer nodded, then nudged Marianne aside, where it was a little quieter. "It was what he did for Mrs. Warren."

"Mrs. Warren?" The spouse of the man she'd met in the Pump Room the other day. The woman who'd been pickpocketed and spent a season in Scotland to recuperate her nerves.

"Aye. I probably shouldn't be telling you this, but after what you did for me here today, I think I owe you." He winked at her. "I'm her doctor, you see. Turns out the man was a bit more than a cutpurse and, well, she ended up with child. She didn't want her husband to know, so Northam here set her up with a plan to visit relatives in Scotland until after the delivery of the child. Little lad came early, I understand, and didn't make it. Sad, really, though probably better for them all."

First Mrs. Strumpshaw's Jamie, then Mrs. Cricklade, and now Mrs. Warren. Mr. Northam had quite a bit of benevolence tucked up his sleeve. She smiled over at him, his head bent in conversation with the magistrate. Somehow, he sensed her gaze, and he lifted his head, returning her smile with a questioning cock of his brow.

She must be sure to congratulate him later on his generous ways. Just when she thought she was beginning to understand him, she was surprised anew.

"That was very kind of him," Marianne said to the doctor.

"Indeed, it was."

"You find Mr. Northam kind, do you?" said a man's voice from behind her.

Marianne turned and came face-to-face with Mr. Shadwell.

Chapter Seven
Pieces of Heart

Mr. Northam had warned her that Mr. Shadwell was here only to make trouble. She glanced back at Dr. Palmer, but he was already gone.

"Have you never wondered why Harby Northam is so interested in your case?" the man asked. "How he, alone, was able to track you down and bring you in?"

"Well, I . . . It is his job, is it not, to find what evidence he can to help his client?" She hadn't really given much thought to Mr. Northam having reasons beyond the obvious. The obvious was already reason enough.

The man nodded, and his untidy hair wisped to and fro as he did. "Perhaps you ought to have a conversation with him. I think there's something he's not telling you." The man glanced over her shoulder. He pulled a small card out of his pocket and handed it to her discreetly. "I'll be at The Three Crowns this afternoon if you want answers." Then he slipped away, out the door.

She glanced down at the card long enough to read the name. Robert Shadwell. The next instant, Mr. Northam was beside her. "What was that about?" He had a dark look on his face.

Marianne slipped the card into her reticule. "What did the magistrate say?"

"Just the usual. Hayter will be transferred to the Taunton jail tomorrow to await the assize."

"So he will be out of Bath. That will be good." She would rest easier knowing he was gone.

Mr. Northam's formidable body parted the crowd as they made their way out to the street. The carriage waited for them a little ways down, and they walked to it in silence. Mr. Shadwell's advice was for her to press Mr. Northam as to why he was so invested in her case.

Mr. Northam closed the carriage door and tapped on the roof that they were ready. They'd gone the length of three buildings before he turned to her and asked, "What did he say to you?"

"Who?" Though she knew exactly whom he meant.

"The man from the jail. Shadwell."

"He said I should ask you how you found me. And why you care about this case."

Mr. Northam gave a nod and then turned to look out the opposite window. Several minutes passed, and he said nothing.

"Well?" she asked.

"Well, what?"

"You know what."

The streets were slow as always, crowded with horses and people. The honey-stoned buildings reflected the yellow sun, and the whole city seemed bathed in gold. But it was plate gold only, for inside each of these dwellings lived real people with real lives. She understood as well as anyone that what went on behind those doors was vastly different than what appeared on the gilded facade.

Is that what Mr. Northam was? A facade? He presented a

fine figure from the outside, but she had very little grasp of what went on inside.

"The man you spoke with doesn't know anything. He likes to make trouble," he said without turning away from the window. "To draw your witness away from Hayter. It is a case I've been following for some time. I had already heard about your misadventure long before Dr. Palmer's encounter with him."

"Why?" There were many cases of highwaymen and marauders. Her case was one in a hundred, although not all of them ended in such a violent way. "And how did you know my attacker was also Bartholomew Hayter?"

He shrugged his shoulders. "It's part of my job. As a barrister, I must keep myself familiar with such things in the event they come up at trial."

This could not be the entire truth. Whatever his true reasons, he was keeping them from her. And if Mr. Shadwell didn't know anything, why did Mr. Northam appear so bothered by him?

She'd seen him play his character perfectly to everyone they'd met thus far, but now he seemed not to have the mask he needed on hand. The look on his face was completely disrobed.

"Mr. Northam," she said. He still had not turned to meet her eyes since they'd begun this subject. It was odd to see a man so thick and strong on the outside suddenly so vulnerable. "I wish you would look at me."

He let out a breath. When he did turn his head, his smile was back in place.

She let it drop. It wouldn't be too difficult to go to the inn and ask Mr. Shadwell herself for the information she wanted. Of course, she would rather hear whatever it was from Mr. Northam himself, but if he wanted to guard his privacy, she would not pry. After all, she well knew the need to keep some things to herself.

"Thank you for your help today. I could not have gotten through that ordeal without your support." She smiled at him so that he might know she did not blame him for his silence, but it only seemed to bother him more.

"Do not smile at me now," he said. "Do not, after all that we have been through, offer now your kindness." Just when she thought she'd seen all of his many faces, now this. His eyes were like a pane of glass, sharp enough to cut but so easily shattered.

"I didn't . . . I'm not . . . I'm sorry."

They had already traveled the short distance back to Green Street. The carriage came to a stop outside her rooms.

He reached for the door, but stopped. "May I be perfectly candid with you?"

"I wish you would." This was what she had wanted all along.

He watched her for a long moment. "Miss Wood." That was all the honesty he seemed able to muster.

"Yes?"

"You have been the most unexpected surprise of my life." His tone gave no indication if that was good or bad. "What I mean is, and please do not think me untoward, but I must speak while I can."

"I'm sure I would never think you untoward."

He didn't seem wholly convinced by her statement, but he went on nonetheless, this time with a voice that reached her soul. "What I mean is, I have never met a woman like you. You have captured a piece of my heart, Miss Marianne Wood, and I don't think I will ever get it back."

She looked down at the broken strings of her reticule. He had spoken with a rawness, an earnestness that made her believe for the first time she was chipping away the gilded facade. What lay behind gave her the smallest hope that at last her long night was ending, that when she turned her face to Mr. Northam, she followed the sun.

"Forgive me. I wanted to tell you this before."

Unmasked

Marianne made her way to the counter to ask the whereabouts of Robert Shadwell. Before she reached it, someone tugged on her elbow from behind. She turned to find Mr. Shadwell. He must have been waiting for her. It irked her that she was so predictable.

"That didn't take long," he said. "I take it Northam did not answer your questions?"

Marianne did not respond. To be so easily anticipated left a bad taste in her mouth.

"Or maybe you didn't have the backbone to ask him?"

Still, she did not answer. This man worked for Bartholomew Hayter and could not be trusted. She would not be handing out any free information.

"No matter. I've got us a table here in the corner where we can talk away from the noise."

She followed him to the rear of the room. The Three Crowns was a decent place. The table was clean, and the inn seemed well cared for.

"So, you've come to learn the truth of Mr. Northam." He had a glass of mead already half gone.

"Yes. I suppose. That is, if you've got anything of truth to say." The chances of getting facts from this man seemed rather slim. Mr. Northam had warned her twice not to listen to him.

"Oh, I've got lots of truth. More than you'll be wanting, so just let me know when you've had enough."

She waited for him to continue, but instead of speaking, he sipped his mead. At last, she realized her mistake. She fished into her reticule for a few coins and set them on the table.

Mr. Shadwell swept them into his hand. "Bartholomew Hayter is Harby Northam's father."

Ridiculous lies, as she had suspected. "We're through here," she said, pushing back her chair.

"'Tis the truth. Northam's not the only one who can do investigating. I've found some things out he'd rather keep buried."

"How can you possibly expect me to believe such a wild claim?" It was the most absurd thing she'd ever heard. As if Mr. Northam could have any connection at all with such a horrible man—a man he wanted to see hanged.

Mr. Shadwell took another swallow of his drink. "He knows I know. Why do you think he wants to keep you away from me? He doesn't want you to find out. It'll turn you against him."

He could not seriously expect her to believe such an outlandish assertion. Mr. Northam had tried to keep her away from Mr. Shadwell, but only because he was trying to help Hayter.

"I can see you've had enough truth for one day." He tossed back the rest of his drink. "I wish you the best with your life and your pursuit of Mr. Hayter."

He scraped his chair back and left.

Marianne leaned forward onto the table. It had to be lies. There was no way Mr. Northam was the son of that man. Mr.

Northam was so kind. So civil. She had come to care for him deeply, even in so short a time as she'd known him.

But to be the son of Bartholomew Hayter. It was unforgivable that he would say nothing of it. Hayter had said nothing either. No glance of knowing between the two of them—at least none that she could see.

It must be lies.

It had to be.

She left the inn and made her way back to Green Street. She barely noticed the lovely structures she passed. St. Mary's Chapel. Queen's Square.

Mr. Northam had been very vague when she'd asked him questions about his family. More than vague, he had not answered a single one. And he had seemed determined to keep her away from Mr. Shadwell. It would also explain how he knew about Bartholomew Hayter's attack on her family and how he alone managed to find her.

It all made sense, and yet it didn't fit together at all. Bartholomew Hayter was also tall and broad-shouldered with dark hair. She'd never once looked at Mr. Northam and seen any similarities between the two, but she'd never considered a need to.

Holy saints. What if it was true?

The moment Marianne entered the house, Mrs. Strumpshaw came running. "Oh, my dear. Mr. Northam has just dropped off the most lovely gown I've ever seen for the ball in the assembly rooms tomorrow."

"Mr. Northam was here?" Her heart pounded at the thought of meeting him. She was not ready for a confrontation.

"No, no. 'Twas a delivery. Now, I've laid it out on your bed so you can see it for yourself."

"Thank you, Mrs. Strumpshaw."

Marianne climbed the stairs, still in shock at the idea of meeting Mr. Northam again. If Mr. Shadwell was lying—which he must be—she should not feel so uncomfortable. But inside, she was wrestling a den of snakes.

On her bed lay a silk gown of silvery blue trimmed in a delicate embroidery of midnight. A pile of matching ribbon for her hair lay beside it, along with a pair of dancing slippers. It was beautiful—and must have cost him a good penny.

Perhaps she should not even attend the ball. The thought of dancing with the son of Bartholomew Hayter sickened her. But it was Mr. Northam. To not attend pulled painfully on the strings of her heart.

She had no proof, no confirmation that what Mr. Shadwell had said was true. She only had his word to go on. But was that not what she'd asked the jury to go on when she gave her testimony today at the inquest? She expected to be believed and yet doubted the testimony of Mr. Shadwell.

The difference was, she'd told the truth.

The only way to know for certain would be to ask Mr. Northam herself. After all he'd done for her, he deserved nothing less. Judgment could wait until she had his word. He might be very good at the wearing of masks, but this was something he could not hide.

She would go to the assembly rooms tomorrow night and let Mr. Northam himself be the one to tell her whether or not it was a lie.

Marianne stood on the dance floor, her dress glowing like moonlight in the light of the many burning candles. The room was filled with people she did not recognize. Until a tall, broad-shouldered man came forward. Mr. Northam. He looked ever so handsome in his dress coat and dark breeches.

He came close, smiling at her like he did that day in Sydney Garden.

He leaned in for a kiss. "Yours is a pretty face," he said, his eyes glowing yellow in the burning fire. A knife glinting in his hands.

"Get off me," she cried, but his yellow eyes only moved closer.

"Miss Wood!"

Marianne opened her eyes to find Mrs. Strumpshaw standing over her. This must be the fourth time she'd come in and woken her from a nightmare tonight. She thought they'd come to an understanding that Mrs. Strumpshaw need not attend her every time she had a bad dream, but the woman insisted. The lack of sleep had to be taking its toll on the older woman.

"Thank you, Mrs. Strumpshaw," she said again, rubbing her hand across her eyes. This was the first time the evil in her nightmares had been anyone other than Bartholomew Hayter.

"Just when I thought you were gettin' over it, and now 'tis worse than ever. Are you sure you don't want me to fetch Mr. Northam? My Jamie's just below stairs, and he can run over there afore you can say pigs in a pie."

"No." Marianne sat up to drink the glass of water Mr. Strumpshaw handed her. "I am well. I'm used to this." She would get out of bed in the morning, as she always did, and pretend she was fine. Because that was what must be done.

Mrs. Strumpshaw gave her a dubious look, then left, her feet plodding heavily on the stairs.

Marianne lit a candle and opened her book. She was nearing the end of the novel, where nearly every person in Adeline's life turned out to be something other than what they appeared. Marianne thought that kind of deceit only happened in novels. Now she must reconsider.

She passed the day quietly in her rooms, partaking of the few books in the library, talking with Mrs. Strumpshaw, and playing several games of backgammon with Jamie. She took her time getting ready for the ball. Mrs. Strumpshaw assembled the ribbons and a strand of pearls into her hair with surprising skill.

When the door sounded with a thud, her heart did the same. Mr. Northam.

She had already decided that if it was true, she would still testify in the trial, but that would be her only contact with Mr. Northam. She could not be friends with him if he was the son of Bartholomew Hayter.

Mrs. Strumpshaw opened the door. It was a footman only. Mr. Northam had sent a carriage to pick her up rather than come himself.

He was looking more and more guilty all the time. He must have known she would seek out Mr. Shadwell and that now she knew. Why else would he avoid her? His final words to her made sense. He wanted to tell her how he felt before she learned the truth. He knew she couldn't bear the sight of him after.

The carriage made its way the few blocks to the assembly rooms. She could hear the music already the moment the footman opened the door.

She stood among the throng. Without Mr. Northam, she had no escort nor a ticket to get in. Perhaps it would have been better if she'd stayed at home.

"Miss Wood," called a woman's voice.

Marianne turned to find Mrs. Cricklade striding forward. She was surprised the lady had remembered her name.

"I see Mr. Northam has abandoned you, but I am instructed to take good care of you." She hooked her hand through Marianne's arm. "Come."

She tugged Marianne though the door, presenting a ticket for her, and walked her up to the ballroom.

"Here." She sighed with pleasure. "Here is the ballroom. I'm never more at home anywhere than I am in a ballroom." She smiled at Marianne. "We must find you a partner." Mrs. Cricklade scoured the room. "Ah. Perfect."

She dragged Marianne around the edge of the crowd until they arrived in front of a man somewhat close to Marianne's age.

"Mr. Fontaine, may I introduce you to Miss Wood? She is in town on business but has taken time to come to the assemblies tonight."

Mr. Fontaine bowed cordially. "A pleasure to meet you."

Marianne curtsied.

"How long are you in Bath?" he asked.

"I leave tomorrow."

"What a pity," he said. He had learned his manners well. A governess somewhere should be very proud. "I had better not waste my time then. Would you do me the honor of the next dance?"

"Thank you." She might as well enjoy herself even if Mr. Northam was not here. Mr. Fontaine seemed genial enough. And easy to look at.

After Mr. Fontaine, it was Mr. Miller. Then Mr. Richards. She'd only had a few turns before Mr. Richards did not appear to take her hand when the steps called for it. Mr. Northam had taken his place.

"I see you are not advertising as a governess this evening," he said.

She did a turn, following the dance. "Where have you been?" He looked better than ever tonight.

"Hiding." He smiled, his mask on and the game in full

play. "But before we discuss all that, I was hoping we could complete the formalities."

The dance separated them for a few moments before coming together for a poussette. "Hello, Miss Wood," he said. "Allow me to compliment you on how stunning you look this evening."

"Is that a formality?"

"Quite the contrary." He took her hand for the turn. "Those are the truest words I've ever spoken."

She let go of him, and they separated again, turning around another couple. He had a way with words and could no doubt charm the socks off a beggar. Had she not spent the majority of the night dreaming of him attacking her, she would have succumbed instantly. But there were things she needed to know first. Truths to uncover.

"There now, the formalities are over," he said. "As is the dance."

She stood apart from him and curtsied. He offered his hand to lead her from the floor, but she refused. "No more games, Mr. Northam, if you please."

He did not look happy. "I know who you have been speaking with, and I know what has been said."

"Then it's true?"

He pinched his lips together. "Yes."

She turned her back on him. How could he? To spend all this time with her. Comfort her. Summon her down from Shrewsbury to help get his own father hanged.

He walked around to face her. "Miss Wood, would you accompany me outside for some air? Perhaps we can talk more privately."

Yes. Air. That was exactly what she needed. And to talk without the music blaring in her ears. She followed Mr.

Northam as he pushed his way through the crush and out into the cool night air. Then she could go no farther. She reached for his arm and pulled him around.

"How could you not tell me he is your father?" It was absurd to think that Mr. Northam could have any connection with the devil, but he had confirmed it himself.

He ducked under a colonnade, and she followed. "I did not know him as a father. Not ever. As you can imagine, Miss Wood, he was not the kind of man to settle down and raise a family. When I was still a babe, my mother married a different man, Mr. George Northam. He raised me as his own, or so I thought."

It was kind of George Northam to take on another man's son. Not all gentlemen would do so.

"When my stepfather died, he left all of his wealth to my mother and his own son, my half brother. This surprised me greatly. It was then that my mother finally explained to me about my real father and told me his name. We didn't fully understand then the kind of man he had turned out to be. There had been no contact whatsoever for the whole of my life."

How awful to be raised believing you are a true son, only to be left with nothing. That must have hurt him deeply. Still, he could have said something. But he had not. He'd lied to her and used her to witness against his own father.

"This does not explain why you've been lying to me." If he lied about this, who knew what else he was hiding? Her trust in him snapped like a rose stem in winter.

"I used my connections with judges and other magistrates to find Bartholomew Hayter."

A couple strolled by, arm in arm. A husband and wife, it seemed, laughing and leaning close. Mr. Northam waited until they passed before continuing, "You must imagine the repulsion I felt to discover that my true father was a monster. That was when I decided to become a barrister and do what I could to right his wrongs." He looked down at the paving stones beneath his feet. "I will, of course, understand completely if you never want to see me again."

"You are a player of games, Mr. Northam. And now I see I am simply another pawn for you to manipulate—a means to an end."

"Miss Wood—"

"You did not tell me the full story of King Bladud, did you?" She pointed an angry finger at him. "About how he tried to fly but landed on Salisbury Church. Because you knew this would be my end also." She had fallen for him, only to find herself pierced through the heart.

"Marianne—"

"I will do what I can to bring Bartholomew Hayter to justice. Not for you. For my family."

"Mr. Northam," called a man from the door. He strode over, bowing respectfully to Mr. Northam. "I must speak with you urgently."

"Can it wait?" Mr. Northam asked.

"I beg your pardon, sir, but this cannot. The magistrate asks to see you directly."

"It is fine, sir," Marianne said to the man. "I was just leaving. Goodbye, Mr. Northam."

He called after her, but she did not turn. She couldn't. No matter how much she enjoyed his company, no matter how her heart tried to pull her back, he was the son of Bartholomew Hayter. She could never forget that.

Marianne set off on foot, not bothering to wait for Mr. Northam's carriage. It was only a few blocks down Milsom Street to Green Street. Her slippers would be ruined, but she hardly cared.

How could Mr. Northam be such a traitor? She'd always known he was hiding something behind his masks, but she never imagined this. She must take her feelings for Mr. Northam and bury them as deep as her family in the cold, hard ground.

The night grew cold, and she wished she'd brought a shawl or a cloak. She hurried on until she reached her front door.

"You're home early," Mrs. Strumpshaw said with surprise. "I hope you enjoyed yourself at the ball."

"As it turned out," Marianne said, "there wasn't anybody there worth dancing with."

Mrs. Strumpshaw stared at her as if she'd just said almond tea cakes weren't worth eating.

"I'm unwell this evening. I think I'll go straight to bed."

Mrs. Strumpshaw nodded. "Very well, dear. I'll bring you up your tea and tonic."

Marianne trudged up the stairs to her room. She made an attempt to unbutton her gown, but she could not reach the lower back. She should have asked Mrs. Strumpshaw to help her undress before going for the tea. She removed the slippers from her feet and placed them on the dressing table. The heel was already in shreds. Then she unwound the ribbons from her hair, coiling them around her fingers and placing them beside the pearls.

It was back to governess for her.

There was not much more she could do without Mrs. Strumpshaw to help her out of her dress. Marianne sat on the edge of her bed then flopped back to wait.

What a disaster this trip had been. At least the inquest had been a success. It would have all been much easier if Mr. Northam had been the antiquated barrister she'd pictured in her head. Long in the teeth, low in the ears.

It was taking Mrs. Strumpshaw a long time. Usually, she had the water boiling and ready to go by the time Marianne was ready for bed.

She closed her eyes. In truth, she did have a bit of a headache.

This is what she deserved after letting her heart get carried away. She should have known better, that nothing good could come from anything associated with Bartholomew Hayter.

Would to God that that man had never crossed paths with her and her family. But then she would never have met Mr. Northam. Even if it had only been for a week, he'd been a light in the dark to her. A quiet port in the midst of a tempestuous sea.

It seemed impossible that such a man could be the offspring of the most vile man on earth. Perhaps she'd been too hasty to dismiss him because of it. But how could she not, when every moment with him would only be another reminder of her loss?

Had Mrs. Strumpshaw completely forgotten about her? Tea did not take this long, and she desperately wanted to get out of her dress.

A hand pressed on her mouth. Marianne's eyes flew open.

She stared into the yellow eyes of Bartholomew Hayter.

Chapter Nine
Strong and Brave

Marianne tried to scream. His hand only clamped down harder upon her mouth. She writhed to get out from under him, but a cold blade stung against her throat and she lay still. This was no dream. He was here. In her room.

"Surprised to see me, pretty lady?"

Marianne could not reply, but he did not wait for one.

"I'm on my way out of town. Need ta tie up a few loose ends afore I go."

She knew it. In her heart, she had always known it would end this way—that the man who'd threatened her from the edge of the trees would one day find her and finish her. She should have stayed tucked away in Shrewsbury. She'd been a fool to ever think she could survive so much evil.

"I warned you, didn't I? I told you ta keep yer mouth tight. But you didn't listen. Now I get ta finish what I started."

He pulled the front of her dress down, exposing the mark he'd left on her two years ago. "Feels good, don't it, ta finally finish something that's been left undone?"

His knife slid from her neck down to the scar. He pressed the steel harder, and the warmth of her blood burned against the cold of his blade. She gasped, but no sound fit between his fingers. This was the end for her.

She tried to find something to defend herself. Her room was barren of any kind of weapon, and even if she had something, she could not reach it.

Her book was there. *The Romance of the Forest.* It was small, but better than nothing. She stretched her hand out, all the while he was upon her, holding her down. At last, she managed to get her fingers around the book.

With all her strength, she swung it at his face.

It caught him off guard. He stumbled to the side, loosening his grip. Marianne rolled away and off the bed. She screamed as loud as she'd ever made a noise in her entire life.

"Help!" she cried. "I need help here!" The house was silent.

Bartholomew Hayter wiped a trickle of blood from his cheek. He grinned up at her. "This will be more fun than I imagined."

Marianne reached behind her, and her fingers closed around her water pitcher. She hurled it at him, but he ducked to the side.

Next, she threw the basin, but it, too, crashed against the wall behind him as he came at her slowly from the opposite side of the bed.

Marianne retreated, matching him step for step. She grabbed for a vase and threw that. He blocked it with his arm, leaving a new cut that created a spot of red through his shirt sleeve.

She was running out of ammunition. Her back was against the window.

He stood before her, blocking any attempt she might make of escape. She pressed back until the panes dug into her.

His knife glinted in the flickering candlelight, then sliced the silk of the beautiful gown that Mr. Northam had given her.

He was nothing like his father. With real evil standing in front of her, the contrast was blinding.

She was reliving exactly the night of her family's death. The moment of every nightmare she'd ever dreamed since that day. At least this time, the nightmare would end. She'd see her family soon enough. When it was finally over.

A crack rang from the doorway, and Hayter collapsed against her, then slumped to the ground.

It took her a moment to catch her breath, then she looked up.

Mr. Northam stood there, a pistol still smoking in his hand. He tossed the firearm aside and crossed the room in three strides.

"Miss Wood. Are you hurt?" He looked her over. "You're bleeding," he said as he pulled a blanket off the bed and wrapped it around her.

She stared at him.

Alive. She was still alive, was she not?

Yes, because the pain in her shoulder was extreme. She'd not felt it before. Mr. Northam was here. And he'd just killed his father.

"Mr. Northam," she whispered. "I think I'm going to faint."

He lifted her into his arms. "It's over now," he whispered. "Over. You never have to fear him ever again."

She leaned into him, and his arms wrapped tighter around her. She lay her head on his shoulder, and he stroked her hair.

"No." She lifted her head. "Mrs. Strumpshaw. Jamie." They could not still be living. Bartholomew Hayter would have taken care of them first.

"Go below stairs," Mr. Northam ordered. "Look for Mrs. Strumpshaw and her son."

Marianne hadn't noticed there were other men present. One of them was the magistrate, Mr. Cranmore. He pulled the door open wider, and Mr. Northam carried her out and into the larger bedroom at the front of the house, then lowered her onto the bed.

"We'd better summon a doctor, I think." Mr. Cranmore had found a linen towel and was pressing it to her shoulder.

Mr. Northam nodded at him, taking over Mr. Cranmore's efforts at stanching the blood.

The shock of Hayter's attack drained away, leaving room for the pain to settle in—a familiar pain she remembered from before. He'd done a remarkable job recreating the past.

"It's all right if I die," she told Mr. Northam. It only seemed fair after she'd already lost her whole family to Hayter in his first ambush.

Mr. Northam smiled at her. His real smile. Not the one he reserved for the jury at the inquest or even the one he saved for Mrs. Cricklade. This was his smile just for her. Like the one he'd given her when she stepped off the mail coach that first day in Bath. "You're not going to die. A bit of sewing and you'll be good as new."

A young man entered. "We've found the mother and her boy. They are a little banged up, but they'll be fine."

Mr. Northam spat out an oath about how Bartholomew Hayter's body would hang from the gibbet till the end of time.

"Do you want to come and check on them?" the younger man asked.

Mr. Northam looked down at her.

She had seen Hayter crumple to the ground. Witnessed the light flicker out of his yellow eyes. Mr. Northam had assured her he was dead and could no longer hurt her. But she would rather eat a pot of stewed eels every meal for the rest of her life than remain alone in a room next door to his body.

"I'll take your word for it," Mr. Northam said. "I'm not leaving her."

The man nodded and left.

"How did he escape?" Marianne asked.

Mr. Northam's jaws clenched. "During the transport to Taunton. He had an accomplice who set fire to the transport wagon."

The front door opened, and footsteps sounded on the stairs.

A moment later, Mr. Cranmore appeared carrying a black leather bag. "I've brought Dr. Palmer. He's on his way up."

Dr. Palmer arrived, out of breath from climbing the stairs on his injured leg.

Mr. Cranmore set his bag down on the dressing table. "I'll go down and see the housekeeper. Get an idea from her what happened and how Hayter got in."

Mr. Northam gave the magistrate a nod, then stood and went to the other side of the bed, giving Dr. Palmer space to work.

The doctor peeled back the cloth, and Marianne gasped. The pain was worse this time; she could feel it in burning waves, searing and spreading to the tips of her body.

The doctor pulled out a bottle of something. "Fetch some brandy," he told Mr. Northam.

Mr. Northam left, returning a few minutes later with a decanter of amber liquid. Close on his heels was Mrs. Strumpshaw, carrying a basin of water and a pile of clean towels.

"Oh, my poor dear," she said. Mrs. Strumpshaw's eye was swollen and bruised, but it didn't seem to affect her smile. "I was scared sick for you."

"Is your Jamie well?" Marianne asked.

"Oh, he's just fine. He's a strong lad." She set the basin down and set to cleaning Marianne's wound.

Mr. Northam poured Marianne a glass of brandy, and she drank it down, grateful for anything that might take some of the pain away.

Dr. Palmer splashed a little of the spirits onto her cut. He might as well have poured a bucket of fire straight onto her heart. She cried out, wishing perhaps that Hayter had finished his deed so her suffering would be over. It took her a few moments to catch her breath, then she found Mr. Northam's face.

He winked and smiled at her. "Strong and brave, remember?"

Right. She had appearances to keep up. But when Dr. Palmer came at her with needle and string, she reached out for Mr. Northam's hand.

He wrapped his large fingers around hers, firm and solid. That single anchor did more to steady her than all the brandy in the world.

It took the doctor nearly half an hour to finish his work.

"I'm afraid this will leave a scar," he said as he packed up his bag. "A worse scar, I should say."

There was nothing to be done about that. A governess had little need for wearing gowns that showed her shoulders anyway.

"I will go and see to the boy now," Dr. Palmer said.

Mrs. Strumpshaw nodded. "Thank you, sir." Then she shooed the men out of the room. "Off you go. I've got to get the miss cleaned and ready for bed."

Marianne let go of Mr. Northam's hand with reluctance. Her business with him was over now. Bartholomew Hayter would not see the noose, but he did meet his just reward. And with the end of Bartholomew Hayter came the end of her connection with Mr. Northam.

Mrs. Strumpshaw put a clean linen wrap around the wound. Marianne was still wearing the silk ball gown. She no longer needed help to unbutton the back, for it was slit from neck to waist. When she slipped it over her shoulders, it fell to the floor.

Mrs. Strumpshaw had her in a new chemise and back in bed in no time. "I'll go make you a draft of tea to help you sleep," she said, gathering up the soiled, ruined clothing and leaving her alone.

Marianne glanced over at the wall separating her from the body of Bartholomew Hayter. Would he come to her in her dreams tonight? It would be a tender mercy if his death in this world also banished him from her nighttime world.

"He's gone," Mr. Northam said, leaning against the doorframe. "They took his body away hours ago."

"Oh." She wouldn't have gotten a wink of sleep all night with his corpse in the next room. "I'm glad to know it."

"May I come in?"

He'd never asked before. But then again, this was the first time he'd entered while she was not either crying out in her sleep or being attacked by a murderer.

"Yes."

He entered and sat in a chair near her bed. "How are you feeling now?"

"Better. It still stings, but it is not so bad." The house was quiet. After all the men clumping around, up and down the stairs, now there was not a sound. "Has everyone gone?"

"Yes. Dr. Palmer left a few moments ago, and the last of the constable's men followed him out."

Marianne looked out the window. The moon was nearly full, resting high in the sky. Its light changed the city from one of gilded walls to silvery stones and diamond windows. He had saved her life—of that there was no doubt—but the cost to him might be hard to pay.

"I'm sorry I ever judged you by your father. It was wrong of me. And I'm sorry you had to kill him. That must have been difficult for you." He'd have to carry that with him the rest of his life.

"It was not difficult at all, Miss Wood. It was an easy choice to make." He scooted his chair a little closer.

"That's right. You and your sense of justice." An advocate for the weak. And she was definitely weak.

He scooted closer still. "I did not do it for justice." He watched her closely, his eyes burning with something deep. She couldn't look away.

His hands rested on the edge of her bed. Marianne placed her fingers on his. He wrapped his hand around hers for the second time that night. Instead of an anchor, this time his touch gave her wings. Perhaps her story was not the same as King Bladud. For now she felt she could fly.

A pool of moonlight streamed through the window, creating a fan of silver on the floor.

"The moon shines bright," he whispered.

She smiled at him. Such nonsense. But she played along, quietly adding, "The stars give a light."

"And I may kiss a pretty girl at ten o'clock at night." He lifted his hand, tucking hers against his chest.

"It's long past ten o'clock, Mr. Northam."

His mouth was inches from hers. "I don't care." He leaned closer.

The moment his lips touched hers, she closed her eyes. The pain of her injuries melted away in the flood of desire that filled her body. His fingers landed on her cheek, then slipped down to the curve of her neck.

Then he let her go, all except her hand, which he held tightly. "Come in, Mrs. Strumpshaw."

Mrs. Strumpshaw entered, her cheeks the color of persimmons. "Beggin' your pardon, Mr. Northam. I've got Miss Wood's chamomile tea concoction here to help her sleep."

If Mrs. Strumpshaw was all aflush, Marianne's cheeks must be ten times worse. What must the woman think of her?

"I have good news, Mrs. Strumpshaw," said Mr. Northam.

The woman nodded without looking up.

"Would you like to hear it?"

She turned around. "Certainly."

"Miss Wood has consented to marry me." Mr. Northam's grin stretched from Bath to Bristol.

"I did no such thing," said Marianne. The very presumption of the man.

Mr. Northam looked at her like he was the one mortally wounded instead of her. "You mean you won't marry me?"

He had far too many airs for his own good. "I will marry you, of course, but I have not yet consented. As a man of the law, I'm surprised you would eschew proper procedure."

Mrs. Strumpshaw handed Marianne her cup of tea. "Congratulations, miss. This is the happiest of news."

Mr. Northam took the cup from her because he would not relinquish her one hand and the other was too painful to lift.

"That will do, Mrs. Strumpshaw. You may go. For I have a keen desire to kiss my newly betrothed one more time before I leave."

Mrs. Strumpshaw's face burned again. She gave Mr. Northam a stern tut-tut as she left the room, leaving the door wide open.

As soon as her feet sounded on the stairs, Mr. Northam set the teacup on the night table.

"From the first moment I saw you in the mail coach, small of stature, frightened, I have admired you. You came to Bath determined to face your greatest fear so that another might have justice. Tonight, when you told me you would no longer play my game, I knew that admiration had grown to something much fonder and I could not live without you." He brushed a strand of hair from her face. "You truly have made me the happiest of men."

"Fine words of flattery," she said. He would always be a player of games, reading people and understanding them faster than they could understand themselves. He knew her before she knew herself, and he'd been right in every assumption.

"Words of truth, I hope you know." He kissed the back of her hand. "When Cranmore told me Hayter had escaped, my only thought was for you. If anything would have happened—" He swallowed hard.

He was not the only one who could read people. She was learning too, and he meant what he had said.

"Yes, Mr. Harby Northam." She let her fingers graze his whiskered jaw. "I will marry you."

He leaned close and kissed her again.

About Julie Daines

Julie Daines was born in Concord, Massachusetts, and was raised in Utah. She spent eighteen months living in London, where she studied and fell in love with English literature, sticky toffee pudding, and the mysterious guy who ran the kebab store around the corner.

She loves reading, writing, and watching movies—anything that transports her to another world. She picks Captain Wentworth over Mr. Darcy, firmly believes in second breakfast, and never leaves home without her verveine.

Visit Julie here:
Website: JulieDaines.com
Facebook: https://www.facebook.com/julie.daines.7

Lord Edmund's Dilemma

By Caroline Warfield

OTHER BOOKS BY CAROLINE WARFIELD

An Open Heart
Dangerous Works
Dangerous Secrets
Dangerous Weakness
A Dangerous Nativity
The Renegade Wife
The Reluctant Wife
Lady Charlotte's Christmas Vigil
Holly and Hopeful Hearts
Never Too Late
Mistletoe, Marriage, and Mayhem

Chapter One

Six bewigged musicians played on, oblivious to the cream of Bath society parading about the Pump Room or sitting in a manner designed to show their *au courant* attire to best advantage. Lucy Ashcroft thought the music especially enjoyable this morning, the crush less so. As the Bath season got underway, more of the fashionable elite poured into town.

The crush thickened as she made her way toward the counter that provided a glass of the famous spa waters to those able to afford a subscription. Lucy found the water disgusting in spite of its reputed health benefits, but the ladies believed they needed a daily dose, and she did not have the heart to say no. She pressed forward as delicately as she could, clutching her subscription chit, as well as Aunt Imogene's, and hoping those serving would be too distracted to notice that this was her third trip. She had no qualms about collecting waters for Aunt Imogene's less fortunate friends who had no subscription of their own. The waters came up from the earth free, after all.

She reached the counter, only to be jostled by gentlemen seeking service. The man behind the counter shot a glance—more of a glare, really—in her direction. It didn't bode well.

The well-dressed gentleman who had taken the place of the corpulent squire to her right must have seen the look.

"I believe this lady was ahead of me," he said. The deep voice, as mellow as the dark chocolate she sipped every morning, echoed through her.

The servant seemed about to argue until he studied the gentleman more carefully. "Of course, my lord," he said with an inclination of his head.

My lord? Suddenly shy, Lucy managed only a quick glance at the man. "Thank you," she murmured. She had an urge to curtsy, but the crowd made that impossible, if not ridiculous. Soon she had her glasses, one for the Dowager Lady Hardy and one for Mrs. Moffat, and began her careful way back through the throng.

"May I assist you with those?" the same deep voice said from behind her.

Heat enveloped Lucy's face, her skin prickling. In the midst of a crowd, both hands clutching glasses of Bath water and her third best dress clinging to her legs, she felt as awkward as she often did when she attempted to mind the children while Stepmama entertained the squire's wife.

"No, thank you. I can manage," she said without turning. A voice in the back of her head—probably her stepmother's—called her a perfect widgeon for not attempting to fix the gentleman's attention. *He's a lord, for goodness' sake.*

The gentleman excused himself to an elderly gentleman who moved aside so he could come around her. "I know we haven't been properly introduced, but your hands are full and you seem like you could use assistance."

Lucy couldn't avoid facing him. His smile, the sort that began with the mouth and infused the entire face with kindness, startled her when she did finally look at him. Little lines around his brown eyes made her think perhaps he perpetually smiled in just such a way. For a titled gentleman, he dressed rather plainly, in black and gray with a simple knot at his neck. She smiled back. She couldn't help it.

"Thank you, my lord, but I am almost to the ladies, and it is just as easy to retain my grip as it would be to hand them over," she said.

He followed her glance to the ladies sitting in their corner—five elderly women obviously on the fringes of society. Not one wore a fashionable dress, and one or two appeared shabby, even to the most casual observer. They were Aunt Imogene's bosom bows, and Lucy considered them her own circle of friends while in Bath. She lovingly referred to them as the Circle when she thought of them.

The man's smile deepened. "I'll leave you to it, then," he murmured. He left her with the slightest of bows as if she, not he, deserved an obeisance.

"Goodness, Lucy, your cheeks are pink!" Aunt Imogene said when Lucy handed over the glasses. Her cronies broke into giggles.

"Who was that gorgeous man?" Mrs. Wellbridge, known to the ladies as Mary, asked, sipping from her glass and peering around Lucy.

"He disappeared into the crowd," Martha, the Dowager Countess of Brookfield, complained. "Lovely specimen, that. Didn't recognize him." Lady Brookfield kept up the pretense that she knew those in the highest circles, but in truth she hadn't been in London in many years and rarely ventured out of her tiny apartments except to join the ladies in taking the water. Lucy was grateful she could at least afford her own subscription, unlike most of the others.

"Well, what did he say?" Aunt Imogene urged.

Lucy obliged the ladies with an explanation. She would

have liked to embroider it for their entertainment, but there was little enough to the encounter.

"A lord?" Anna Moffat gasped. The woman seemed even thinner than she had when Lucy first arrived in Bath. Aunt Imogene doubted her friend got enough to eat and regularly sought creative ways to feed her from her own modest funds.

The same could be said for Lady Hardy, a baron's widow who never joined in the banter. She stared down at her half empty glass. Lucy understood how Mrs. Moffat, a spinster, might be reduced to such circumstances, but couldn't fathom Lady Hardy's family neglecting her so. The woman never spoke about them. She rarely spoke at all.

"He did fill out his trousers, I'll say that. No padding there," Lady Brookfield remarked with a knowing expression. "Don't you think so, Lucy?" she added to the general amusement of the company.

Lucy's cheeks burned. "I was too busy balancing the glasses to notice, my lady," she replied.

When the conversation turned as it inevitably did to aches and affronts of old age, the benefits of the waters, and the necessity of daily dosing, Lucy let her mind wander. The encounter with the gentleman, she thought, would give her something to dream about.

When Stepmama insisted that Lucy deserved a holiday in Bath, she had no doubt meant it kindly. Stepmama was never unkind, but sending Lucy away also left her with one less mouth to feed and time to concentrate on the marriage plots she wove around her own daughter, Eliza.

"Only think, Lucy. Perhaps you'll find a husband in Bath," her stepmother had said. Did she understand that being thrust upon Aunt Imogene narrowed Lucy's social circle to women of advanced age? Perhaps.

There were assemblies here as well, but attending with Aunt Imogene or Mrs. Wellbridge—the only two of the ladies who could also afford a subscription to the assembly rooms—Lucy found herself a wallflower, consigned to the chairs in the corner where the dowagers sat. A husband in Bath? Unlikely, but she could dream.

She let her thoughts drift back to her encounter with the man with a lovely voice. When she did, it wasn't the state of his trousers she remembered, but his kind smile and the web of little laugh lines around his eyes.

The Marchioness of Waringford pinned her youngest son with a glare he knew well. "Really, Edmund, how long can it take to fetch a simple glass of water? I should have sent Hildegard," she said, referring to her companion with a sniff.

Lord Edmund Parker, long used to his mother's complaints, stood stoically at her side and said nothing.

"Who was that girl who importuned you? I don't recognize her as anyone we should know," the woman went on.

"I have no idea," he replied. He had briefly considered following the young woman to the group of elderly ladies she so obviously cared for, but it would have been rude, if not intrusive. He had no one to introduce him. She had the appearance of an upper servant of some sort. *A companion, perhaps*, he thought, glancing at Hildegard. Yet she intrigued him for reasons he couldn't quite say.

His mother produced a dramatic sigh. "Bath society isn't at all what it once was. They admit any sort here. One almost regrets that frail health forces one to take the waters. Thank goodness the higher class baths and assembly rooms cater to the better crowd."

Mother is as frail as an ox, he thought. *She comes to Bath to consult with the other harpies, lest she miss an opportunity to shore up her position at their head.*

The marchioness downed her water, gave an imperious glance around, and, having decided she had made sufficient impression for one day, announced, "We will leave now, the company being less than it ought." She raised a hand to her son, who dutifully assisted her to rise.

She moved toward the massive double doors, a frigate in full sail, and Edmund followed ruefully in her wake, hands clasped behind his back. The little group of older women who still huddled in the shadows between two of the massive arched windows distracted him.

His mother sensed his pause and turned. "I knew Lady Brookfield had fallen, but I didn't realize how very low. How pitiful for a dowager." She said the last word in tones she might have used for a vile disease. Edmund's mother enjoyed her status and loathed the idea of ceding it to a daughter-in-law. Lady Brookfield might be a mere dowager countess, but the marchioness reveled in her full control of the marquess's household.

He watched the young lady he had assisted lean forward to listen to one of the women. She made a picture of gentle sweetness that held his attention. *What ties her to these women who so obviously have fallen into difficult circumstances?* he wondered. *None appear able to afford a companion. Is she a daughter or a niece, perhaps?*

"You are gaping like a fish, Edmund. Kindly cease," his mother snapped, drawing him away. "Come along. We've had quite enough for one day."

But would the young woman be here again tomorrow? The thought that she might brought a smile to his face. Perhaps he might enjoy this forced sojourn in Bath after all.

Chapter Two

"You really ought to be more careful, Edmund. Dressed as you are, you could be mistaken for a servant following after a little nobody like that." The marchioness waited until they were safely in the confines of her carriage before resuming her verbal assault.

"What is wrong with my appearance?" he asked. "I thought your dearest hope is for me to become a curate, and I can hardly—"

"A curate? How appalling! You know full well your father has other ambitions."

"The Archbishop of Little Riding?"

"Don't joke about such things. It will be a trivial matter to ensure a place for you on the archbishop's staff as soon as you are ordained, a proper springboard for your career. He is displeased, you know—your father, not the archbishop, although His Grace will begin to wonder soon enough if you don't act. Do you wish for Canterbury to take personal offense after all your father's efforts?"

"We've been over this before." They had been over it daily since they left Waring Park on this miserable holiday. "I have no desire to offend the archbishop, but I wish Father hadn't acted without speaking to me."

"Nonsense. You've always known you were for the church. We've made that clear since you were a boy."

The church. Fate of every third son. Charles—Viscount Philmont—the heir, Nathaniel the soldier, Edmund the cleric. His brothers had each done their duty, to their cost. Charles and his family lived at the family seat under Father's thumb, and Nathaniel? After lingering for a month when they brought him back from Spain, he lay buried in a soldier's grave, dutiful to the end. Family demanded that Edmund do his duty as well; he just couldn't bring himself to it. He tried hinting at his true ambition, but both of his parents ignored him. Did it matter how he lived his life now that Charles had a second son to put more distance between Edmund and the succession? He thought not, but his father had other ambitions.

He had no answer for her, at least none he hadn't voiced this past month.

"You've always been a worry, too dreamy for your own good, too lost in books. Your father tried letting you run free in London last Season to do what all young men do—to no avail, he said." She smirked at him slyly and went on in a faux whisper, "I heard him tell Philmont you never pursued the first ladybird."

"Mother! You shouldn't even hear such things."

"Needs must when a mother worries. Your father does too. He asked Philmont if he should question your, ah, predilections."

Edmund colored and looked over at Hildegard, who sat perfectly still, staring at her hands as if a shocking conversation was nothing to her. It probably was. He turned back to his mother and choked out, "And what did Charles tell him?"

"That he had reason to know you liked women perfectly well but were too pompous to have truck with soiled doves."

Am I pompous? he wondered. *I'm as hot-blooded as the*

next man, but not so much that I would take advantage of a woman. Charles talks as if virtue was a failing.

"All that sober uprightness," his mother complained, shaking her head. "You belong in the church, Edmund. Accept it and get on with it. But please, improve your appearance. The better sorts of clerics wear serge and linen. You look like an impoverished scholar."

"I might like that," Edmund mused.

"Better clothing?"

"The life of a scholar, except many of them do as little good in the world as ambitious churchmen. I'm afraid I don't have that in me, Mother. If I seek ordination, I will do parish work. Father needs to tell the archbishop his wayward son is not available."

The glare this speech received would have melted tin, but Edmund Parker was made of sterner stuff. He had spent most of his freedom in London frequenting a clinic for the poor on the fringe of Seven Dials. Traveling to or from there by night was not for the faint of heart, but he'd done it many nights, coming home smelling of gin and hoping word reached his father that he had been out carousing. If the marquess knew how much Edmund admired the physicians who toiled there thanklessly or the compassion he had developed for the ladies of the night who came there desperate for help, the old man would have flown into a rage.

The marchioness bit her lip and glared out the window, leaving Edmund to his dilemma. Would they tolerate a gentleman physician in the family? Perhaps, but only if he devoted himself to the megrims of the upper ten thousand, and only then grudgingly. Edmund had no interest in that whatsoever. *What else interests you, Edmund?*

The only other thing that came to him had joyful eyes and a kind heart. He wondered how he might arrange an introduction. His mother seemed to know at least one lady in her circle. *Perhaps I can trade on that scant acquaintance. How hard would it be to call on Lady Brookfield?*

Lucy and her aunt walked the final few blocks to her modest house alone after leaving Norma Wellbridge in the company of grandchildren at her comfortable suite above her son-in-law's offices. The others, of course, turned off earlier, walking together toward a shabbier section of Bath where Lady Brookfield managed a small apartment with a sitting room and the others rented sleeping rooms in boarding houses.

"I wish Agnes had accepted my invitation to tea." Aunt Imogene sighed.

"Lady Hardy? It's early. She may yet change her mind." Lucy bit the inside of her cheek in thought. Her aunt invited the woman daily. She accepted precisely every third day, which Lucy suspected was the most often her pride would allow. Tea included cold meats and fruit on days she accepted—Aunt Imogene's effort to get good food into her friend. "Is there any other way we can help her?"

"There are only so many days the baker can contrive to make her believe eight pence worth of stale bread and buns can be had for a ha'penny, though Mr. Fields has been very cooperative."

Happy to take Aunt Imogene's subsidy more like, Lucy thought.

"Mrs. Wellbridge is keen to attend the assembly this Thursday," Lucy said, turning the subject to one more enjoyable. "Martha loves to watch the dancing. She says music feeds the soul."

"Will her daughter and her husband come this week, do

you think?" Lucy hoped so. Mrs. Philmont had a lively humor, and her attendance gave Lucy respite from her elderly circle of friends.

"Unlikely. Martha says their youngest has the croup."

"With four little ones, she rarely has time for assemblies," Lucy replied. *More's the pity.* As much as she wished for Minnie Philmont's company, she envied her. She would much rather spend her days with children than with the dubious joys of the baths, the assemblies, and the Pump Room.

They walked in silence the final steps. Aunt Imogene's maid of all work opened the door, bobbed a curtsy, and waited patiently while they removed bonnets and cloaks.

"Martha thought you might be especially keen for Thursday's assembly as well," Aunt Imogene said.

"Why would that be?" Lucy's unfeigned confusion amused her aunt.

"Why, your young man might be there, of course." The older woman's eyes twinkled.

"Really, Aunt Imogene! We encounter people every day when we go to take the waters. A moment of kindness hardly makes him my young man! I don't even know his name."

"He's newly arrived, or we'd have seen him there before. He'll be at the weekly assembly. I have no doubt." Aunt Imogene dropped into her comfortable chair, the one close to the fire with her embroidery nearby. "No doubt at all," she murmured.

Would he? The thought, once planted, ruffled Lucy's serenity. She had been content to sit quietly while her aunt and her friend enjoyed the bustle around them, but oh, how she would love to dance every dance. The Master of Ceremonies occasionally urged a gentleman her way. Bath being overrun with the invalid, the elderly, and the lame, her partners were rarely young or vital. With the assembly two days away, she could only dream. *What would it be like to dance with a handsome young man with kind eyes?*

Chapter Three

A pale girl with large, sad eyes responded to Edmund's knock. The harassed-looking woman on the ground floor had assured him that this apartment on the third floor belonged to Lady Brookfield. It had taken some effort to ferret out the address at all. The neighborhood, once he found it, had been rather poorer than he anticipated—poor, but not squalid. It looked safe enough. *But how on earth does an elderly lady manage the stairs?* he wondered.

The girl frowned and admitted him. "We don't get much company save Mrs. Crane and Miz Ashcroft," she said. She stared at him, uncertain what to do.

"Would you announce me to Lady Brookfield, please?"

"She be in there," the girl said, pointing. "You kin announce yersel'." She turned and walked toward the back of the apartment.

"Susie? Who is here?" a quivery voice asked from the direction the girl had pointed.

Edmund squared his shoulders and entered the small sitting room. He had lied to his mother when he told her his destination. He hated lies, but he was about to tell another one, possibly several.

"Good afternoon, Lady Brookfield," he announced with a perfectly correct bow. "Please excuse my unannounced call. I am Lord Edmund Parker. I believe you are acquainted with my mother, the Marchioness of Waringford. When she noticed you at the Pump Room this morning, she insisted I call and bring you her regards."

The woman blinked several times. A shrewd light replaced her puzzlement, and she smiled at Edmund. "Did she now? How kind of Hester. Is she well? I hope her presence in Bath doesn't signal illness," she said sweetly.

Edmund gathered from this that the woman knew full well his mother visited Bath every year and further that she had never once called on the dowager countess or invited her for tea. "Minor complaints only," he replied. "She is well enough." *Healthy as a horse.*

The two of them held eyes, each assessing the other, until Lady Brookfield appeared to reach a conclusion. "If you would ring that bell next to you, I'll have my maid bring refreshments," she said at last.

At the tinkle of the little bell, Susie shuffled in. "What?" she asked.

Lady Brookfield blushed at the rudeness and, Edmund suspected, her straitened circumstances, but he would not for the world let on he noticed anything amiss. The countess rose and had hushed words with Susie in the hallway. Edmund suspected she directed her to use fresh tea, rather than reuse leaves, and felt a pang of regret. He couldn't embarrass her by refusing.

When she returned, she sat delicately on the sofa. "You say you noticed me in the Pump Room this morning. Everyone who is anyone takes the waters here."

"Indeed, disgusting though they might be."

Lord Edmund's Dilemma

She cackled at that. "Yes, but the water brings one thing no other remedy seems to have."

"What is that, my lady?"

"Hope, boy, hope." She met his smile at that, and for a moment, they were in accord.

Susie teetered in with a tea tray then, tongue between her teeth, and Edmund put a hand out to prevent disaster, placing the tray with its chipped teapot and mismatched cups on the table in front of Lady Brookfield. Susie scurried out, and the dowager countess began to pour with all the grace of a grand lady in the finest drawing room, which of course she had once been.

She handed Edmund a cup, lifted hers, and watched him slyly over the top of it. "So, young Lord Edmund, suppose you tell me the real reason you are here."

Edmund's face burned. The lady may be elderly, but she wasn't a fool. He took a swallow of surprisingly decent tea and set the cup down. "When I noticed you this morning, my mother gave me your name. Pump Room staff gave me your direction."

"And?" She took another sip and raised an eyebrow.

"A young lady sat with you and your friends."

Her lips twitched, and he feared for a moment she might tease him about which of the ladies could be described as *young*. "Miss Lucy Ashcroft," she said. "The niece of a friend and kindness personified."

"Yes, I could see that. I attempted to assist her, but she insisted she didn't need my help. The thing is, Lady Brookfield, I'm going to be in Bath for some days, and I can hardly approach her, even in so public a place as the Pump Room."

"No," the old woman murmured. "I should say not. Some

men wouldn't hesitate, though, even with an innocent like Lucy."

"I would never! The thing is, Lady Brookfield—"

"You would like an introduction."

He let out a deep breath, relieved. "That's it, exactly. I will see her every morning, if I accompany my mother, and I'd like to offer her my assistance."

"And your company?"

"That too." He grinned at her.

"Lucy is an excellent child. I don't know if I should. What do you have to say for yourself?" Her shrewd eyes bore into him.

He hadn't expected this. The unwed son of a marquess, even a younger one, generally fended off importuning mothers; he didn't often have to prove his worth. "Well," he said at last, "I'm young, healthy, unattached. My pedigree is—"

"Long, exalted, and stable enough, but what about *you*, boy? Are you the heir?"

"No! My brother Charles has that privilege, and he has two sons. I can't even call myself the spare at this point."

"Are you for the army? Clergy? Or do you plan to fritter your life away in London like most of your fellows?"

Edmund's heart sank. The countess skewered him as badly as his mother. What could he say? His chin rose defensively. "I haven't decided." At her stare, he relented. "I've finished my theological studies. I'm to the point of ordination, but it is a big step. I haven't made any commitments."

"I assume your parents expect it."

He nodded miserably, and the old woman surprised him by patting his hand. "Don't let them push you, my boy. Don't do it unless you can put your heart in it." She sat back and sipped more tea. "She won't like it, you know."

"I beg your pardon?"

"Lucy Ashcroft is respectable. Daughter of a baronet, but that won't serve. Your mother will want an earl's daughter, if not higher, to bear her grandchildren."

"I'm not planning to sire children, Lady Brookfield. I just want to be introduced so I can chat with the young lady." He shifted uncomfortably at the turn the conversation had taken.

"Oh, you'll get around to siring children eventually," she replied. "I'll introduce you to our Lucy, but you treat her respectfully, do you hear? If you don't, you'll answer to me. Now eat one of those biscuits."

He looked down at the two ginger biscuits on a rose-patterned plate. *I can't take her food. Taking her best tea is bad enough.*

"Eat up! A young man like you needs sustenance."

He watched her closely. She may live in difficult circumstances, but she didn't look hungry. *I can't insult her either.*

Edmund took a nibble of the stale biscuit and smiled at his hostess. He would see Miss Lucy Ashcroft tomorrow, and this time she would talk to him.

Lucy brought the daily glass of water to Aunt Imogene first, as she always did, and the ladies insisted she take the second, as they always did. She would have preferred to have nothing to do with the disgusting beverage, but the Circle believed firmly in the healing properties of the vile stuff and refused to budge from their position that "a young woman can surely put the benefits to even better use." What those uses might be was left tactfully unspoken. Gagging down the last swallow, Lucy started to rise to retrieve another round of glasses when a familiar voice interrupted her.

"Lady Brookfield, how lovely you look today!" The man with the deep, rich voice approached their little group with a sunny smile. Anyone's approach was remarkable—fine company generally ignored them all—so the sound of a handsome young man pronouncing compliments in Lady Brookfield's direction left Lucy gaping.

"Lord Edmund, how delightful to see you again," Lady Brookfield replied archly.

What is she up to? Lucy wondered, but she didn't have time to consider the matter. The interesting young man beamed at the women, studiously avoiding Lucy's eyes, and then back at Lady Brookfield expectantly.

"May I introduce you to my friends, Lord Edmund?"

His smile broadened, and Lady Brookfield proceeded to do just that, beginning with Lady Hardy, who looked up long enough to nod an acknowledgement and then looked back at her hands. Lady Brookfield introduced the others in order, from Aunt Imogene to Mrs. Moffat to Lucy last of all, a mischievous twinkle in her eye.

"And this is Miss Lucy Ashcroft, daughter of Sir William Ashcroft of Little Hocking in Herefordshire."

If Lord Edmund's smile intrigued Lucy before, it stopped her breath when he turned its full force in her direction.

"I'm honored, Miss Ashcroft," he said. Before Lucy could respond, he went on, "Ladies, may I be so bold as to bring up another chair to join you?"

Lucy bobbed up like a cork on a wave. "You may take mine, Lord Edmund. I was just about to seek Bath water for Lady Brookfield and Mrs. Wellbridge."

"Excellent! I'll come with you, and we can serve the rest of the ladies as well." He followed her before she could think of an excuse to prevent it. She wasn't sure if she was more worried about revealing the extent of the ladies' poverty or her mild deception in using her subscription for them. When he offered his arm, she thought it churlish to refuse, but her mortification increased with every step. When they approached the counter, she hesitated.

Nothing for it but the truth, Lucy. Let him think what he may. "There's a slight problem. I only have two subscriptions," she explained in a pained whisper. "The others..."

His eyes crinkled up in the way that fascinated her when he smiled. "I suspected so. You needn't fear I'll embarrass them—or you. We'll make two trips."

The servers filled Lucy's request without hesitation or raised eyebrows. For once she didn't have to wait while they tended to others. She accepted Lord Edmund's company as a gift, if only for one morning. He carried one glass so she could take his arm. When they returned to the Circle and handed their glasses to two of the ladies, he leaned in and asked, "What do we do now? Fetch the other two or allow some time to pass?"

Distracted by his breath on her ear, Lucy couldn't answer at first. A timely "ahem" from Lady Brookfield brought her down to earth. "It's best to allow some time to pass. The men get busy and don't question how many glasses I need," Lucy whispered back.

Edmund conjured up a chair, although Lucy had no idea how he managed it, as the Pump Room was filled to capacity. He sat and listened patiently to the elderly women's usual talk of ills and megrims. He even added the occasional, "My mother has exactly the same..."

Just as Lucy began to wonder about the unnamed mother, he gave her a knowing look with a raised brow so that they stood as one to go in pursuit of drinks for the other two ladies. They returned in companionable silence without mishap. Lucy couldn't escape the feeling he meant to ask her something, but they approached the Circle before he could.

"Lovely, dear," Mrs. Moffat said when she took her glass. "You are such a kind girl, Lucy."

"Lord Edmund," Lady Brookfield broke in. "Mrs. Crane and Mrs. Wellbridge were just discussing their plans to attend the Thursday assembly."

Were they? From the befuddled looks on their faces, Lucy suspected not. *What is she up to?*

"I, of course, don't bother with that nonsense," Lady Brookfield continued, "but Imogene and Mary derive some benefit from watching the festivities. Our Lucy will attend as well." She flashed Lucy a glance, leaving the girl puzzled as to how she should react to that pronouncement.

Edmund struggled to keep from laughing, especially when Mary Wellbridge jumped in gamely. "Why yes, Lucy loves the music, don't you, dear?"

Five pairs of eyes watched Edmund expectantly. Lucy's eyes dropped to her lap as hard as her heart fell into her stomach. She very much feared her face had turned bright red.

"As a matter of fact, Lady Brookfield, I obtained my subscription to the Assembly Rooms just yesterday afternoon. Isn't that a lovely coincidence? I'll be able to have a comfortable coze with Mrs. Crane and Mrs. Wellbridge . . ." He paused—*for effect*, Lucy thought when she couldn't resist a glance up at him. "And with Miss Ashcroft, of course." His smile lit her from within. "Perhaps," he said as if he had just thought of it—something Lucy very much doubted, "you would save a dance for me, Miss Ashcroft, me being new to Bath." She couldn't take her eyes from him.

"I—"

"Of course she will," Lady Brookfield answered for her.

Lucy smiled back at him. She couldn't help herself. "Of course I will," she murmured. *A dance! This lovely man wishes to dance with me!*

Something in the distance caught his eye, and his smile dimmed. "I'd best take my leave now. Thank you, ladies, for making me welcome. Mrs. Crane, Mrs. Wellbridge, I will see you at the assembly."

"Miss Ashcroft, I, ah . . ." He flicked a glance in the same direction as before. Lucy followed the direction and saw a formidable woman glaring back at her. Edmund went on, "I will look forward to tomorrow night." He bowed and left them, leaving Lucy breathless once again.

"Who is that dragon glowering at us?" Mrs. Moffat asked.

Lady Brookfield waited until they all attended her words. "That would be the Marchioness of Waringford. Lord Edmund's mother."

Angels have mercy! He didn't look like the son of a marquess. He didn't look like the son of that horrid woman either. Lucy's heart sank. Any *tendre* she may have harbored died as quickly as it began. There could be nothing between plain Lucy Ashcroft and the son of the Marquess of Waringford in any universe she knew. A sad sigh escaped her.

At least I'll have my dance, she thought.

Chapter Four

"Darling boy, I have no energy to travel to that wretched Pump Room. I shall rest here in our modest lodgings," the marchioness groaned the following morning, sniffing a lavender scented handkerchief. The curtains in her sitting room had been pulled, casting her in shadow.

If this townhouse is 'modest,' I'm a monkey, Edmund thought. Their Bath lodgings lay toward the end of the Royal Crescent nearest the spa. They were modest only in comparison to the marquess's London mansion.

"I'm sorry to hear you are unwell. I am happy to go myself and bring the water home," Edmund told her.

"That won't be necessary, my dear. I sent a footman."

He couldn't see her in the dim light, but he suspected that if he did, her expression would hold more than a little calculation. The previous day she had ripped into him over his visit with the ladies—or to be precise his "particular attention to that nobody," Lucy Ashcroft. Edmund, however, could be just as calculating. "In that case, I'll leave you to Hildegard's care."

"What will you do with yourself?" his mother asked with an edge to her voice.

"I believe I shall take a walk. Bath has many sights I've not yet seen."

He didn't entirely lie to her. Two hours later, he walked south along Stall Street in the direction of the river and Imogene Crane's residence. If he failed to mention that he went first to the Pump Room where he secured Mrs. Crane's permission to walk Lucy home, his mother didn't need to know. The aunt came with them, of course, but as they progressed, she seemed to fall farther and farther behind, always within eyesight.

After his third attempt to begin a conversation resulted in a one-word response, Edmund feared his efforts to become acquainted with her had come to naught, until he hit upon another topic.

"I thought Lady Hardy looked peaked this morning. Do you agree?"

Her eyes, he noted, were a particularly vivid shade of blue, lit from within by excitement. He noticed this because she looked directly at him with a wide-open gaze at his mention of Lady Hardy. "Yes, worse than ever today. I wonder if she ate this morning. Some days she does not, Aunt Imogene and I are certain on the point, and yet there is a limit to what one can do when the woman's pride throws up a barrier to more."

Her meaning didn't penetrate his mind at first, fixated as he was by the sound of her voice. It had a gentle, throaty quality that he found entrancing. The words themselves, however, came into focus soon enough, and he stopped in his tracks and spun around to face her, horrified. "She doesn't eat?"

"Some, of course. The question is, how much?"

"Has she no family?"

Her bright eyes dimmed. "She has a son, at least. Aunt

Imogene told me there was some sort of falling out with his wife, and they shunted Agnes off to Bath. Her rent is paid, but he otherwise ignores her."

The compassion in her expression transfixed him. "How horrible for the lady," he murmured, conscious only of the beautiful woman looking back at him. The only sign he saw that she recognized his intense scrutiny was a slight bloom of pink in her cheeks.

Lucy pulled her eyes from his. "Dr. Barry believes she may have an illness as well, but he cannot be certain if poor nutrition is the underlying cause of it or just making it worse."

"Dr. Barry?" Edmund asked, offering his arm again so they could proceed, concerned about this so-called doctor. As a city of invalids, Bath teemed with charlatans. He worried that some quack might have gotten his claws into poor Lady Hardy, who couldn't even afford to eat properly.

"Yes. He conducts a free clinic close to the embankment."

Free clinic? Edmund's heart began to pound. Memories of his time in London added excitement to what had been mere skepticism about the doctor. "Tell me about this clinic, Miss Ashcroft."

Lucy described premises near the river frequented by dock laborers, poor working mothers, and those like Agnes Hardy, who were "abandoned by those who ought to care."

"Is this physician one of them—the laborers, I mean?"

"Do you mean to ask if he is in trade? No. He's a gentleman. He attends Aunt Imogene in her home as well."

Something she said came back to him. She said "shunted off to Bath" as if she understood how that felt.

Edmund cleared his throat, preparing to ask what puzzled him most. "How is it you are in Bath with only your aunt for company?"

A smile as heartwarming as it was brief flashed across her

face before she turned her gaze forward. "No one could come with me. My younger sister caught a fever from one of the children just as Stepmama plotted her London season. They gave me little enough to do, and it seemed wise to get out from underfoot."

Younger sister? Lucy didn't have a London season. Edmund would bet a quarterly allowance on it.

Before he could ask, she continued, "Elise is my stepsister. Her mother's grandaunt offered to sponsor her; otherwise Papa could never have afforded it. We are comfortable enough, but with six little ones and dowries to provide, London was beyond our reach. It is a tremendous opportunity for Elise."

She sounded genuinely pleased for her younger sister. *What a generous-hearted lady!* He bit his tongue to keep from blurting out a rude question: *Has a dowry been set aside for you?* He hoped her father cared enough to provide for her but suspected that with another sister and six more to provide for, any wedding portion would be small.

Lucy went on, unaware of his thoughts. "Stepmama worried about me, I think. Bath looked to her like a consolation of some sort, and Papa's Aunt Imogene seemed delighted to have me."

Of course the aunt was delighted. The entire ladies' circle is delighted. She waits on them. She coos over them. She worries about them. She lights up their life.

"And how does Bath look to *you*?"

She glanced at him all too briefly and then forward. "Like a holiday, of course. Something new and interesting. Sooner or later, I'll go home again, and Stepmama will be happy for my help with the little ones."

He had no answer for that. The streets narrowed, and they reached a modest townhouse flush against several equally undistinguished but respectable dwellings. Edmund looked for Mrs. Crane and felt no small amount of relief to see her rounding the corner. He bowed, tipped his hat to the ladies, and set off across town to the Royal Crescent with his hands behind his back and his mind lost in thought.

What would it be like to take a wife? That extraordinary thought sobered him. *I have no business wondering about any young lady's dowry. Father will likely turn me out without a penny when I thwart his plans. What then?*

By the time he reached his mother's townhouse, he convinced himself it would be a mistake to pursue Lucy Ashcroft's attention any further. Nothing could come of it. Still, he had promised her a dance. *One dance won't hurt, will it?*

Chapter Five

Lucy's gown, a pretty sprigged muslin in ecru, may have lacked embroidery or lace ruffles, but she thought it complemented the blue of her eyes, especially when Aunt Imogene produced a soft woolen shawl in the same shade of blue as the forget-me-nots that dotted the gown. The muslin had been a gift for her holiday. She made the dress herself from fashion plates Stepmama found, but she had never worn it.

Peering in her looking glass, Lucy thought she looked as fine as ever she had. Rosettes she had fashioned from blue ribbons adorned her hairpins, and her mother's single strand of pearls rested elegantly against her skin. The neckline of the dress didn't plunge as deeply as some she had seen at the assemblies, but the modest opening made her feel sophisticated. *Good enough for Bath society*, she thought. *If only I have good reason to wear it.*

She might never dress up quite so much again, but if she was to have a dance with an attractive young man, she wanted to look her best for it. If she didn't, she had the joy of looking her best. She tried not to let Lord Edmund's abrupt departure that morning worry her.

"Do you think he will come?" she asked her aunt, turning from the mirror.

Aunt Imogene, who had been clucking over her preparations, beamed at her. "Whyever would he not? He requested a dance, and he doesn't strike me as the sort of young man who would break a promise."

"His mother may forbid it. She looks formidable."

Aunt Imogene's laugh warmed Lucy. "She does indeed, but Lord Edmund is a grown man. He certainly knows his own mind. Besides, if he's the sort who lets his mother rule his life, would you want his attention?"

Lucy knew full well the power families could wield when they chose, money being chief among the weapons they might employ, but far from the only one. Loyalty, the primacy of family ties, custom, and habit all came to bear for those with modest means as much as those with more. Her own presence in Bath gave testimony to that.

"It's only a dance, Aunt Imogene. He may choose not to upset her over such a trifle."

"Lucy! Don't you want to dance with the man? He certainly seems eager to fix your attention."

"He did earlier," Lucy said glumly. "I'm afraid I may have been too honest about our family circumstances. The closer we got to home, the quieter he became, and when we reached the door, he rushed off as if he couldn't wait to get away. So please don't spin any fairy tales about Lord Edmund Parker. We may not see him again." At her aunt's crestfallen face, she rushed on, "I will not be castaway over one forgotten dance, Aunt. You are not to worry. I will enjoy myself this evening. Perhaps Mr. Hunter will ask me to dance again."

Aunt Imogene gave an unladylike snort. "He's old enough to be your father."

"Perhaps." Lucy grinned. "But he doesn't step on my toes."

"We'd best be off before we're more than fashionably late, young lady. You don't want to be the one to stand up that young man of yours."

"Lord Edmund Parker is merely an acquaintance. He is not my young man!"

"So you say . . ."

An hour later, Lucy scanned the assemblage for any sign of her "acquaintance" but found none. Mr. Hunter had indeed asked her to dance, and the rigors of the steps brought roses to her cheeks. The skinny son of a barrister, whose clammy hands she remembered from previous outings, had been eyeing her for ten minutes, and she feared he would request a dance as well.

Before he could do so, however, a ripple of excitement went through the throng, and Lucy saw the Marchioness of Waringford poised in the doorway, surveying the company with a haughty gaze before acknowledging the master of ceremonies, who bowed so low Lucy feared his nose would scrape the floor. The marchioness paraded forward to the place of honor the master had hurriedly prepared for her. Only then did Lucy see him.

Lord Edmund stopped in the doorway as his mother had, but his eager survey of the room had none of his mother's arrogance. Lucy had only ever seen him dressed plainly before, usually in the same gray suit. Tonight, he dressed entirely in black, aside from the pristine white linen of his shirt and the exquisitely tied neck cloth. She could barely breathe just seeing him, and then he met her eyes, and her breath stopped completely, only to come back in a swift intake when he walked toward her.

His eyes held hers while he made his way to her. She

couldn't have looked away if she tried. She didn't try. When he stood in front of her and smiled down at her with eyes that reminded her of the same rich chocolate as his voice, she almost melted. He bowed, breaking eye contact, and reality descended.

"You grace us with loveliness tonight, Miss Ashcroft," he murmured.

She had little experience with men's fashion, but even Lucy could see that both the material and the cut of his clothing were of the first stare of fashion. His suit alone must have cost the moon. She felt like a sparrow in her new gown by comparison. She blushed, flustered, and blurted out, "And you look magnificent."

She wanted to sink into the floor. Ladies did not comment on a gentleman's person!

The laughter in his eyes bore no mockery. He leaned closer and whispered, "Do you like my finery? I'm trying to appease my mother."

Lucy blinked and glanced across the room only to see the marchioness glaring at them. "Oh my. It doesn't seem to be working."

He ignored her concern, although it must have been obvious. "Shall we dance, Miss Ashcroft? Between us, we will quite put the company in the shade in all our finery," he said, extending a hand to lead her out.

She took it and forgot the marchioness entirely.

Edmund thought Lucy Ashcroft a perfect lady from the tips of her toes to the delightful rosettes in her glorious hair. Her graceful movement through the steps of the dance enchanted him, even as the light in her eyes held him fast.

The dance ended much too soon, and she sank into a

perfect curtsy as he bowed, his eyes never leaving hers. They rose and stood, grinning at one another rather longer than was proper before he offered her his arm to return her to her aunt. When he looked around, he saw more than one pair of eyes watching them with a speculative gleam. He didn't dare look in his mother's direction.

When they approached Mrs. Crane, he saw that Mrs. Wellbridge had joined her and that both ladies positively beamed at him. His heart sank. He had tried to tell himself sternly that he needed to have a care lest he give Miss Ashcroft expectations he could not meet. It seemed he was too late. The aunt and her cronies, at least, already had expectations.

Edmund greeted the two women politely before bowing over Lucy's hand. "Thank you for honoring me with a dance, Miss Ashcroft," he said with perfect politeness. He tried to ignore her puzzled expression when he hurried away. *Who can blame her for being confused? She must think I go from hot to cold in an instant.*

When his head cleared and he realized he was walking in his mother's direction, her thunderous expression made him veer off toward the punch bowl, where a number of gentlemen stood in clusters watching the dancing. He nodded politely and took a glass of punch, drank deeply, and grimaced.

"Not the finest, is it? Not as weak as I hear they make it at Almack's, though," a man said.

Edmund had to laugh. He had tasted the fare in the hallowed halls of Almack's and he had to agree. "No, but I think they may have slipped Bath water into it."

The gentleman looked around furtively and moved to block Edmund from view of the crowd. He produced a small flask and raised an eyebrow. Edmund smelled gin, but thought it couldn't be any worse than the punch already tasted. He nodded, and the man tipped a helping into Edmund's cup.

"I'm John Oates," the stranger said, holding out a hand.

"Edmund Parker," Edmund replied, shaking it.

"That would be Lord Edmund, I believe," another man put in.

"For my sins, yes," Edmund answered.

The men stood shoulder to shoulder, watching the next dance form. "That Ashcroft girl is a pretty chit," Oates murmured without looking at Edmund.

Pretty? She's glorious, Edmund thought. He didn't answer the man. He watched a skinny boy lead Lucy out. *Not one other lady here comes close to her.*

"Looks like that barrister Oliver's boy wants to cut you out, my lord," one of the men said to universal laughter.

"He'd ought to be dancing with yon pathetic set," another said, pointing toward the far corner and setting off more ribald chuckling. Edmund followed their eyes to where three plain girls sat with identically bored expressions, hands folded in their laps, obviously lacking partners. *Why aren't any of you leading them out?* he wondered.

When the next set formed, a man old enough to be Lucy's father led her out. Not one of the men hiding by the punch bowl made an effort to ask a lady to dance.

"The Ashcroft girl has danced every set so far. You've put her into fashion, my lord," one wag exclaimed.

"Lucy Ashcroft is a fine girl," Oates said, pitching his voice for Edmund alone. "A baronet's daughter. She would make a fine wife for a barrister or a squire. I hear she won't come with much of a dowry, though. Men care about that." His knowing look irritated Edmund, who put his empty glass on the table.

"Thank you for the fortification," he said, and he set out toward the sad young ladies in the corner.

Lord Edmund's Dilemma

Edmund led out each of the wallflowers, one by one. His attention did little to improve their popularity, but his kindness seemed to cheer them. One, he discovered, was a governess, another the daughter of a physician, and the third a vicar's niece. All seemed pleasant enough, but none particularly held his attention.

Lucy danced every set, and men surrounded her between sets. Was she always this popular? The men's gossip had implied otherwise. He watched her every step, unable to keep his eyes away, obsessed with the grace of her dancing, the wonder of her form, and the way gold highlights flickered off her honey-brown hair in the candlelight.

He led the third young lady, whose name he could not recall, back to her seat, determined to leave before he made a bigger cake of himself. He bowed absently and started across the room, studiously avoiding a glance in Lucy's direction.

His mother greeted him with a sour expression. "Thank goodness. I thought you would never stop dancing. Has Bath run out of pathetic spinsters?" she snapped. He distracted her long enough to take their leave.

"At least you spread your consequence around," she groaned when the carriage door closed. "Dancing with those creatures at least reflected on your kindness, exactly the sort of reputation one expects of a man of the cloth."

"Every man can be kind if he chooses," Edmund murmured, lost in his own thoughts.

"It would have been more effective if you didn't keep staring at that Ashcroft chit."

"I did no such thing. I danced with her as I had promised. That was all."

"Any fool could see the way you watched her, Edmund. It will not do. People will believe you've formed some sort of attachment! You mustn't let that happen."

Too late, he thought morosely. He feared he had fallen in love and had no idea what to do about it.

Chapter Six

The marchioness attended the Pump Room the next day without her son, leaving Lucy downcast. She could hardly storm up to the woman and demand to know his whereabouts.

Aunt Imogene and Mary Wellbridge met bright and early that morning to gossip over every detail of the assembly on their way to the Pump Room. They regaled the others with Lucy's "triumph." It hardly felt that way to Lucy. Lord Edmund danced with her once and left with a curt bow. One moment he had been smiling warmly and the next he looked like he couldn't get away fast enough. She determined to put him out of her mind and relegate the entire experience to a pleasant memory.

The following day was little different, only this time she did not see the marchioness either. *Perhaps they returned to London*, Lucy thought, determined to put the entire interlude behind her. She went about her customary trips to fetch Bath water for the ladies, but couldn't help wishing Edmund would appear, especially when she trooped back to the counter the second time.

"May I help you with those, Miss Ashcroft?" His familiar

voice set her heart racing. She couldn't reply over the lump in her throat, but she happily handed over one of the glasses.

"Is your mother unwell?"

"I think she is fine, but perhaps a bit weary. We walked about the Crescent Fields yesterday. Her companion told me she simply wanted to sleep late and recover," Edmund said wryly, the lines around his eyes crinkling up with good humor. The open park that faced the Royal Crescent wouldn't constitute an exhausting journey to any of Aunt Imogene's friends, let alone a healthy woman of middle age.

Lucy's lips twitched. "She isn't used to walking, I think," she said, remembering the immense carriage that carried her to the Pump Room every morning.

"Unlike you," Edmund agreed. "I thought perhaps I might walk you home again."

She looked at him fully then. Sadness lurked in his kind eyes, and she didn't know what to think about it. The temptation to brave another walk felt overwhelming, yet she feared another lift of spirits dampened by an abrupt change of mood. She had no idea what troubled the young man, but she longed to comfort him. *If we walk, might he tell me?*

"Thank you for the kind offer, but no," she responded at last. "I promised Dr. Barry I would visit the clinic this morning." The remembered errand provided a comfortable excuse.

When a flame of excitement drove the darkness from his eyes, her heart soared. "I help him as I am able every week," she went on. "There are always children to entertain, older ladies with anxiety to soothe, bandages to roll, or tidying to do. I wish I could go every day, but Aunt Imogene begs me not to overdo."

"May I go with you?" he asked, his anxious expression telling her the answer mattered to him a great deal.

"I suppose so, but I should warn you. It's a poor clinic. The conditions may be unfamiliar or uncomfortable—not at all what you are used to."

"You might be surprised by what I am used to," he responded with a lift of his eyebrows.

They supplied the Circle with their daily dose, and Edmund asked Aunt Imogene if he might accompany Lucy.

"Oh, that would be perfect!" the old woman said. "I do not wish to see any more of that place than I must, and I dislike having Lucy go alone, but she will insist on it."

"I'm needed, Aunt Imogene, and I try to repay Dr. Barry for his kindnesses." Her face heated under the power of Edmund's obvious approval. There was more to this man than dancing.

Soon the two of them walked along in companionable silence. She spoke when they turned toward a commercial district near the river and conditions looked bleaker. "Tell me. What are you so familiar with that I might be surprised, Lord Edmund?"

"You may think me some sort of society fribble, but I am not."

"I never thought that!"

His smile might have lit Bath. "Oxford dominated most of my time these last years."

"You're a scholar?"

He shrugged. "I like studies, but no. I'm a third son—or I was—Miss Ashcroft. Theology is the fate of us all."

"You're to be ordained." It wasn't a question.

"Yes. Perhaps. I can't decide. My parents expect it. I can't bring myself to do it."

She waited patiently, mulling over his words. Even the sons of powerful families bore the burden of family expectations. After a while, he stopped walking and turned to her.

"My father's idea of the clergy is about power and influence. He has arranged an appointment to the Archbishop of Canterbury's staff. I've told them I won't do it. If I must be ordained, I want a parish." He searched her face, and Lucy wondered if he could see into her soul. "I'm not meant to be a society preacher, Miss Ashcroft. I would seek a small parish or urban mission if I had to. My parents do not approve of either choice."

"So you haven't spent your time cutting a dash across the *ton*?" she said, swallowing.

"Oh, I did my time in London. You've seen my finery, so you can be certain I know my way around a ballroom. My parents would be appalled to know I spent most of my nights—"

Embarrassment caused pink blotches to rise up his neck and over his cheekbones when he went on, "Not that I did anything I'm ashamed of. Quite the contrary. They just don't understand."

She thought he meant to say more, but he took her arm abruptly and began walking.

What had he been about to confide? She didn't have time to ask him, because they had arrived at the clinic.

Horace Barry managed much with very little. His clinic impressed Edmund from the first moment when the man looked up from examining an old man's wound to sag with relief at the sight of Lucy. She managed the quickest of introductions before running off to do as the doctor bade her. His reaction to Edmund held less welcome.

"I don't have time for the curious, Lord Edmund," the man said, indicating the crowd waiting for attention with a hand holding a lancet.

Lord Edmund's Dilemma

"Parker, please, and I agree, you do not," Edmund replied. "How can I help?"

A snort was the reply. "Can you drain an abscess, Parker?"

"Yes." Edmund almost laughed at the gape-mouthed response. "I spent some time with David Cartwright's clinic last year, mostly observing, but he taught me the essentials."

Barry handed him the lancet. "Get to it, in that case. Others need me." He started to walk away. "Good man, Cartwright," he said over his shoulder.

Edmund soon had the wound cleaned. He found bandages in good order. Supplies were meager, but well-organized. He even found a bit of honey he hoped would help heal the wound. He had doubts. He already knew a patient as elderly and under nourished as the one before him healed slowly, if at all.

"Keep this clean whatever you do, and come back next week so Dr. Barry can have a look at it," he said, tying off the bandage. He knew cleanliness for this man might be a futile goal, but he had to urge it.

"Are ye th' new doctor?" the old man asked. He didn't wait for an answer. "Barry needs help, even if ye aren't one."

"I'm just visiting Bath."

"Pity," the old man said as he walked off, shaking his head.

"Here's a scraped knee for you, Lord Edmund." Lucy's voice startled him. He had been staring after the elderly patient.

"Scraped knee?"

Lucy shrugged. "Dr. Barry said to bring her to you," she said apologetically.

Edmund smiled down at a small girl in a dingy gown that looked more like a sack than a dress and probably had been.

He lifted her to the table and began to inspect her knee. The cut looked deeper than a mere scrape. The child was lucky someone brought her in—and that there was a clinic to come to.

Hours flew by after that. One task gave way to another, and Edmund took what came his way. Once or twice he caught sight of Lucy, notebook in hand, talking to waiting patients, cleaning up, or restocking supplies where she could.

Late in the afternoon, it occurred to him that he hadn't eaten since breakfast and didn't care. Then he realized belatedly that Lucy hadn't eaten either, and he did care about that. *Her Aunt Imogene will have my hide for not taking better care of her.* He washed his hands and went in search of Barry.

"I need to get Miss Ashcroft home," he told the doctor.

"How long will you be in Bath?" Barry asked with no preamble.

"I haven't decided."

"We can use your help, I won't lie to you. I'm here on Wednesday morning and Saturday all day," he said. "I have other patients the rest of the week. I have to support my family," he added apologetically.

Or he would be here every day, Edmund had no doubt.

Barry went on sardonically, "Not that I charge fees, of course. God forbid people should think that I'm in trade!"

Edmund knew the method. Clients left a discreet stipend, sometimes specified by the physician's friend or assistant, with his hat and cane. All involved avoided the taint of trade.

"You're able to support a family like that?" He hoped the doctor didn't take offense at the question he blurted.

Barry stared at him long and hard. "Well enough, if the lady doesn't require a Season in London and silk gowns." *The* lady, not *his* lady. He had answered the underlying question.

Lord Edmund's Dilemma

A man could support a wife if he lived modestly and worked hard. Edmund could do both.

Edmund left the clinic with much to consider.

Chapter Seven

The walk home from Barry's clinic confused Lucy. Lord Edmund didn't speak for several blocks, and she could think of nothing to interrupt his preoccupation. She almost thought he had forgotten her, except that he took her hand in his and held it all the way home. The warmth that flowed between them reached her heart and left her breathless.

He spoke without warning when they approached Corn Street, startling her after his long silence. "You are accustomed to living modestly, aren't you, Lucy?"

She wasn't sure what shocked her the most, his use of her given name or the odd question. "Of course," she answered. "But you already knew that." He seemed to have nothing else to say. Embarrassed, she blurted out, "There's no shame in it."

"Of course not!" he responded hotly. They stopped under a low-hanging linden tree, and he turned her to face him. "It's just that—"

He never finished what he meant to say. He just stared into her eyes for so long that Lucy lost track of time. When he swayed toward her, she thought he meant to kiss her, and the anticipation sent the most peculiar feelings through her to heat her insides and pool in her lower belly.

Just as abruptly, he stepped back and offered his arm properly. "We'd best get you home, Miss Ashcroft," he said as if he hadn't just made free with her given name.

The next morning brought gray skies and little prospect of pleasurable activity. Sundays with Aunt Imogene tended toward rest and quiet. Mrs. Moffat came to dinner after church as she often did, although she protested vociferously that she would return the invitation "as soon as I am able."

Lucy and her aunt knew that day was unlikely to arrive and expected no such return. They were in total agreement that those with more had an obligation to share with those with less. They convinced Lady Hardy to come occasionally, but only when the entire Circle assembled at Aunt Imogene's table. This Sunday they did not.

Cook presented a simple but satisfying dinner, the sort of meal that enabled her to make twice as much as needed, enough so that Aunt Imogene could press the remaining mutton and potatoes on her friend, assuring her, "We'll never eat all this. You do me a favor, truly."

After a few hours of pleasant conversation during which Lucy read to the older ladies from Shakespeare, Mrs. Moffat took her leave. Lucy would have preferred to read from the novel she kept at her bedside, but Aunt Imogene deemed novels inappropriate for Sunday. Lucy privately thought some passages of Shakespeare were no more appropriate, but she didn't argue.

Aunt Imogene applied herself to her needlework while their maid of all work lit the candles in the sitting room. Lucy took one in her hand and begged to be excused.

She went to her room, intending to read from the lovely romance on her bedside before sleep, but an hour later the book lay unread on her lap. Instead of reading, she replayed every moment of the previous day—or at least every moment she spent with Lord Edmund Parker. His mercurial mood changes continued to puzzle her.

Memories of that moment in the shelter of the linden tree left her restless and overheated; sleep eluded her. When Aunt Imogene sent the maid to wake her early in the morning, she prepared to face the day wondering if she might see him again or if she would come to any clarity if she did.

Dreary weather that matched her mood made their routine walk to the Pump Room uncomfortable. When they arrived, she saw no sign of Edmund or the marchioness and chided herself for letting her night fantasies drive her to search for him. He had never promised her he would be there—had promised her nothing at all, she had to admit. *He's bound to leave Bath sooner rather than later. His mother will see to that much, if nothing else.*

The rest of the Circle arrived shortly after. They gathered at the same time they always did and sat in the same corner as they did every day. This particular Monday morning, Lucy had none of her customary cheerfulness. She found herself out of sorts and resentful, imagining how her life would stretch out, one day exactly like the other, caring for these ladies—sweet though they may be—until she herself sank into dreary spinsterhood.

"Do you need help, dear?" Mrs. Wellbridge asked when Lucy rose to fetch the second set of glasses. "You look peaked."

"No. I don't need help. I do this every morning," Lucy snapped. She trudged off toward the counter, unhappy with herself and remorseful.

Her mood took an abrupt turn halfway there when Edmund rushed up to her smelling of rain. "I'm sorry I'm late!" he said.

Her treacherous heart soared, in spite of her efforts to

keep it anchored to solid ground. She needed no flights of fancy. "I wasn't expecting you," she lied.

"The ladies always expect their waters at this time. I can't leave their angel of mercy unprotected," he replied with a grin.

Lucy couldn't control her expanding smile.

He sobered abruptly and reached into a pocket. "Do you think the ladies would object if I gave them these subscription chits I found?"

"Found?" Lucy asked with a raised brow.

His bland expression didn't change. "They can't object if they don't know."

He insisted she take the extra chits, and she couldn't resist his kindness any more than she could help admiring how he charmed the workers who served them.

"I thought you weren't coming," she told him while they made their way back to the Circle. "I see that your mother isn't here again."

"My mother hasn't recovered from the sight of me when I arrived home from Dr. Barry's clinic on Saturday. The dirt on my jacket gave her palpitations, and the blood on my waistcoat made her faint—or so she claimed." His eyes danced with amusement.

Lucy gasped and turned to him. She ought to have known his family wouldn't approve of her taking him to such a place. "I'm so sorry, Lord Edmund. I didn't intend to trouble the marchioness. If I had known you had skills, I could have warned you that Dr. Barry would coerce you into helping. Is that what you tried to tell me? About the way you spent your days in London that would upset your father?"

His mood shifted, as it so easily did, from cheeky to sober. "I'm afraid so. I spent days observing at Cartwright's clinic. It began after my brother Nathaniel died of his wounds in spite of good care. I began to wonder how the ordinary soldiers fared and then how poor families managed. That led me to Cartwright. I'm afraid it isn't how my father expects his son to spend his time."

Or his mother either, she thought. "Was your clothing quite ruined?"

"My valet reacted in horror, but he managed to remove the stains, as well he should have. For what my father pays him, he ought to be able to work miracles."

Lucy scolded herself silently. Of course he had a personal servant. What man of his class did not? *And yet, he spends his time in clinics for the poor. No wonder he confuses me. He's full of contradictions.*

"Will you stay away in the future?" She didn't ask her real questions: *Will you leave Bath soon? Will I see you again?*

"Goodness no! You can't keep me away now that I've met Barry. Next time, though, I'll bring a change of clothing." The cheeky grin had returned.

The change of clothing soothed his valet but did nothing to calm his mother. The second time he visited Barry's clinic she flew into a rage.

"We will not coddle this foolish start of yours, Edmund. People of your rank may direct their man of business to support such concerns out of charity, but we do not visit the filthy places."

"I don't 'visit,' Mother, like some sort of tourist. I assist Barry in his—"

"Assist?" she shrieked. "Never say you lay hands on those creatures!"

Edmund stood his ground. "I do and I will. I tried to tell

you I have no future in the clergy. My path lies in medicine. I'm certain of that." He realized the truth of it deep in his heart. He had crossed a bridge and wouldn't go back.

The marchioness ordered, cajoled, insisted, and finally, turning puce, declared, "No son of mine will stoop so far beneath him!"

"It isn't beneath me to do good with my life," he retorted.

"We will see what your father has to say to the matter," she concluded. She raised her chin and refused to speak to him further.

Lucy and Edmund settled into a comfortable pattern for the next two weeks. He joined her with the ladies every morning save Sunday, and he accompanied her to the clinic each Wednesday and Saturday.

Other days, he walked her home. When he began reaching for her hand while they walked, she kept her gaze straight ahead but didn't pull her hand away. The feel of her delicate fingers in his gave him hope.

Sundays, he accompanied his mother, fuming even on the Lord's Day, to Bath Abbey for services. Lucy and her aunt, he discovered, worshiped elsewhere.

When Lucy inquired about his mother's conspicuous absence at the Pump Room, he changed the subject. He didn't want to lie.

At no time did he mention Lucy to the marchioness either, in spite of his growing conviction that she would play a role in his future. He feared his mother would thunder down on Lucy and the ladies before he had a chance to discern his path forward.

The Circle, as Lucy called them, had come to expect his participation in their morning ritual, and he rather enjoyed the way the entire group beamed up at him when he arrived.

When the day came that Lucy greeted him blushing a fiery red, he realized the ladies had not only developed expectations of their match, but also bedeviled Lucy about it.

He trudged home in misery that day. He knew two things for certain: he loved Lucy Ashcroft, and he ought to declare himself. Yet how could he speak to her until he was certain he could support her? He could think of only one way out of the morass that gripped him: he had to speak to Dr. Barry more directly about his hopes and fears. He plucked up his courage and approached the man, offering dinner at one of the finer hotels.

"Well, Parker," Barry said when their plates were cleared and their glasses refilled, "I don't think you brought me here to discuss beefsteak, as good as that one was. What is troubling you, my young friend?"

Edmund peered into the ruby liquid swirling in his glass and tried to gather his thoughts.

"Well?" Amusement gave a lift to Barry's voice.

"Can Bath support another physician?" Edmund blurted out. "That is, if it were possible and didn't take ten years and—"

"Slowly, slowly. One question at a time. The first is easy. Bath is a haven of the invalid and elderly. Physicians are always in short supply—particularly honest and able ones."

Edmund breathed in slowly to calm himself, relieved that Barry didn't take his ambition as a threat or competition. "What would it take to develop a practice?"

"You're getting ahead of yourself. You have to study first. Have you completed your university courses?"

"Certainly. Oxford."

"Greek and Latin, of course. What about lectures on medical science, few and far between though they may be?"

"For the past year, yes." Edmund felt embarrassed. "My

parents intended me for the clergy, and so my studies primarily focused on theology, but after observing with Cartwright, I couldn't stay away from the lectures."

"You already have rather more clinical experience than many of the sprigs who come out of the lecture hall to be licensed without ever seeing a patient," Barry mused. "Can anyone there serve as a reference for you in this matter?"

Edmund pondered the question. "Stallings," he said at last. "I certainly pestered him with questions." He grinned ruefully. "I took to following him to his premises after lecture."

"Cartwright also, I presume, and myself, of course. If you wish to practice in Bath, you could avoid the Royal College of Physicians and those London hospitals. The bishop here can license you for local practice. Your charity work will weigh in your favor."

Edmund sat up straighter. Could it be that simple? "I'll write to Stallings and Cartwright immediately!"

"One other thing. It would help if you observed for a period at the General Hospital here; it may, in fact, be necessary."

"For how long?" He slumped back in his seat.

"Months. A year. You can get yourself set up during that time. I gather there is some pressing desire to move quickly." When Edmund didn't respond, Barry went on, "I presume this has something to do with Miss Ashcroft."

"The medicine, no. I will pursue that in any case, but the urgency, yes. It has everything to do with Lucy Ashcroft." The marchioness always insisted any talk of money reflected on the speaker's poor taste and bad manners; however, something in Barry's manner encouraged trust.

"They don't approve—my parents, that is—and if Father doesn't approve . . ."

"He won't support you," Barry concluded.

"I'm dependent on him for my income, at least until I make a start."

"Families like yours generally provide their sons with other sources of income. Does your father control them all?"

"I own a small estate in Devon from my maternal grandfather."

"You could set up a family there," Barry pointed out.

"The house is small and needs repair before I could live in it. It would take what little income comes from the land and rents to make it habitable. There would be insufficient funds to feed them."

"But your father might help, in that case," Barry said.

"Not if I defy him about the archbishop," Edmund replied. "What would I do with myself marooned in the country? I would have to give up medicine."

"Villages need physicians as well, though the income, I fear, is meager." Pity gave Barry's words a somber tone.

"How can I ask Lucy to be content as the wife of an impoverished country doctor? I might not even afford more than a single servant to help her in that crumbling country house," Edmund went on miserably.

"That brings us back to Bath and establishing a practice. You don't think your father will assist you at the beginning?"

"Then least of all. He'll want to vent his disapproval." The marchioness had already dispatched at least two heated letters to London, but no reply had come to Bath. He still had no idea where he stood with the marquess.

"From what you say, you aren't without assets, but you'll have to live frugally."

"I can't ask the lady to accept deprivation for my sake."

Barry bit his lower lip. Edmund suspected he hid

amusement. "A noble thought," the doctor said, "but perhaps you ought to ask the lady what she thinks first."

He pondered Barry's advice well into the night. He should ask her, he concluded, only when he knew for certain how bad it would be. He had to put it to his father first. He had to be absolutely certain how he stood.

Chapter Eight

The Circle began to linger longer every morning after they had taken the waters. Edmund had a way of spreading joy, and Lucy suspected they had all fallen in love with him. They teased her mercilessly about *her* Lord Edmund, but she thought they had each taken him as one of their own. Mary Wellbridge openly flirted, Anna Moffat simpered, and even Aunt Imogene played coy. Lady Brookfield sat up straighter and acted more vivacious than she had in all the time Lucy had known her. She topped many of Edmund's amusing anecdotes about the *haut ton* with ones of her own. Only Lady Hardy held back.

The morning after Edmund's dinner with Barry, he leaned over Lucy's chair to whisper in her ear that he had something to tell her later. Then he put the Circle in stitches with a story involving the archbishop's terrier and the Countess of Ambler's drawing room. Mrs. Moffat laughed until tears rolled down her cheeks. Lady Brookfield made a ribald remark about the countess's butler. Aunt Imogene and Mrs. Wellbridge giggled. The ladies' laughter warmed Lucy's heart until Lady Hardy slumped back in her chair.

Edmund's cheerful manner disappeared, and he leaned toward the stricken lady. "Are you well?" he asked.

Lucy, alerted, reached for the lady's hand. It felt cold as ice. The woman's unfocused eyes frightened Lucy, and the incoherent sounds she made alarmed her more.

"Loosen her clothing, Lucy," Edmund ordered. He laid two fingers on Lady Hardy's wrist and pulled his watch from its pocket.

The familiarity hardly registered. Lucy hurried to do as he bade, unbuttoning the top of the stricken woman's gown and pulling it away from her neck. The worn fabric tore slightly when she did.

"Her pulse is faint," Edmund said. "We need to get her to a more private place," he said looking frantically around the Pump Room. "Oh, hell! Let's take her to Barry." He scooped the elderly lady up without apologizing for his language and strode toward the door.

Lucy took leave of the rest of the ladies, who stared after her with stunned expressions.

"Hurry, Lucy dear. Bring us word as soon as you can," Aunt Imogene called after her.

She ran after Edmund with Lady Hardy's reticule and cloak. When they arrived at Barry's premises, the doctor realized the gravity of the situation immediately. Edmund, still carrying his burden, followed him into his examining room, and the door shut firmly behind them, leaving Lucy to fret in the reception room.

The reception room boasted a modicum more comfort than the free clinic with its wooden benches. Patients could choose from the threadbare couch, a settee that listed unevenly, and several wooden chairs, not one of which matched another. Lucy stood against the wall.

Barry's regulars, who did not seem to be in crisis,

gradually drifted away as time passed, some grumbling that they would come back later. Finally, Lucy shared the room with only a young mother whose feverish son slept in her lap and a fern drooping in a pot by the window. Neither had much to say.

The door to the physician's examination room stayed closed. Lucy hoped her sense of time had slowed with worry, because she hated to think Edmund and Dr. Barry had actually disappeared with her friend several hours earlier. She had come very close to the limit of her endurance just before the door opened, and Edmund gestured for her to come in. The young mother glowered when Lucy disappeared into the inner rooms.

They faced each other in the dim hallway, the narrow passage forcing them to stand close together.

"Tell me! How is she? May I see her?" Lucy demanded.

Edmund took both of her hands in his. His thumb made little circles on the top of her left hand, but she doubted he even realized he was doing it. "She had an attack of apoplexy. I thought—" He swallowed hard. "What I thought doesn't matter. I have much to learn. Barry rates it minor. He believes she will recover given time and enough to eat."

"She starves herself!" Lucy said hotly.

He nodded, anger transforming his normal good cheer. "Her son should be horsewhipped. The apoplexy may have more to do with her age, but starvation made her vulnerable and will certainly impact her recovery."

"What happens now?"

"Barry has some patient rooms. She will stay for several days for Barry to assess how much damage the attack caused and for us to make sure she eats."

"She won't take charity, Edmund. Aunt Imogene and I have tried, you must know that."

"She won't have a choice, or rather, her choice is here or the charity ward at the General Hospital. We need to feed her while we can."

They found her sleeping when they looked in. Mrs. Barry had dressed her in a loose, comfortable gown and put her in bed. Lucy spoke with the physician's wife in hushed tones, assuring her that she would not be without help. Mrs. Barry slipped out to take a look at the woman with the child.

Convinced her friend would be well until morning, Lucy left Lady Hardy's cloak and reticule and let Edmund lead her out. "Dr. Barry sends his thanks. He left to call on a patient," he told her.

"You knew what was wrong immediately, didn't you?" she asked while he helped her with her cloak.

"Yes, but not what to do about it—and I wasn't certain how bad an attack we witnessed. Barry knew. He handled her brilliantly. I have much to learn."

"You said that before—that you have much to learn. Do you intend to study, then?"

"That's what I meant to talk to you about today. My degree is finished, and I have a year of medical lectures behind me. Barry thinks I can be licensed based on that and my clinic time."

A dozen questions rushed like bees into Lucy's mind. For a moment, she could only stand in the narrow passageway to Dr. Barry's premises and stare at the man she had come to care for. His proximity and the spicy aroma of his cologne got in the way of coherent thought.

His eyes never left hers. "What is it, Lucy?"

"Aren't the teaching hospitals in London?" she whispered.

"That isn't entirely true. Barry thinks the bishop can

license me to practice here, especially if I put in some time observing at a local hospital."

"You would stay here in Bath?" She sounded breathless even to herself and trailed off in a self-conscious fluster, wondering if Aunt Imogene would let her stay indefinitely. *Can he hear the hope in my voice? He must think me forward.*

He turned to the door and offered his arm, leading her out to the street. "It isn't quite that simple," he said at last. "I have to get references from lecturers at Oxford and from Cartwright. Barry, of course will help. Even if I'm licensed and all goes smoothly, I'll have to find rooms and obtain equipment and supplies. It will be very dear."

Lucy didn't stop walking with her eyes forward, but she screwed up her brow, puzzled. *Edmund is wealthy, isn't he? How can he worry about costs?* The answer came to her in a rush. "Your parents won't like it. Will your father put stumbling blocks in your way?"

"They will hate it, and yes. I think it likely he will cut off my funds." He turned sharply toward her. "I don't mind for myself. I don't need luxury, and I want to stand on my own."

"But to set up a practice..."

"It may be difficult to do that or—or anything else," he finished in a rush and continued walking.

Lucy tried to tame her unruly thoughts, afraid to believe he might mean a wife or to hope it might be her.

After a moment, he stopped again. This time, he faced her and went on, "I can't speak further until I know exactly how I stand. Mother wrote to Father asking him to intervene when she knew I was helping at Barry's clinic. She wrote twice, but he never replied. I must go back to London to confront him. I can't make plans until I know. Do you understand, Lucy?"

They had come to the edge of Spring Garden, thick with

bushes. He pulled her out of sight of passersby and cupped her face with his hands. He studied her face as if it held the secret to his life. She hoped it did.

He scrutinized her with such intensity she thought he might scorch her face. She could hardly breathe, much less answer. When he groaned and lowered his head for a gentle kiss, he chased the last of her thoughts away. His lips touched hers softly, moving first to one side and then the other. She returned the favor, mimicking his motions with ones of her own.

He must have liked it because he put his arms around her back, pulled her closer, and opened his mouth to nibble her lower lip. She moaned and opened her mouth to him. He moved his open mouth across hers, sending sensations exploding in her entire body. He lifted his head and let his hands slide down her back before he dropped them to his side.

"I have to speak with my father, Lucy. Do you understand? I can't—"

She put two fingers on his mouth to silence him. "I know," she sighed. "Do what you must."

They walked to Aunt Imogene's home in silence. In the morning, he was gone.

Chapter Nine

Lady Hardy fussed when Lucy brought in a tray at dinnertime. "Can't 'ford pay," she complained. In the week she had been Dr. Barry's guest, her speech had improved, and her grumbling signaled that she became more her old self every day.

"Hush, my lady. Dr. Barry ordered me to feed you this supper, so eat it you shall," Lucy replied, unable to hide her smile. Lucy fed her every night and could therefore judge the tiny steps by which her friend improved day by day. She missed Edmund horribly and threw herself into the work to keep her mind occupied. It proved a mixed blessing.

The medical practice reminded her of Edmund and his ambitions, and it brought him closer when she worked there. He had departed for London without saying good-bye or stopping to see her, and he had not written to her.

"I should say not!" Aunt Imogene had pointed out tartly. "Lord Edmund is too well behaved to correspond with a young lady. It isn't done, Lucy, you must know that. He would have to travel all the way to Herefordshire to ask your father's permission to do that."

Lucy wished he might be a little less honorable for once,

but no letters were forthcoming. When the second week passed, her worries increased. She wondered if he really had been hinting he might pay his addresses to her when he returned. His parents would never approve. They would want an earl's daughter, at least.

Long days in Barry's clinic or at his practice caring for Lady Hardy left her exhausted, but happy. *If Edmund could begin such work and I could help him . . .* The thought lodged in her heart—her dearest dream.

The days crawled by, and her worst fears began to dominate her heart. *Has he fallen into London's delights so deeply that he lost his interest in being a physician and Bath no longer draws his attention? London ladies are so much more sophisticated than I am.* The very worst came to her every night when she stared into the dark. *Has he forgotten me?*

"I'm well. You must let me go home," Lady Hardy insisted at the end of the second week. Dr. Barry told Lucy to do whatever she could to keep the old woman there for a month, until she was strong enough and better nourished.

Lucy handed her the spoon and held a bowl in front of her. They had progressed to a richer stew from the basic broths of the beginning. The woman's hand shook when she gripped the spoon and tried to dip it into the stew, leaving splatters on the towel Lucy had placed on her front. "Let me do that," Lucy said gently. She began to spoon the stew into the woman's mouth.

"Miss Ashcroft, please come." Mrs. Barry stood in the door, looking worried.

"I'll be right back," Lucy told Lady Hardy, laying a comforting hand on her shoulder.

"What is it?" Lucy asked, coming into the passageway.

"Someone wants to see Lady Hardy," the physician's wife explained.

It couldn't be Aunt Imogene or the other ladies. They came in turns at noon to help and hardly needed to ask. Her heart leaped. *Edmund?* "Who is it?" she demanded.

"A man claiming to be Baron Hardy, her son. He is pacing the reception room like an angry bear."

A stout, bluff-looking man with coarse, close-cropped, brown hair and a square face spun on well-shod heels when they entered. He wore a brown suit much rumpled from travel and a plainly knotted neck cloth.

"Where is my mother?" he demanded.

"Baron Hardy?" Lucy asked.

"Who else would I be? I've been told she's here."

"Your mother has suffered apoplexy. We're caring for her here," Mrs. Barry told him.

"She hasn't seen you in several years," Lucy began.

"Neither here nor there, and not anyone's business. And who are you?" he shouted.

"I am Miss Lucy Ashcroft, Lady Hardy's friend."

"That man mentioned you. Some kind of hanger-on, are you?"

"I beg your pardon? Your mother lives alone with only the kindness of friends to keep her from utter ruin."

Baron Hardy's face had reached an alarming shade of red, whether from anger or shame, Lucy couldn't tell.

"If, as Miss Ashcroft says, she hasn't seen you in some time, my lord, your appearance may be a shock. In her fragile condition, you could cause a setback." Mrs. Barry spoke with her head high and hands clasped in front of her.

The baron drew in several large breaths, pulling himself under control. "I did not come here to harm the woman. I came here to see her condition for myself, as a son ought.

When that Lord Edmund Parker insulted me in my own home and told me—"

"Edmund came to see you?" Lucy gasped.

"Pushed in and accused me of failing in my duty—falsely, I might add. Where is my mother?"

Lucy straightened her back and tipped her chin. "Lord Edmund Parker doesn't lie, Lord Hardy. Did he tell you your mother lives in dire poverty? That she hasn't enough to eat? That the only reason she didn't die was because her attack happened in front of friends?"

Baron Hardy's mouth tightened to a thin line. "Show me to my mother," he ground out through stiff lips and stalked toward the door. Lucy scurried to slip in front of him and hurried down the hall.

"Lady Hardy," she said with a forced smile when she burst through the door, "someone is here to see you." The baron followed on her heels.

"Penrod!" Lady Hardy pushed up on her elbows, eyes wide with shock. Lucy turned to chastise the baron and found an identical expression on his face.

"Mama?" Lord Hardy groaned. "What has happened to you?" He dropped to a chair at her side.

"Is it truly you, Penrod? I thought you forgot me as soon as you abandoned me."

"Abandoned you? You and Mildred couldn't get along, and we agreed Bath was best, did we not? I never abandoned you. I left Mr. Jenkins instructions . . ."

"You never wrote," his mother cried, tears flowing, "and it took all of the pittance you sent me to pay for my room. I had naught for food the last of each quarter. How could you leave me like this?"

"That devil Jenkins told me you had a respectable suite of

rooms—even asked for more, and I gave it willingly," he sputtered. "I don't understand this."

"But you never answered my letters." She cried harder. "I begged and begged you . . ."

"I didn't get any letters. How did you send them?"

"I—" Lady Hardy's voice cracked. "Oh, God. I gave them to Jenkins to send you. I had no coin for the post."

Lucy put a hand to the wall to steady herself. "We would have posted them for you, my lady. You know Aunt Imogene would have."

The lady turned her head away. "I won't take charity," she whispered.

Baron Hardy took his mother's hand. "I'm sorry, Mama. Jenkins is a scoundrel," he said.

Lucy thought the man might have checked instead of trusting his man of business, but she kept her counsel and opened the door to leave.

"Miss Ashcroft, may I have the honor of calling on you and your aunt tomorrow?" Baron Hardy asked.

She retrieved her card from her reticule and gave it to the man. "We take waters at the Pump Room in the morning. Your mother knows our habits," she told him. By the time she left, he had begun to feed his mother awkwardly but with determination.

Lucy walked home with a surge of pride. *Edmund visited Baron Hardy—and did a thorough job of it! What else has he done these past weeks?*

Chapter Ten

Edmund watched Michaels pack a valise and tried not to interfere, even though he had already dispensed with the man's services. The valet meant it kindly and took pride in his work, for which the Marquess of Waringford paid him well. However harsh Edmund's father might choose to be with his son, he would not fail to pay a servant.

"Here you are, my lord. Bare necessities for your journey," the man said with a frown. "Shall I have a footman carry it to the foyer?"

"I believe I can handle it," Edmund responded, containing his amusement. "I will have to from now on, won't I?"

Michaels shifted from one foot to another, an uncharacteristic sign of agitation. "If I may be so bold, sir, I shall miss being in your service, even if—"

"Even if I take less care of my appearance than a gentleman ought?" Edmund finished with a twinkle.

"As her ladyship says, my lord. I wish you well in your work. Medicine is a noble calling, if not an activity in which fashionable gentlemen generally participate."

Edmund had no response to that pronouncement. Being a physician ranked low in the social ladder, a few short steps above the unthinkable—engaging in trade. Michaels leaned forward to whisper nervously, as if he feared being overheard, "It's a noble thing you do, and make no mistake."

Edmund took his leave before they both became maudlin, and carried his valise to the front door, where the butler informed him, with a ferocious frown of disapproval, that his hackney had not yet arrived.

Another expense, he thought, mentally husbanding every penny, *but I can't walk to the coaching inn in a timely fashion.*

"Is His Lordship in his study?" Edmund asked and, upon being assured his father was indeed in his office, set off in that direction.

His mother had taken to her bed after the final row and would not speak to him. *You would think I proposed to disappear into Africa and go native,* he thought. *Or open a gambling den, although she might approve of that one.* She vowed never to set foot in Bath again, which, all in all, might be for the best.

"Enter," his father growled in response to his knock. The old man scanned Edmund's traveling coat and suit with distaste, a familiar response.

"My transport should be here momentarily. I wanted to take my leave."

"Come to face me, have you? I'll give you that. Have you informed Philmont?"

"I wrote to Charles last night. It is in the morning post." He left unspoken the fact that Charles had urged him to follow his dreams the previous summer. Parental wrath on Charles's head wouldn't help Edmund one iota.

"I'm not dying. I'm removing to Bath. I'll see Charles again," he went on. He didn't ask whether or when his parents would receive him again.

The marquess grunted. "There's no turning you from

this road, is there." It wasn't a question. The old man shook his grizzled head and scowled ferociously. "I won't wish you well. Don't expect it."

The odd statement took Edmund aback. "I wouldn't expect it. You made your disapproval plain. I wish you well, Father; I hope we meet again before too long." He hesitated from old habit, waiting to be dismissed.

The marquess laid a fisted hand over an envelope on his desk. "If you can't make us proud, at least don't disgrace us in Bath. Gossip travels, and your nephews would suffer." He glared without wavering at Edmund, who had no response to this outburst, but he held his father's gaze without shirking. It was his father who looked away. He shrank a little, picking up the envelope and holding it out.

"Go on, take it," the old man said. "There won't be more. If you fail, let it be on your head." He picked up a pen and made a show of going back to his work.

Edmund held the packet for a long moment before tucking it in his coat. "Thank you, Father," he said.

The marquess did not look up, and Edmund took that for the intended dismissal. He didn't look at the contents of the envelope until the hackney pulled away from his parents' house. When he did, he found a generous portion. It didn't constitute a fortune, but he thought it enough to purchase a modest house suitable for medical offices. He closed his eyes against tears that threatened and let hope—and gratitude— push out the grief he had harbored. His father loved him.

The stiff seat of the hackney provided none of the comfort of his mother's well-sprung carriage, but Edmund leaned against it happily. The road to Bath lay open before him.

I have one more stop to make first.

When weeks turned into a month without word from Edmund, Lucy trudged home from Lady Hardy's new apartment with sagging shoulders, thoroughly dejected.

She continued to attend the lady daily, even after Baron Hardy moved his mother to a set of rooms near Mrs. Wellbridge and his affairs to a new man of business suggested by Aunt Imogene. Relations between mother and son remained strained, but they both agreed it was best if she remained in Bath. He left with a promise of regular visits.

His offer of a small stipend for Lucy—"a token of gratitude for your kindness and generous friendship"—stunned her, but she accepted it eagerly. Nursing Lady Hardy gave her a sense of purpose. Her growing competence in the task gave her pride. Life as a physician's wife would suit her perfectly. Of that, she had no doubt, but the thought drove her spirits into the ground.

If only Edmund came, I might actually be happy, she thought, climbing the steps to her aunt's townhouse.

"A letter come for you, miss," the maid, Erma, said, taking her cloak and bonnet. "I put it on the mantel in the sitting room."

Edmund? Heart racing, Lucy hurried into her aunt's tiny sitting room and grabbed the folded bundle of paper from the simple wooden mantelpiece in the center of the room, avidly scanning the address. Her heart sank. She dropped into a deeply cushioned chair.

"Lucy, dear, I heard you come in. I—Oh my. Bad news, is it? You look despondent," Aunt Imogene clucked with concern, seating herself beside Lucy.

"It is from Stepmama, of course." Lucy held the unopened missive by one corner and waved it in the air, too miserable to care.

"Your patient, then? Has Agnes taken a turn for the worse?"

"No, she is right as rain, improving every day."

"What, then?"

"Mrs. Wellbridge stopped to see Lady Hardy. She had been to see Dr. Barry and brought fresh potions for our patient." She drew breath to continue, the words sticking in her throat. "She saw Lord Edmund."

Aunt Imogene sat up straight. "Lord Edmund? Back in Bath? Was she certain?"

"As certain as can be without actually speaking with him. She noticed him near the Pulteney Bridge walking toward Dr. Barry's premises, which she had just left. He didn't see her."

"Why—" Aunt Imogene began but did not complete the thought.

"Why has he not called or even appeared in the Pump Room? I asked myself that all the way home. Perhaps he has no wish to continue the acquaintance. Perhaps his parents have forbidden it."

Lucy stood up and paced to the window, staring out as if she might conjure Edmund from the ether and bring him to the door. She heard Aunt Imogene order tea without turning to look. The older lady believed tea healed all ills.

"Come sit and read your stepmother's missive. Perhaps there is happy news from Little Hocking."

Lucy looked at the papers in her hand. She did not care to read Stepmama's words gushing over Elise's coming Season but knew her aunt would give her no peace until she did.

The letter showed signs of a difficult journey via the mails. A muddy footprint gave evidence of it falling at least once. Indeed, when she opened it, the message appeared to have been written at least two weeks before. She scanned it quickly.

"Do tell, Lucy. Don't dawdle over the thing," Aunt Imogene urged. "That frown tells you found more news not to your liking."

"Elise is not to have a Season after all," Lucy gasped. "Her illness delayed any hope of London before the Little Season, and now even that is not to happen. She has accepted an offer with Papa's blessing, but Stepmama is not pleased. She is quite put out, in fact."

"Why on earth?"

"Stepmama had such hopes for her eldest, and now Elise has accepted a man she met at a local assembly. Stepmama describes him as 'merely a farmer,' and calls his cousin—who is an earl, no less—as 'distant as the moon.'" Lucy smiled sadly at that exaggeration. "Oh, Aunt, can't you just see Stepmama's dramatic sigh, arm protectively across her eyes, moaning about ungrateful children?" She mimicked the thought, bringing a disapproving glare.

"If he is Elise's choice, then surely you must be happy for her!" Aunt Imogene said.

"I am—truly. If he is worthy, rank doesn't matter." Lucy dropped the paper, scrunched between both hands, into her lap. "Elise married! I wish her every happiness." Her lip twisted a bit, and she returned her aunt's concerned gaze. "Very well. I confess to envy, Aunt, at least a bit. I won't let it color my love for my sister, do not fear." Her heart felt as if a giant hand had ripped it out and squeezed it. *I let myself hope, fool that I am.*

"Why do I suspect there is more?"

"There is. Stepmama wishes me to return home. She writes, 'If Elise must do this thing in the village, we will make the best of it. I will require your assistance, Lucy, if we are to put on the wedding breakfast that reflects our consequence. Come home as soon as you can manage the thing.'"

"She means *you* will put on a wedding breakfast to impress the neighbors. That hardly seems fair to me," Aunt Imogene sputtered.

Lucy moaned silently. *It isn't. Merciful angels; it is not fair, but I'll do it for Elise.* "I shall have to notify Lord Hardy that I can't continue to accept his kind stipend."

"Never say you plan to give in to that stepmother of yours!"

"How can I not, Aunt Imogene? Would you have me wait until Papa orders me home? From the looks of this missive, I have already been delayed well past when she expected me to respond. No, I think it best if I simply pack my things and go."

"But, Lucy dear, what if—"

"Don't weave dreams of fairy silk, Aunt Imogene. I will send the butcher's boy to arrange transportation and pack immediately."

Every step toward her room felt like one more step toward dreary spinsterhood in Little Hocking, caring for Stepmama's ever-growing brood, brightened only by visits to Aunt Imogene. *Even that will not lighten my life if Edmund is here but has no wish to see me.*

Chapter Eleven

The too-small gilded chair offered to Edmund forced him to stretch his legs out, only to pull them back. He struggled to be still while the clock ticked and he waited.

"The ladies will be ever so glad to see you, my lord," the little maid had chirped. "Especially Miss Lucy. She said—" The girl clapped a hand over her mouth at that and hustled off to fetch Mrs. Crane, closing him in the claustrophobic sitting room.

He didn't want Mrs. Crane. He wanted his Lucy. After a full half hour elapsed, however, he wished either one would appear. His fantasy of his true love greeting him at the door and throwing herself into his arms lay in ashes. He couldn't tell how long it had been since the maid left, but it felt like hours.

"Oh, thank the angels you are here, Lord Edmund." Mrs. Crane bustled into the sitting room still wearing her cloak and bonnet, cheeks red and breath heaving. "I was at Mary Wellbridge's bemoaning the news when Erma sent word you were here. I'm so sorry you had to wait. You may still be in time, but you will have to hurry."

"Hurry? I beg your patience, Mrs. Crane, but I don't understand."

Lucy's aunt wrung her hands. "You came to call on Lucy, did you not? She's gone. That stepmother of hers has ordered her home to assist with her sister's wedding. She left for the coaching inn an hour ago. God knows how soon the coach will depart."

Leaving? "But I—"

"Don't gape, boy. There isn't time!"

She didn't have to tell him twice. Edmund left the house at a sprint in the direction she gave him.

He skidded into the inn yard to see the mail coach pulling out onto the road north. He had no time to ask if it was the coach to Herefordshire. Grateful for congestion on the road, he reached the horse's heads while they still kept to a slow pace, grabbed on to the harness, and shouted to the driver to stop.

"Trying to get kilt, are ya? You best have good reason, you," the driver glowered, but the vehicle halted.

Edmund didn't wait to answer. He yanked the door open while the driver shouted at him to stop and called inside, "Miss Lucy Ashcroft?" No one answered. His eyes adjusted to the gloom, and he could see for himself. She wasn't there. He slammed the door shut and turned back to the inn, the driver shouting rude curses behind him.

He didn't plan to wait for the next coach to Herefordshire. He would hire a horse, a luxury he could ill afford. *She said she would wait*, he told himself angrily. *Now I will have to follow her all the way back to—* "Lucy!"

"Edmund?" The source of his hopes and frustrations blinked back at him across the room. She stood with a valise at her feet, dressed for travel.

He strode across the room, prepared to berate her for

leaving him.

She pounced before he could speak. "Perhaps you wish to explain why you left me with expectations and then sent no word for over a month."

"I did not give you expectations! How could I when I wasn't sure of my situation? I was careful not to." His face heated with the memory of that kiss. *Of course she had expectations, you bloody fool.* "Lucy, I'm sorry I took so long. I went to Oxford first to seek out Stallings for an endorsement. The old rip made me wait three days while he grilled me on my knowledge, but in the end, I got what I wanted."

She stood in silence, her chin up, as if to say, "That accounts for *three* of the days . . ."

He glanced around, seeing avid stares in every direction, and lowered his voice to a whisper. "Lucy, this is hardly the place for this conversation. Can we go someplace private?"

"When did you return to Bath?" she demanded again. "And why didn't you call?" Her voice cracked on that last, and his heart did as well, and he understood his error.

"It's easier to show you," he answered, picking up her valise and pulling her by the hand. She scowled at him once, and he thought she would object, but she followed him.

He led her as rapidly as he could without tripping toward the neighborhood near the Pulteney Bridge until they stopped in a street lined with stone houses, an identical row of modest residences several years old, each with the same white door three steps above street level.

"Edmund, slow down and tell me what this is about!"

They stopped in front of number twelve, a house with the knocker removed. Dead flowers filled pealing boxes, and the window frames needed paint. Edmund pulled a key from his pocket and unlocked the front door, holding it open for her. Her eyes grew wide staring up at the house and back to the door.

He reached for her in exasperation and pulled her inside the empty house. Scraps of paper littered the dusty floor of the foyer. He had hoped to clean the place up first, but so be it!

"The rooms at street level are big enough. I can build a surgery in here," he began, walking into a room obviously intended as a sitting room. "The drawing room across the foyer can serve as a waiting room."

Lucy, who had been gaping at the fireplace, spun around. "Your father approves of your plans?"

"Hardly! He's cut me off. 'Until I come to my senses,' he says. But I know my heart. I've met with Dr. Barry, and he agreed to take me on as an apprentice. Barry says Bath can well support a hundred decent physicians—-it supports enough charlatans."

He sobered then and gathered both of her hands in his. "Father has cut off my allowance and made it clear no more assistance will be forthcoming, but he gave me enough to purchase this house. I have to succeed—or fail—on my own."

Compassion shone through Lucy's eyes, her own feelings consumed in sorrow over his family's rejection. He cleared his throat, discomfort making him shy.

"I own the house outright, and a small estate in Devon. It provides little income, but enough I think to pay for the household. This floor will make a surgery, and the upstairs is large enough for living quarters." He searched her dear face and found only confusion. "I should be able to set up a household, although life will be lean for a few years until I'm a full physician and begin to build a practice."

I'm babbling. No wonder she looks confused. "If you are worried about my parents, I think they'll come around in a few years, particularly once there are grandchildren."

Lucy paled, shocked at his words.

He shook his head. "I'm bungling this." He reached for her where she stood still as a statue.

Grandchildren? She blinked rapidly, her thoughts a jumble. When he took her hands and pulled her closer, she couldn't think at all.

"Lucy, don't you see? Before I encountered a certain determined lady at the Pump Room, I floated through life, aimless and confused, allowing my parents to dictate my dreams. When I met you, the pieces fell into place for me. I—" He groaned and glanced upward. "Damn it, Lucy!"

Arms gentle but determined, he pulled her flush against his chest, holding her firmly in his arms. His mouth covered hers in tender salute that gentled and teased along her lips. She gasped, surprised by his impetuous behavior, but shock gave way to a tentative response. When his exploration of her mouth and neck continued, an instinctive need to mimic his actions took over. She slipped her hands up to his neck and into his thick black hair, holding him close.

He pulled away at last over her whimper of protest and nestled her head against his shoulder. After a shuddering breath, he rasped, "I will take that answer as a yes."

Yes? Lucy stiffened. She put both hands on his chest and pushed. He let her go immediately. "My dear Lord Edmund. I don't recall being asked a question. How could there be an answer?" She lifted her chin and attempted to glare. She suspected from the laughter in his eyes that she was unsuccessful.

Edmund gave a dramatic bow and dropped to one knee in front of her. "Miss Ashcroft, I present my humble self as a candidate for your hand in marriage. I realize my means are not of the highest, but I offer this hearth and home—" He gestured at the room dramatically with one arm. When Lucy tried to interrupt, he held up a hand and shook his head, cleared his throat and went on, "I must make you aware that a physician's wife must be his partner in all things. Hard work will be required." Again, he silenced her with a raised brow and pointed glare. "Please allow me to finish." At that pronouncement, Lucy's laughter spilled over, but he continued anyway, "Will you do me the honor of—"

Lucy dropped to her knees and kissed him, finally silencing his ridiculous speech and knocking him over in the process. "Yes. Yes. Yes. Of course I'll marry you," she said between kisses to his chin, his eyes, his cheek, and back to his tempting mouth.

Edmund rolled over and pulled her to a sitting position, gripping her hand with his. "That's the reaction I rather hoped for in the first place," he said, laughing. "We need to wed soon before there is much more of this delightful activity."

Lucy bit her lip. "Banns take three weeks. It will take at least that long to plan a wedding."

His smile melted her heart. "You'll want to prepare a dress, plan a breakfast, and invite the Circle to attend."

She nodded as he pulled her to her feet. "But there's more. Stepmama has ordered me home to Little Hocking, Edmund. I don't want to step on Elise's day." Another thought struck her hard enough to make the color leach from her face. "Papa!" she said. "We need to ask my father's blessing."

His grin broadened. "Didn't I say? We have his enthusiastic blessing. That is another thing that kept me away. The road to Little Hocking gave me a miserable time."

"You spoke to my father?" she gasped.

"Of course. I wanted to do it properly—" What else he might have said was drowned in a flood of more kisses. At least this time they stayed upright.

"There's more," he said, smiling against her mouth.

She pulled back to blink up at him. "From Papa?"

"Yes, but mostly from your stepmother. She is quite in a dither, even though I made it plain the marquess and marchioness would not attend our wedding. She thinks perhaps Bath is a more suitable venue for the wedding of an exalted person such as myself."

"Your parents won't attend our wedding?"

"*Persona non grata*, remember? Your stepmother will have to be content with my brother, the viscount. He and his family will assuredly attend."

"But here in Bath?"

"At this very moment, they are preparing to bring Elise, her betrothed, and your charming gaggle of younger siblings to Bath by the end of the month, after I made it clear I would brook no delay. We'd best warn your aunt about the coming invasion."

"You've thought of everything!"

He looked around the room and ran the hand not cradling hers over the back of his neck ruefully. "Our house isn't exactly ready for you, Lucy."

"'Our house.' I like that. We only need a room or two to start. A kitchen, a sitting room, a bedroom." Heat flushed her cheeks. "Can you show me the rest? It's the place where we will care for people, care for one another, and, God willing, care for our children. We'll be happy here, Edmund, I'm sure of it."

And so they were. Doctor Lord Edmund Parker and his wife and helpmate cared for the elderly and infirm in the house at number twelve while raising a brood of six children in the upper stories and enjoying visits from their many relatives. They followed their dreams into contented old age, still together at number twelve, even happier than Lucy predicted.

THE END

About Caroline Warfield

Traveler, poet, librarian, technology manager—award-winning author Caroline Warfield has been many things (even a nun), but she is, above all, a romantic. Having retired to the urban wilds of eastern Pennsylvania, she reckons she is on at least her third act, happily working in an office surrounded by windows while she lets her characters lead her to adventures in England and the far-flung corners of the British Empire. She nudges them to explore the riskiest territory of all, the human heart.

She is the author of the Dangerous Series, set in the Regency Era, and the Children of Empire Series, set in the late Georgian/early Victorian era. The second series follows the lives of the children of characters in the first.

You can find her at www.carolinewarfield.com

The Fine Art of Kissing in the Park

By Jaima Fixsen

Caroline Warfield

OTHER BOOKS BY JAIMA FIXSEN

Fairchild
Incognita
Courting Scandal
The Reformer
Power of the Matchmaker
Dark Before Dawn

Chapter One

The house in London belonged to Grandmama, but the place looked more like Christopher's every year. Thick political treatises had crowded out the traveler's accounts in the library, and modest Sheraton furniture supplanted the unseemly baroque. It was an elegant, stylish place—home now to both of them.

Neither Caroline nor her elder brother had reason to expect Grandmama's arrival that wintry evening, though Caroline, who'd advised against decorator depredations, welcomed Grandmama with a clearer conscience, beckoning her into the hall away from the icy draft. "Come inside," she said. "You must be half froze!"

Grandmama, hugging her furs close, couldn't clasp Caroline's outstretched hands, but she offered a thin-lipped smile.

"We didn't expect you in town." Christopher was too flummoxed to offer more than the obvious.

"Clearly not." Grandmama frowned at the Japanese marquetry box perching where her bust by Nollekens used to be. "I'd like my room, please." Behind her, the housekeeper's face took on the expression of an agony-stricken saint.

Caroline moved to the rescue. "It will take a few moments, I'm afraid. Come warm yourself in the drawing room." Over Grandmama's shoulder, Caroline met the housekeeper's eyes, signaling her to remove Christopher's things from the principal bedchamber. *Hurry,* she mouthed.

Of course Grandmama understood. "You may supervise the unpacking of my things, Caroline. I'd like a word with your brother."

Excluded by a firmly closed door, Caroline didn't hear their discussion. She turned her attention to other problems. The sheets in the linen cupboard were acceptable, so long as Grandmama never discovered Christopher used better ones. Caroline could bring over the flowers from her own dressing table. With the card left off, Grandmama wouldn't know they were from Robert—which would be best, as she'd never taken warmly to Caroline's fiancé. Caroline fetched the fussy ornaments Grandmama loved, lately relegated to the guest chambers, swept up her brother's remaining books, and headed downstairs to hurry along the hot water bottles—just as Christopher emerged from the drawing room muttering under his breath about Grandmama's profanity.

"I always said you shouldn't take her room, Kit," Caroline reminded him.

"She hasn't been to London in years! Why she must descend upon us now—"

Caroline hushed him and steered him into the library, where he could solace his pride with books and a brandy. "Let me handle Grandmama. You must get ready for this evening." Caroline didn't want anything upsetting him.

She settled Kit at his desk, shelved the books that had been in Grandmama's room—organized by topic, year, and author—and found her grandmother seated in the armchair nearest the drawing room fire, waving her lacquered stick at

Caroline's dog. Caroline dashed forward, scooping a growling Ormonde off the hearthrug.

"In all the bustle I forgot Ormonde likes to come in here."

If Grandmama had struck him . . . Caroline ran her hands over his forelegs and head, and he stopped quivering, going soft in her arms. In the next days, she'd have to keep him and Grandmama away from each other.

"When are you going to train him? He's a menace."

"He's still a baby." Caroline sat on the sofa, holding her dog close. "I imagine he takes exception to your shoe buckles." They flashed in the firelight on the toes of Grandmama's outmoded, high-heeled shoes. "What brings you to London?" Caroline asked.

"John Coachman and these catastrophically bad roads." Grandmama recrossed her ankles, and Ormonde tensed.

Rubbing the spaniel's belly, Caroline set to work soothing them both. Grandmama only snorted when Caroline reported Kit's selection to two parliamentary committees—in his first term!—but Caroline guessed she was pleased. Grandmama was less pleased when Caroline insisted she warm her insides with tea instead of brandy. Nevertheless, she accepted a steaming cup, grumbling that she could hold her liquor very well and that she'd never met such a pack of insufferables as the younger generation. Caroline served her a slice of frosted lemon cake, which soon vanished. Her own piece, she crumbled into bits and fed them one by one to Ormonde.

Informed that Kit's initiatives in the house included a water closet and a closed stove in the kitchen, Grandmama gave signs of reluctant approval.

"And a new chef," Caroline added. "French. You'll enjoy the way he prepares the poultry."

"Still entertaining the world? You shouldn't let your brother make free with your money."

Caroline wouldn't restart this old argument. "I like hostessing. Our parties are as much for my sake as Kit's."

"Does that stuffed shirt of yours often dine here?"

"I don't know who you mean," Caroline lied, unwilling to hear criticism of Robert. If she listened to her grandmother, she'd be waiting for some dashing but pedigreed seventeenth-century cavalier. Such men existed only in novels and old portraits. Caroline had decided long ago that romance was out of fashion. This was the age of reason, and she was no porcelain shepherdess. She had a great deal of affection for Sir Robert Symes, who, if all went well tonight, would soon be a cabinet minister. Besides helping Kit's career, as Sir Robert's wife she'd have plenty of meaningful work—dinners, drafting memoranda, perhaps even watching key debates in parliament... Robert was a methodical man, but an excellent speaker.

"Chosen a wedding date yet?"

"The way you feel about him, I'm surprised you're always pressing for one," Caroline returned evenly.

"After two and a half years, I'm surprised you haven't forgotten," Grandmama said. "I would."

Caroline ignored this, tickling Ormonde, who was restless.

Kit joined them once he'd changed his dress for evening, and Caroline took the opportunity to shut her dog in his basket. Grandmama turned sharp again, and Kit, never good at appeasement, only grudgingly performed the courtesies, taxing Caroline's skill at domestic diplomacy.

"I'm so pleased with Kit," she said, hoping to force a smile from Grandmama. "Member for Penryn at the same age as our father." It meant a good deal to them both.

"*He* was a Tory too," Grandmama said glumly.

The Fine Art of Kissing in the Park

"Wish Kit well, won't you?" Caroline urged. "It's not every night your grandson dines with the Prime Minister."

Grandmama was less impressed than Caroline had hoped, and positively scowled when a noise in the hall made Kit start for the door saying, "That'll be Robert."

"I'll be only a moment," Caroline said and followed her brother. He didn't hear her silent approach—even if Grandmama's teetering pumps were still in fashion, Caroline was too tall for anything but flat-soled slippers—and started when she hissed, "You didn't tell me Robert was coming!"

"Thought I mentioned it the other afternoon."

"I don't recall it," Caroline said, falling in beside him.

Kit shrugged. Robert was ahead of them, standing by the front door. Kit grinned at him. "Think this is it?"

"Difficult to say." Robert stretched his neck inside his starched collar.

"I'll be thinking of you all night," Caroline told him. "He wants you to replace Aldridge. I can feel it."

Robert took her hands. "I hope so, but one never knows. He might want Kit."

"Yes, in a year or two." She smiled at her brother. Since winning his seat in the election four years ago, he'd moved from the backbenches, but a seat in the cabinet was premature. Robert, a ten-year veteran of the House of Commons, would have this vacancy. She hoped.

Feeling Robert's arms stiffening, Caroline freed her hands. After the first moment of greeting, Robert never seemed to know what to do with them, and she didn't like making him uncomfortable. "Good luck." She smiled at him.

He shifted his feet. "If you're right, we'll have to set our minds to choosing a wedding date."

"I would like that." Pushing for a date had always seemed lowering, but fresh from Grandmama's company, with Robert on the brink of success, Caroline couldn't resist this little nudge.

"Good idea," Kit put in. "Our grandmother's arrived, and if I know anything, she's been giving Caroline an earful. Doesn't approve of long engagements."

Caroline gave him a sharp look, which he ignored.

"Upset the countess, have I?" Robert smiled at Caroline sympathetically. "Don't let her sit up too long. Not healthy at her age. And don't you wait up either. We'll be late."

Keeping back a warning not to broach too many bottles—she'd learned politicians accomplished nothing without sufficient quantities of wine—Caroline let her brother plant a kiss on her cheek on his way out the door. Robert hesitated, his eyes on the hat clutched in his restless fingers, so Caroline leaned forward, making it easy for him. His lips brushed her hairline. "I'll come see you in the morning," he murmured. "We'll get things settled."

"I'd like that," Caroline said again.

Robert donned his hat. "Until tomorrow, then. Give my regards to Lady Lynher."

Grandmama wouldn't want them, but Caroline kept silent.

"Come on, Robert!" Responding to Kit's impatient summons, Robert bowed and followed him into the cold. The draft swirled around Caroline's ankles, prickling her bare arms. There would be frost tonight.

In spite of the chill, Caroline lingered in the hall. *Let him do well.* One wish would serve both men. Though she knew it was foolish to hope too much, she wanted the post for Robert and for Kit to make a good impression tonight. If her father were still living and still in politics, Kit's progress would be easier—but then, his ambitions might be milder too, though he'd always been conscious of his position as the son of a younger son.

If all went as planned, tomorrow morning Kit would grin at her as Robert fiddled with his watch fob, blushing as he shared the good news. Perhaps a wedding as soon as February...

Ormonde barked, protesting his imprisonment. She'd better let him out. It would give her an excuse to cut short the coming tête-à-tête with Grandmama.

"Did he kiss you good night?" Grandmama asked. Reading the answer in Caroline's prim lips and arching eyebrows, she snorted again. "A peck on the cheek," she said disgustedly.

"Forehead." Caroline bent to free Ormonde, who frisked past her and ran a circuit of the room.

"Even worse. Man's a dead bore."

"Please remember I'm engaged to Sir Robert." Caroline pursued Ormonde behind the chair.

"Trust me, I've tried to forget. Are you sure he hasn't?" Grandmama drew her feet in just as Ormonde dashed by. Caroline caught him and lifted him up.

Two and a half years *was* a long time, but then Grandmama wouldn't understand. She'd never forgiven Caroline's father for turning Tory or understood Kit's ambitions to succeed him in the House of Commons. Why waste money on elections when, for much less, you could buy a commission in the army?

Caroline petted Ormonde's ears, giving herself time to find calm, watching a chunk of coal drop off the grate, its orange glow fading. Kit liked Robert, Uncle Warren liked Robert, she liked Robert. Grandmama's approval was hardly necessary. "I will like being married to a cabinet minister," Caroline told her. "And it will be useful for Kit." Grandmama would understand that. She might read novels, but she'd made a dynastic marriage herself. "I'll take Ormonde outside, put him to bed in my room, and then you and I can have a game of cards?"

As she'd predicted, Grandmama accepted this program. In the interest of peace, Caroline let Grandmama beat her.

Kit found her in the early morning, chalk-faced with smudges under his eyes. It was long before breakfast and unlike him to intrude in her room. Caroline sat up and pulled the sheets around her. "What's wrong?"

"I'm sorry, Caroline."

"He was passed over?" Caroline sighed, telling herself it was no good cutting up over it. Resigned, she climbed out of bed and pulled on her dressing gown. "Perhaps next time." Her voice was steady, her eyes on the tying of her sash.

Kit shook his head. "No, they gave him the post."

"Then why—" Caroline looked up. Her brother looked quite ill. "Ought you to sit down?"

Kit slumped into her chair. He was rumpled, stubble darkening his chin, wearing the same clothes he had left in. Just returned, then.

"I take it you both drank too much?"

He bit his lip. "Got a trifle out of hand," he finally admitted. "Went on long after dinner. I should have . . ."

Caroline folded her hands.

"John Cavendish began it. Rode a horse up the front stairs of the club. Robert tried and—"

"He'd never do such a thing." Robert was entirely too sensible for pranks like that.

"Said he'd do it. There was no stopping him." Awful

pleading filled Kit's eyes. And pity, sharp enough to make her look away.

Caroline pulled the neck of her dressing gown closer, blocking the cold. "Is he badly hurt?" She must go to him, if he wasn't too embarrassed.

Kit swallowed and ran a hand through his hair. "He's dead, Caroline. Neck broken."

She shook her head, dimly aware it was increasingly hard to breathe. She must have misheard. "Broken?" Dead was an unthinkable word to pronounce. She smoothed her hands down her dressing gown.

"It was so sudden. Nothing to be done." Kit's eyes fixed on hers, making it impossible to look away or keep disbelieving him. Certainty settled on her slowly, but it was too heavy to shift. Her empty hands were clumsy, too thick and stiff to move.

"I see."

Robert looked away, walking shakily to the window. "I'm so sorry, Caroline."

"Not your fault," Caroline replied mechanically. Robert would never be a cabinet minister. Or her husband. He was gone. "Thank you for telling me." They were her words, but they sounded like they came from someone else.

Chapter Two

Sixteen months later

Caroline was not pleased with the town of Bath. She was not pleased with the weather, though the view from the windows showed a clear spring sky. She was not pleased with the neat row of houses across the way or this bland one they'd rented on the corner of Camden Place and nowhere.

If Robert were living and she were his wife, she'd have purpose, place, and presence. But Robert was gone, the time for mourning past. Unattached at age twenty-four, she'd become a liability, a spinster. She'd hoped to find a match this spring in London. Kit had promised, but Uncle Warren had overruled, saying, "Someone has to stay with Grandmama."

Someone meant her, especially from Uncle Warren, and Kit had agreed. If Caroline didn't go to Bath, Grandmama would ambush them in London, and he couldn't very well keep her out of her own house. It wasn't convenient for him to be troubled with her just now. Caroline could rejoin him in the fall or next year's Season. She'd be twenty-five then—a fact that only accelerated her scattering thoughts.

Spinsterhood wasn't a terrible fate in London, where she could hope for a remedy. In Bath, you couldn't step anywhere without meeting a dozen of the tribe: toothy ladies with intellectual hobbies going three times a week to the library, jilts and jilted trying to live down the infamy, girls who were girls no longer, having missed their chance. Had she? No. She had sufficient fortune to buy a man, if it came to that. But she wouldn't. Robert had been an ambitious man, one she'd been proud of until the humiliating debacle of his death. Unfortunately, there were fewer acceptable choices at her age.

Times like this, she wished it were possible to explain to Robert how she'd been wronged. Youth had slipped by, and she, falsely secure in her lengthy engagement, hadn't troubled to think what would happen if the thing didn't come off. Only concern for her marketable assets kept her from grinding her teeth.

She had no appetite for breakfast. "I'm going to walk Ormonde," she told Grandmama and collected Ormonde's lead. Ormonde himself was trickier to find, but Caroline discovered him at last behind a tall-backed sofa, dismembering one of Grandmama's gloves. Pocketing it for discreet disposal later, she knotted the lead to his collar, and he took off like a rocket, barely waiting for the knot to be tied, slowing only to a gambol once they were outside the house.

Mincing around a puddle, he spotted a shiny black beetle, ate it, then anointed the nearest lamp post. He sniffed every one of the others until he spotted a scrap of paper lying in the street and lunged. Caroline urged him forward with a tug on the leash. He'd spent too much time yesterday in his basket because Grandmama hadn't wanted him loose in the carriage.

"Ormonde!" He stopped and looked at her, tongue lolling. Caroline smiled, for in spite of the glove, his quivering excitement was unfailingly cheering. She'd have gone mad this last year without him.

The early hour spared them the stares of genteel strollers

in stately parade to the Pump Room. Caroline wasn't looking forward to joining that, but Bath was less stuffy this early, with society abed and the sunrise making the houses blush. Watching a hopping warbler with yellow patches, Caroline forgot her dislike of this mannerly paradise, quaint and clockwork in rules and calendar.

The bird, a cheeky, fat fellow, lighted on a railing, rousing Ormonde to frantic complaint. Startled, the bird flew off, but Ormonde didn't hush. Fearing he'd soon wake whoever slumbered behind the nearest windows, Caroline hurried him around the corner, slipping into a long, unladylike stride.

She stepped off the flagway and onto the street, in case Ormonde was tempted to snuffle the sleepy-eyed dairymaid walking the other way. Behind them walked a blue-coated physician with serious, slanting brows. Except for the bird, no one paid her and Ormonde any mind. Ormonde dashed left and right, but mostly onward to the Circus, then the Crescent, and on to the park, where he would make certain the squirrel and bird populations were properly routed.

"One of these days you must acquire some manners," Caroline murmured. Ormonde yipped happily in reply, straining for the trees. Caroline let out a chuckle. "Grandmama will like you better when you learn to be more sedate." Perhaps that was hoping for miracles.

He was too flighty to come off the lead this morning, so Caroline let him tug her about the park. Ormonde slighted an elm, then charged after a squirrel who'd dared reveal his presence. Caroline was warm beneath her cloak and probably red in the cheeks when she saw her bootlace straggling onto the grass. She bent to tie it, fumbling in her haste. Ormonde's ears pricked.

"Stay," Caroline warned, but he ignored her. Caroline

groped for the leash just as Ormonde bounded across the grass, the lead slithering behind him.

"Ormonde! Come!"

As ever, it failed to check him. Soon he'd be out of sight. Caroline broke into a run. She was only halfway across the lawn when he vanished into the trees.

When she reached them, there was no sign of him. "Ormonde!"

She found two morning walkers startled by her shouting, but no brown-and-white dog, not even by a patch of toadstools, organisms Ormonde usually found reason to attack. Anxious now, she hurried around trees and hedges, calling without real hope. He could have run through the park altogether and found his way to the river or—

There. In the shade of a tree, Ormonde yelped and wriggled in a man's arms.

"Let go of my dog!" Caroline said, marching towards him. Instead of setting Ormonde onto the ground, he bent his head and whispered something. Ormonde went still.

"This scrap's yours?" the man asked.

"Yes. I've been looking everywhere." She stretched out her hands, but Ormonde nuzzled deeper into the man's shoulder, leaving white hairs on his coat.

He chuckled, speaking to the dog. "I know she's lovely, but are you acquainted with her?"

"He only occasionally sits on command," Caroline said, terse and blushing. "Answering questions is beyond him."

"How can I be sure he's yours?"

Caroline frowned. He couldn't mean it. Yes, there were creases around his mouth and eyes, but she couldn't tell if they were precursors to a teasing smile. His firm chin and the thread of white scar barely visible above one eye made her think he wasn't joking. "Who but his owner would want him?" she asked, exasperated.

"I'm rather taken with him. Seems a capital fellow." He bent his head to the dog again. "How about it? Will you come have a snooze on my hearth?" As he spoke, he stroked Ormonde's ears, eliciting a whine of ecstasy.

Time to put a stop to this. "A kind offer, but—"

He glanced up at her with an amused smile. "I didn't think I was inviting you. However, if you're willing—"

Caroline choked, unable to reply.

"She blushes perfectly," he murmured to Ormonde. "If she really belongs to you, then perhaps—"

"Let me have him." If she wasn't reasonably certain he was thinking about having *her* on his hearthrug, she wouldn't hesitate to snatch Ormonde. As it was, she couldn't touch him, let alone wrestle away her dog. "Please."

"His name is Ormonde?" the man asked. "Where did that come from?"

The rapid switch made her pause. "Named for James Butler, first Duke of Ormonde." Kit had liked the idea of naming the dog after a statesman, and Caroline hadn't wanted to call him Pitt.

"And you want him back, even though he's so faithless? Careful now. You might get your heart broken."

Caroline's eyes narrowed. What could he know of broken hearts? "I'm not afraid, I assure you," she said coolly. "He's young and high-spirited is all. My brother gave him to me."

His expression changed to a rueful grin. "I should have known this dog would get me in trouble. Will your brother call, offering me a choice of swords or pistols?"

Caroline's brows lifted in mock astonishment. "I hardly think so. I'll forget this by luncheon, so long as you give back my dog."

His smile turned calculating. "Is that a promise?"

"Assuredly."

"Then you may have him. If you pay his ransom first."

Ransom? Caroline felt her eyes go round—maddening, when she was resolved to exhibit only icy disdain.

He shifted Ormonde to one side. His joints—hips, knees, little fingers, even—moved with a swagger. "I'll give you this dog. For a kiss."

Not a peck on her forehead, Caroline was sure. In the thirty-one months of their engagement, Robert had never been this bold.

"Only because you swore you wouldn't tell," he explained. "It'll be our secret. I mustn't soil my reputation."

His reputation? Caroline seethed.

He lowered his voice, glancing left and right. "You see, I have a sister. If she ever heard, she'd roast me, but you looked too charming. I couldn't resist."

Shameless flattery, and yet . . . the way he looked at her, she believed him. He'd taken an immediate fancy to her—an experience entirely new. She felt unbalanced, ready to squeak, blush, or beg, but there was vitality running through her too. She'd cling to that. Caroline raised her chin. "First, give me the dog."

"For a moment, I thought you'd say he wasn't worth it."

She'd surprised him. She nearly laughed, it felt so marvelous. "Only just. My dog, if you please."

"You won't cut and run?" He looked younger now, the raffish edge gone.

Caroline shook her head.

"Then I'll take you at your word."

He released Ormonde into her arms and smiled expectantly, forcing Caroline to duck her chin and drop her eyes.

The Fine Art of Kissing in the Park

"This is secret," she said, playing for time. He stepped close—close enough she could sew on his coat buttons if she'd cared to. The top one hung a little loose. "I can't do it when you're watching me," Caroline whispered.

His lips parted, and his eyes fell shut. Released from paralysis, Caroline lifted up Ormonde, who lapped his wet tongue all the way up the man's lean cheek.

He recoiled in surprise, but Caroline was already running, Ormonde yipping as he bounced in her arms. Behind her, the man broke into laughter. Caroline threw a glance back—he was wiping his cheek with his handkerchief. "Serves you right! Next time, be more specific!"

He said something, but her heartbeat was too loud to make out the words. She didn't stop or look back again until she reached the house on Camden Place. The street was quiet, nearly all the window shades drawn. She was back in the land of rules again, straight and strict and immutable as geometry.

A safe place to be, she thought.

Jack Edwards watched her go. Yes, she was a fine one, but that did not give him permission to flirt with her. He couldn't have thought she'd really kiss him. He might allow himself to imagine questionable things about lovely young ladies, but such games weren't supposed to intrude on reality.

In the normal way of things, he was more disciplined—he was the respectable one in his family! Laura must be rubbing off on him; his sister was a rogue if there ever was one. If she'd witnessed this, she'd laugh herself to tears and tell him he had an unfortunate touch. "Kissed by a dog! You can do better," she'd say.

Well, she hadn't seen, and he'd never tell her. No one but the lady herself and Ormonde would know.

His walk had tired him. It was time to go home. The distance was far enough his ears should stop burning before he arrived. Shrugging off his self-consciousness—which didn't work, but it was worth a try—Jack set off in the opposite direction, going around the trees until he emerged in front of Bath's Royal Crescent. The house was on the left. Quietly, Jack let himself inside, hoping for solitude. No good. Henrietta Arundel—his hostess—was sitting on the bottom stair with her middle son on her lap.

"You're out early this morning." She didn't look up. Little William frowned, deep in concentration as his mother buckled his brown leather shoe. Henrietta never cared about dignity. It was one of many things Jack liked about her. She was a beautiful woman, but the strain of the last month had left her pale and tired.

"I like mornings," Jack said. "But may I say I think this hour too early for you?"

"Nonsense." She finished with the buckle and slid William off her lap. "I wasn't ill. You don't fill out your clothes yet."

Jack smiled. Useless to remind her of the long hours she'd nursed first her sick children and then him. The influenza had been bad this year.

"I promised Laura you'd rest." Few women could command from the stair-carpet, but Henrietta managed it.

"I'm in no danger," Jack murmured.

"Not anymore." Henrietta laced her fingers together and slid them over her knees. "You were gone an awfully long time. Still not sleeping?"

"Not well," Jack confessed. "I'm up with the sun, but that's long been my habit, so I won't have you writing to Laura. She worries too much as it is."

The Fine Art of Kissing in the Park

When he'd succumbed to the infection just as Henrietta's boy William finally turned the corner, his sister had feared the worst—and it had been a near thing. Worn down by the fight to save Henrietta's children, he'd been delirious for days. Laura, due to deliver her second child and quarantined in the next county, had gone wild with worry. Once Jack was well enough to get out of bed, she insisted he come with the Arundels to convalesce in Bath. It was a course he didn't mind recommending to patients, but for himself...

There was work to do in Suffolk. Nine had died while he'd been ill.

Jack wasn't a new doctor. A surgical apprenticeship in His Majesty's Navy, his studies in Edinburgh, another two voyages as a naval physician, and three years as a country doctor had taught him to save those he could and not to blame himself too much for the others. But surely some of those nine would have recovered had he been there to tend them, instead of alternately sweating and shivering in a sickbed himself. If he'd rationed his strength . . . Well, Henrietta's oldest, Laurence, would have survived, but not William or the baby.

He should have sent for another doctor to help at the start of the outbreak. Lord Fairchild, Henrietta's father and Laura's father-in-law, had sent for one immediately once Jack fell ill. It had only taken a day and a half to bring Dr. Fielding to the district, but with so many patients in crisis, it hadn't been soon enough, though Fielding was a gifted physician. Jack liked him, enough to leave him in charge when Laura, backed by her husband and all his family, insisted he accompany the Arundels to Bath. Jack was tired, but coming here felt like cheating. He ought to face the families he'd failed. Nine new graves in the churchyard—eight, he corrected, for Mrs. Larkin's baby hadn't yet been christened. Jack hadn't asked where they'd buried the little girl, knowing they'd be taking it hard.

Time enough for that. Fielding would manage things, and if Jack hadn't been so convinced he was invincible in the first place . . . Henrietta said one of the reasons he must come here was so he could break his habit of overwork. So far all he'd done was nurse a tendency for brooding. But how did one apologize for a failure like that?

"Maybe you should have walked longer," Henrietta said. "Since you've come in, you've turned sad again. I was encouraged when I first saw you. You had your smile back. Of course, before you returned I was afraid you'd fainted in the street."

"Was I gone that long?" Jack asked.

"You were. And Andrews said you took no breakfast. Will you have some now? I expect it's gone cold, but we could—"

"Later. I'm not hungry. I'll take a look in the nursery. Where's Percy?"

"Feeding the baby." Taking William's hand, she helped him up the steps one at a time. Jack followed her. The nursery was on the second floor. William had only managed the first flight of stairs before but conquered all of them today.

"What a champion!" Jack said to encourage him. "I'd say you're ready for an airing, wouldn't you?"

William, older than his years, merely nodded.

Inside the nursery, Henrietta's husband, Lord Percy Arundel, was reading classics to his oldest son while balancing the baby and a feeder. He broke off long enough to glance at them and smile. "Halfway done!"

"The milk or Thucydides?" Jack asked.

Percy proffered the half-empty bottle. "We've still got a pile of history to go." Seeing his wife's severe look, he added, "I'm only summarizing."

The Fine Art of Kissing in the Park

Laurence, in most ways a typical lad of six, had taken the book and turned back the pages to study a tinted engraving. His other white, fine-boned hand clutched a lead grenadier. He needed an airing too, from the look of it.

Jack listened at the boys' chests and counted pulses—William liked to help hold his watch. In the erratic gaiety of the nursery, he forgot his earlier blue mood and the madness that preceded it. When at last Henrietta and Percy relinquished the children to the nursery maid, they trooped down together to the drawing room, Henrietta talking over her shoulder at Jack, linked to her husband's arm. Jack suggested they take a drive in the afternoon, and the children could have a short runabout.

"What happened on your walk this morning?" Henrietta asked. Jack nearly stumbled.

"Nothing," he said, knowing his reaction had already given him away.

"You looked better than I've seen in a long time," she insisted. "And you've never been one of those types who extol the restorative powers of nature."

"Maybe he is now," Percy said. "It's a fine day."

Henrietta dismissed her husband's reasoning with a look, settled herself into a chair and tucked up her feet. "What made you happy?"

"I enjoyed my walk. That's all." Embarrassing to admit the rest and besides, he'd told Ormonde's owner he'd keep it secret.

Ignoring her husband's warnings, Henrietta probed again. "Jack, you know I'll just keep asking." Beside her, Percy's face made silent apology.

"Fine! There was a young lady. I helped her find her dog,"

Jack admitted, hoping to lay the matter to rest. Confessing that much seemed acceptable.

A huge smile spread over Henrietta's face. "And?"

Behind her, Percy sketched a line across his throat.

"That's all. She was lovely, with quite an endearing dog, but I never learned her name." Jack pulled a random book from the shelves and sat down on the sofa—*Introduction to the Study of Bibliography.* Oh God.

"What does she look like?" Henrietta asked.

Percy cleared his throat. "My love, I think Jack prefers to leave the subject alone. He's on holiday."

Henrietta snorted but said nothing.

Resigned to his penance, Jack opened the thick volume to a "succinct account of the different substances employed for manuscripts and printed books," beginning with stone. If nothing else, he'd learned today that Percy's books, and ladies wandering through the park, were both best left alone.

Henrietta had detected Percy's potential as a husband from the very first, and nothing in their years of marriage had caused her to revise this assessment. Percy was surprised, the following morning, when she asked him to escort her to the Pump Room, but he didn't quibble—one of many proofs of his sterling worth.

"You're scheming again," he said as he took her by the arm to descend the front steps.

"Nonsense." The row of houses arced away from her, pale as pearl against the blue sky and the lovingly tended green. "Isn't this lovely? Aren't you glad we came?"

Percy ignored this. "Should I worry for myself or for Jack?"

The Fine Art of Kissing in the Park

"There is absolutely nothing to worry about," Henrietta assured him.

"As bad as that?" He chuckled.

"It's simply a matter of improving probabilities. I'm conducting an experiment."

"Yes, with people."

"That's the best kind," she told him.

"Just what are you trying to do?"

It was only a quarter mile from the Royal Crescent to the Upper Assembly Rooms, according to the agent who'd let them the house. Henrietta knew her husband for a good walker, venturing out daily to clear his thoughts. He lagged today, moving well under his usual pace, wanting an explanation from her. Very well. "I want to flush out this young lady Jack met in the park."

"We're bloodhounds today? Bath's a small place, but I think our chances of finding one girl are small. We don't even know what she looks like."

Henrietta shook her head. "She'll find us."

"You really think so?"

"There's a strong possibility." And she knew just how to raise Jack's chances. Her reasoning, after all, was very simple. She'd never mention it to Percy, but Jack was the ideal corsair lover: dark and tall with a fading scar, the aristocratic bearing of his French forebears, and the magnetism of his sister, a former actress. Any young lady who wasn't already attached—as she was, quite happily—would be intrigued by him. And Jack was hiding something. The meeting hadn't been just a simple passing in the park.

They made their way around the Circus and turned on to Bennett Street. Bath might no longer be England's foremost resort, but the buildings of the Upper Rooms hadn't been convinced of that. Basking in the morning sun, they welcomed visiting notables—and if these persons were less exalted than in former years, they were too dignified to notice.

"You never felt it necessary to come here before," Percy muttered.

"The boys weren't sufficiently well for me to leave them," Henrietta said innocently. "This is expected." From her reticule, she fished out the clipping she'd taken from the newspaper and read: "Visitors are asked, on Arrival, to insert their Names and Places of Abode in the Book kept for this Purpose at the Pump Room, enabling the Master of Ceremonies to comply with his Wishes and the Expectations of the Public."

"I see." But he looked skeptical.

"Trust me. She'll find us in a week." Henrietta passed blithely under the columned entrance and brought her husband inside. Pretending interest in her surroundings, she paused. A moment later, her hopes were fulfilled.

"Arundel? Is that you?"

They turned, confronting a trio of Bath tabbies. Henrietta smiled. She felt her husband swallow.

"Lady Margaret. It's been an age."

The shortest one, brittle and lacy as a snowflake, closed her fan and beckoned them closer. "You were in long shirts, then. It's good to see you, Percival."

Henrietta let her husband make introductions. Besides Lady Margaret, there was a dowager countess and another lady Henrietta thought was the aunt of a bishop. Her teeth were false, and her skin gray as a wet November. As Lady Margaret reminisced about a young Percival—"Such a trial to his mother. Everyone called him Chuckles!"—Henrietta excused herself.

"I'll put our names in the book," she whispered. Her

fingers were tingling with excitement when she picked up the pen. Should she put Percy down for the card room? The extra money would be worth his consternation. Good wives were always loving, but not always kind. As for the dress balls . . . Yes, they'd do those too. Poor Percy. This wouldn't be much of a holiday for him.

In flowing, untidy script, she wrote both her and her husband's names, then tapped the pen against her chin, delayed only seconds by her expiring conscience. Jack wouldn't like this; he might even be furious, but she'd take the risk. With more care than before, she wrote Jack's particulars. Instead of the name he habitually used, Dr. John Edwards, she put down the name he'd long forsaken: *Jacques-Marie Phillipe Leon Edouard Lecroy-Duplessis, Comte D'Aiguines.* And added their address in Bath.

If Jack's mysterious young lady had any gumption at all, she'd find them.

Chapter Three

Rakish fellows who ransomed dogs for kisses couldn't be trusted. Such a man was capable of anything and best forgotten. Unfortunately, Caroline found the forgetting difficult—only because the experience was so singular, she told herself. If life were not so tedious just now, she could have banished him from her mind without any trouble.

A loud clap at her ear made Caroline start. It was Grandmama, smirking behind her shoulder.

"Woolgathering? Again? We have callers."

Caroline put away her half-finished letter. "Forgive me. I didn't realize there was company." Grandmama was anxious to make her presence known now that they were settled in the house. Resigned, Caroline accompanied her to the drawing room, where she made the acquaintance of Mr. King. The Master of Ceremonies of Bath's Upper Rooms was correct in dress, speech, manners—genial too, without being too much of a toady. He was happy to welcome the Dowager Countess of Lynher back to Bath and tell her with whom she might wish to renew her acquaintance.

"Lady Margaret Derwent is resident these past six weeks and intends to stay out the summer. The Misses Palmer, of course. They have a house on Laura Place. You may recall—"

"Cats, both of them," Grandmama whispered to Caroline. "Never married."

"General Rockford—"

Grandmama chortled. "Now he was a handsome blade back in the day."

"A friend of yours?" Mr. King asked, but Grandmama only twinkled. He left after Grandmama promised to put their names in the subscription book, a duty they performed the following morning. Circling in the Pump Room's revolving exhibition, Caroline's mind wandered while Grandmama picked apart the characters of the other visitors in scarcely heard asides, happy as Ormonde when he got into the butter.

Caroline recognized most of Bath's gerontocracy, but it wasn't her set. Nor had she any wish to acquaint herself with the put-upon lady's companions and the daughters-too-plain-to-be-puffed-off. The best and brightest were in London doing the Season; classing herself with these hapless souls was depressing. She did exchange greetings with one former friend, Emma Barnes, come to Bath to recover from a difficult confinement, but that was uncomfortable. While she didn't envy Emma her husband, it was past time she had one of her own. More and more Caroline recognized the grim and frightening prospect of being left behind.

No sign of the rogue from the park—not that she was looking. She was simply being careful.

They walked around again. Grandmama twittered while Caroline fought back her yawns. Perhaps tomorrow she could plead off and walk with Ormonde instead. They needn't go to the park. They could look in the shop windows on Milsom Street—if she didn't mind risking the other shoppers' necks. Ormonde's erratic darting made it almost certain they'd trip someone. Smiling vaguely at another lady with gray, crimped curls, Caroline decided it was beneath her to avoid the park simply because she'd met trouble last time. She scanned the room again, but he wasn't there.

Perhaps he didn't move in polite society.

Over the next two days, she endured a music concert and calls to and from Grandmama's friends. She wrote a long letter to Kit and a shorter one to Uncle Warren, saying Grandmama was in excellent health and spirits and in need of no one's company. Only Kit wrote back, saying he'd been introduced to Miss Matilda Clarkwell. Caroline didn't know the girl but recognized the fortune. Preoccupied with Miss Clarkwell, Kit answered none of her questions about removing to London. The only man she spoke with on her early morning walks was General Rockwell. He might have been dashing once, but his face had hardened into a leer.

Then, after an afternoon of gossip with Grandmama's friend Lady Margaret, she saw him again. She almost didn't recognize him, for her attention caught first on the dainty lady beside him wearing an alarming shade of blue. She was coaxing along a solemn boy of three or four, who was dragging a stick along the iron railing in front of the houses. The lady laughed, making the man's head turn.

Yes, it was him. Same jaw, same eyes, same smile. Caroline tensed. His unguarded face made the fondness he felt for the lady in blue emphatically plain.

"Who's that?" Caroline sounded half strangled. Surprised, Grandmama followed her gaze.

"I'm not certain, but it looks like Lady Arundel. Haven't seen her in years." She laughed. "I remember her. Aware to the inch how pretty she is and bold as brass. Dresses terribly, though."

The man was laughing with her, saying something in reply, but any moment they'd resume walking.

"Don't let them see us!" Caroline hissed, seizing Grandmama's arm and wheeling them in the direction of the green.

"What's got into you?" Grandmama asked. "Yes, he's handsome, but that's no reason to— Have a little countenance, Caroline!"

"Shh!" With her arm firmly in her grandmother's, Caroline marched across the street, away from the houses of the Royal Crescent. Her mind turned several cartwheels, then righted itself. Arundel. "Who's the gentleman?" Because the rogue was definitely not Lady Arundel's husband. Caroline remembered him.

"Don't know him from Adam. But Arundel's just over there." With a slight jerk of her head, Grandmama directed Caroline's attention to a stooped-shouldered man in front of them on the lawn. He also had a young boy beside him, and there was a nursemaid too, toting a baby. Lord Arundel knelt on the grass, examining something in the palm of his hand. It was too small for Caroline to see, but the boy was riveted.

Caroline cast a furtive glance over her shoulder.

Behind her, the rogue scooped up the boy with the stick, lifted him onto his hip, and went up the steps of a house. Lady Arundel followed, turning back to wave to the rest of her family, who didn't notice. Caroline's breath came easier.

She remembered Lord Arundel, a staid fellow who'd somehow brought the most entrancing girl of the season to the altar seven years ago. Christopher had talked of it, one of the disappointed number. Caroline was seventeen then and only just going out to parties—small ones hosted by political families who'd been friends of her father.

Grandmama had complained then too, bitterly animadverting on Uncle Warren and Christopher's continual politicking. They were turning Caroline into a bluestocking. "What kind of husband will that get her?" she sniffed.

None, as it turned out.

Caroline cleared her head with a blink and a quick breath. Thoughts like these weren't helpful, and Grandmama was eyeing her.

"Do you know these people?"

"Not a one," Caroline said, knowing it was no way to fend off Grandmama's probing. "Will you be all right to go home in a chair? I just remembered an errand I must run in Milsom Street."

"I'm sure I can manage." Her eyes held questions, but these Caroline ignored. She got Grandmama a chair and took off in the direction of the shops on Milsom Street. Once the chair was out of sight, Caroline changed course and hurried to the Pump Room, heading straight for the subscription book. She flipped back a page.

Mrs. Minerva Fitzmorris, Colonel Redmond, Mr. and Mrs. Edgerton . . . There. Three names in a single, showy handwriting, but one leaped out at her, long enough she read it twice to be sure. No wonder he'd been so outrageous that morning in the park. A French Comte could be excused—or even expected—to behave in just such a fashion. It was still unforgivable, but now she found herself wondering where he'd got that faint line of a scar and how many women he'd utterly ruined.

He likely made the process quite pleasant. Best stay clear of him. He'd probably kissed scores of ladies in public parks.

Jack told Henrietta he felt out of place at dress balls, as well as balls of every other sort. This in no way deflected her. It was Monday night, and they were going to the ball at the Upper Rooms, and what's more, he would dance.

"You know how," she said, as if that settled it.

He couldn't tell her there was someone he meant to avoid. Henrietta already made too many arch comments about the young lady he'd "helped" in the park. It had only been a few days since that incident and, as everyone who was anyone would attend this evening's ball, chances were good she'd be there. It was too much to hope she'd left town.

They walked to the assembly rooms, Henrietta and Percy talking in lively and elusive terms about some wager—Jack didn't want to know what. Couples. He lagged behind, trying to convince himself this command appearance was a blessing in disguise. At least he'd get it over with. When he saw her, he would simply look away—assuming she didn't first—and they could pretend nothing had happened. Nothing had, which was a pity, because he would have liked kissing her. But play like that was for courtiers, not earnest physicians like him. You'd think the navy and medical school would have trained such quirks out of him—and most of the time, they had.

"Why are you scowling?" Henrietta asked. "You're allowed to have a little fun."

He had, four days ago, and tonight it was going to get him in trouble. He felt it like the change of wind in the air. Wary, he followed Percy and Henrietta inside.

The rooms were crowded, and there was considerable jostling before they made their way to the cloakroom. Henrietta's enthusiasm was undimmed. Shedding her cloak, she righted her headdress, seized her husband's arm, and set off for the ballroom. Allowing the crowd to separate them, Jack meandered through the Octagon to the card room, pretending to watch the play.

"Would you care to join?" One player looked up at him. He had jaundiced skin and overlarge rings on his hands.

"Thank you, no. Just enjoying the game in passing." Jack moved on through a cloud of tobacco smoke. Eventually though, Henrietta found him. Informed that she was parched with thirst, he accepted the inevitable and took her to the tea room for lemonade. Of course after that, he had to dance with her.

Not that he minded so much. She was good company. Even if he wished she'd exert herself in other directions, she was spending considerable effort on him.

"You look fine tonight," he told her as they took their place at the bottom of the set.

"I know. So do you."

"A necessity. I shouldn't like to embarrass you."

"Hmph." She glanced out the corner of her eye. "If only I could take the credit for you."

The first strains of a reel silenced them. Jack counted time, watching the fellow beside him so he'd know when to start. His memory of the steps was rusty. Except for infrequent capering after dinners at his sister's, he hadn't danced since a long-ago Gibraltar ball.

The first time they changed partners, he turned left instead of right, but corrected the mistake before the musicians advanced to the next measure. Marking time again, the lead couple chased down the line, linked arms, swung right and left, and they all began again. Bow, step forward, turn, and join hands. One step forward rising up on the toes, then a step back and letting go of Henrietta's gloved hand. A sweeping stride on the diagonal, joining hands, and walking past a dark-haired lady in blue. Next came a girl in yellow with bouncing curls, then a slight one too timid to meet his eyes. He gave them only cursory glances himself, his attention on the steps, so he didn't notice the girl from the park until she was in front of him, taking his hand.

His step faltered, but he avoided a mistake, skimming to her side. Now he didn't have to face her, but there was still a chance, through their joined hands, she'd detect his feverish pulse. Jack stared at the backs of the couple in front and schooled his features. She circled around him, gliding like a prima donna amidst the ballet corps. When the pattern of the dance brought them face-to-face again, she looked through him.

Keeping his face pleasant enough to avoid attention but distant enough to discourage conversation, Jack made it to the end of the set. It was typical of his luck that almost immediately upon arrival in Bath he'd mishandled the lady who turned out to be the most beautiful one in town. Inwardly shaking his head at such folly, Jack took Henrietta's hand and led her off the floor. "Who was the lady with the pink sash?" he whispered.

"I'll find out." She was off before he could stop her, leaving him to buttress the pale, classically decorated wall. He shouldn't have asked. At this point, it was better not to know.

Henrietta returned quicker than he expected. "Well spotted," she whispered, shielding her mouth with her fan. "The lady is Caroline Trenholme, niece of the Earl of Lynher. She's worth twenty thousand pounds."

Jack could have cursed. No doubt he looked like the worst kind of fortune hunter. Why couldn't she have been a rector's daughter? Not that she looked like any rector's daughter he'd ever seen. They didn't wear that many jewels. She had pride in the set of her mouth. Perhaps that was what first beguiled him. She was Quality and knew it. He was lucky she'd merely made him kiss her dog instead of summoning the watch or reporting him to the network of Bath gossips.

Jack ran his tongue over his teeth behind closed lips. Unless she had. He'd been too unsociable thus far to know if he was being shunned. "Henrietta—" No. He couldn't think of a way to explain.

Miss Trenholme was on the same side of the room, barely twenty feet away. He mustn't look at her.

Boiling fury or icy rage? Caroline wasn't certain which was stronger, only that she was trembling, too angry for original thought. *How dare he?*

He'd shown nothing on confronting her, not a twitch of an eyebrow, not a single sideways glance, not a flicker of recognition, nothing but a hesitant step—and he'd made several throughout the set. She'd counted three. The humiliation of being ignored was worse when she considered the care she'd taken tonight with her appearance. Unable to help herself, she'd put pearls in her hair and dressed up her décolletage.

"Did you not enjoy the dance?" Grandmama asked once Caroline had thanked and dispensed with her partner.

"It was ripping."

That earned a look. Caroline didn't normally use slang.

Caroline tapped her closed fan on her lips. In spite of herself, she'd imagined their next meeting—a chance encounter in a dim corridor behind the cloakrooms or a meeting in early morning half-light at the park. She'd even toyed with the idea of kissing him—and he was too smooth or too bacon-brained to remember her!

"You look like you're about to do something rash."

Probably. "You see that gen— That man there?" She indicated with the tip of her fan.

"The one we saw in front of Lady Margaret's?"

It was always a mistake to underestimate Grandmama. Caroline nodded an eighth of an inch. "I want you to bring him to me."

Grandmama smiled. "You're growing to be an interesting girl. Consider it done." Looping up her trailing shawl, Grandmama soared off, nodding once at a brocade-covered bench supporting Lady Greyhurst on the opposite side of the room. Familiar with her family's social shorthand, Caroline went there to wait.

It didn't take long. Somehow in passing, Grandmama gathered Lord and Lady Arundel and Caroline's quarry into her train. A pomaded dandy stepped aside to let them pass. From her end of the room, Caroline moved forward. As her grandmother stopped to present Lady Arundel to that shameless roué General Rockwell, Caroline attacked the flank.

"I looked Grandmama, but I didn't find your brooch. I'm quite sure you didn't have it on when we left the house."

Grandmama gave her a sharp look. Subterfuge was perfectly acceptable, just not the kind that made her look like an elderly widgeon.

"What is it like, ma'am? Let us help you look," Lord Arundel offered.

Caroline stopped attending. The Comte d'Augines was looking at her. Carefully, she traced her fan from the corner of her mouth along her bottom lip. He stiffened.

"—Not worth the trouble. I expect my granddaughter has remembered right *this* time," Grandmama said.

He smiled, so slight it was a secret. Caroline didn't feel angry anymore. She was glad she'd chosen the pearls.

"—I never liked the brooch anyway." Changing theme as smoothly as a concert pianist, Grandmama said, "General Rockwell, you've met my granddaughter, but I don't think Lord and Lady Arundel have. Miss Caroline Trenholme."

"So glad to make your acquaintance." Caroline curtsied.

"And this young man is?"

Caroline leaped to fill Grandmama's leading pause. The

admiration in his eyes counted for something, but he didn't deserve an easy time of it. "We've already met. It is a pleasure to see you again, Monsieur Comte."

Unexpected silence greeted her words. Lord Arundel looked daggers at his wife, and General Rockwell stuttered, "I thought you said your name was Edwards."

Edwards? She couldn't be mistaken. She'd seen his name in the book, sharing the same address as the Arundels. Edwards was just a part of that litany of names, chanting singsong in her head this past twenty-four hours: *Jacques-Marie Phillipe Leon Edouard Lecroy-Duplessis, Comte D'Aiguines.* But whoever he was, he'd gone as still as a waxwork.

"I was born Jacques-Marie Duplessis," he said at last. Caroline frowned, for he was shortening considerably. "But it has been many years since I was called that. I never think of myself as Monsieur Comte." The last two words were twisted with mockery.

Grandmama flinched. "Don't tell me you are a Republican."

He laughed, and the tension around them slackened. "Hardly that. But after fleeing the slaughter in France, I learned my name didn't matter so much as paying the grocer's bill. I consider myself fortunate in my profession. I am a physician."

And poor, evidently. Come down in the world and obliged to work, and she'd exposed him. Caroline had never blundered this awfully.

"But Miss Trenholme is correct. I have had the pleasure of meeting her before." He turned to her, his expression indecipherable. "How is Ormonde? He hasn't run off again?"

"My dog." Caroline stammered, explaining herself to the company. "I—"

"Does a simple doctor rate well enough to beg one of your dances?"

Anything to escape these goggling stares. "Thank you. It would be a pleasure."

He motioned, and they moved off together. He didn't offer his arm. Caroline pressed her lips together, waiting.

"Where did you get that name?" he asked.

Here, at least, she deserved no blame. "It was written with Lord and Lady Arundel's in the subscription book."

He tightened his lips. "Henrietta."

Before the tide of color rose too high in her cheeks, she apologized. She knew enough to be wary of French titles; often they weren't what they seemed. "Forgive me. I hadn't thought—"

Unexpectedly, he smiled at her, a slow widening of lips that made her feel awkward. "I just realized you've been looking for me."

"Looking out for you," Caroline corrected hastily. "There's a difference. It only seemed prudent."

"Hmm." They walked on, past a lady in an *eau de nil* overdress and plumes, around one of the white pillars of the colonnade. "I fear I've disappointed you," he said. "Since you expected *Monsieur Comte.*"

"Don't flatter yourself. I—"

"No untruths, Miss Trenholme. Whatever else I might be, I'm honest. I wasn't going to intrude on your notice tonight, even after I saw you in the dance. If not for Lady Arundel I would have hid in the card room all evening, and since that morning I've ceded to you and Ormonde all the territory of the park. I was willing to make up for my misdemeanours by leaving you be. If you truly wanted to avoid me, you could have. Instead you searched out my name in the subscription book, and, if I'm not mistaken, staged a meeting between us using your grandmother. It was cleverly done, but I'd lay my life you planned it."

Fine, then. She wouldn't deny it. "If Duplessis is your name, I don't see why you don't use it. The truth is, I am disappointed. I don't normally befriend doctors."

"I believe you."

"Offended?"

Braced for insult or icy reproof he surprised her instead with a grin, and the skirmish she was losing didn't seem to matter anymore. She'd wager her garters he was glad she'd found him. "I'm not offended," he said. "Even though you know better, you want to dance with me."

Caroline couldn't reply. Her pulse beat in her throat.

He leaned close to avoid brushing shoulders with a uniformed gentleman and murmured, "This is hopeless, you know." Caroline swallowed. There was something about whispers. They felt almost like a touch.

"Why?"

"I've not the stature to match you. And you are too . . . prudent for me."

Prudish, he meant. Caroline's eyes narrowed. "Just what did you think we might be to each other? Are you married?"

"No."

"Betrothed?"

He shook his head.

These were uncharted waters, but she plunged ahead. "Nor am I. So flirtation is entirely permissible." She took a breath, pretending a sangfroid she didn't feel. "I thought you had some interest in me, but if it was merely Ormonde . . ."

"No."

"Then we are agreed." Saying it, she felt tremendous relief.

"I've never agreed to flirt with anyone before," he said.

Nor had she, but he didn't need to know that.

"It seems very formal," he said. "But if flirting is allowed—"

The set was forming, a boulanger, but he thought her a prude, and she wanted very much to prove she wasn't. "Do you mind forgoing our dance?" Caroline asked. "I'd like to fetch my shawl."

Chapter Four

He hadn't thought it at their first meeting, but perhaps this woman knew what she was about. Ignoring the suspicion that he was sailing into trouble, Jack followed her, keeping twenty paces back. She moved with assurance that enticed but didn't entirely convince him. This coolness couldn't make him forget the befuddled suspicion he'd provoked last week in the park. Maybe she just liked to tease. Entirely possible, given how last time he'd ended up with a kiss from her dog.

Less sure now, Jack followed her into the warren of cloak and serving rooms. Without a glance back, she disappeared behind one of the doors. After a discreet interval, Jack let himself in. He was crowded by wine crates and empty cake trays... and her, leaning against a stack of boxes not six inches away from him.

Dark and dusky in the uncertain light, she looked more sophisticated than she had the other morning.

"Why are you here?" Jack asked. If she was treating this like a dare...

"Bath? It's where they keep dowagers and spinsters."

She was willfully misunderstanding him. Very well. "Which one are you?"

"Not a dowager." Her eyes flicked over him. "Why are you here?"

"The spinsters." He stepped close and lifted his hand to her cheek. She took a quick breath, then settled into his cupped palm. Her skin was warm. So often his training made him notice only symptoms: faint scars, nearsightedness, the curves of badly set bones. She was much more than pupils and a pulse. "May I kiss you?"

Her eyes, falling heavily, flew open. "Why else are we here?"

Why, indeed? He closed the last few inches.

They couldn't count on remaining undisturbed for long—which was a good thing, Jack told himself, abandoning the idea of putting a wedge beneath the door. He bent and kissed her lips once more, swift and soft this time. "You should go," he whispered.

"Yes." She smoothed her hands over the front of her gown.

Jack nodded at the curl trailing over her shoulder. "We should fix that. No, let me." He was glad of any reason to touch her, and the lack of a mirror made an excellent excuse.

"Thank you." Tidy again, she edged past him, stopping at the door. "That was lovely."

"May I call tomorrow—to see Ormonde?" he added when she hesitated.

"Come early." She had a slant in her smile.

Jack grinned. "Until then." He ducked his head to study his hands, purposely nonchalant, and listened to her go. Unable to follow anytime soon, he examined the labels on the wine bottles, squinting to make out the letters. Not inferior, but nothing to boast about. Rather like him.

He wasn't sorry. Clearly, neither was she. But alone with his thoughts, Jack knew he was in trouble. Much as he enjoyed the taste of her mouth, there was something daunting about her ambition. *I don't normally befriend doctors*—said after she'd laid a trap for a count. An ideal flirt, though, since his heart was safe from a lady like that.

Not that she'll keep you for long.

But holidays were for temporary enjoyments, for pleasures. And Caroline was too shrewd to injure herself heart-jousting. No reason conscience should trouble him.

Caroline was dancing when he returned to the ball room. Percy and Henrietta, thankfully, had parted from her grandmother.

"What were you thinking, putting that absurd handle of mine in the subscription book?" Jack asked.

"It's your name," Henrietta said.

Jack snorted. "I barely remember using it. You make me look like a hanger-on, some worthless braggart—"

"If I had a title from the reign of King Henry the Fourth—"

"You do," Percy interrupted. "What Jack calls himself is his business. My dear, you shouldn't have done it."

Henrietta huffed. "The title was bait. And it worked. You like her."

What's not to like? Jack thought. "And she found a plain country doctor when she was looking for a count."

"That didn't stop her from agreeing to dance with you." Henrietta's eyes narrowed. "There's rouge on your shirt points." Reading Jack's expression, she lowered her voice. "Miss Trenholme wouldn't be human if the title didn't intrigue her. But once she gets to know you, your title—or lack of it—will be immaterial."

Jack didn't share Henrietta's faith in humanity. Or in Caroline Trenholme, who was lovely, but . . . "No. Not her." Jack shook her head.

Percy gave a weak smile. "I'm inclined to agree with Jack. The Trenholmes are very high in the instep. Her uncle—"

"That old gudgeon!"

"Henrietta!" Percy's whispered reproof quieted her.

"All right." She turned to Jack, her eyes contrite. "I'm sorry if I've made things difficult for you. Trust me. It will come aright. If it hasn't already." The corner of her mouth hitched up, revealing her dimple. "You were gone quite a long time with her."

"Just taking some refreshment," Jack replied. "Don't offer much here, do they?"

"It's best not to come hungry," Henrietta told him archly.

"I'll remember."

Percy folded his arms, glancing between them. "Well, if you're both satisfied, may we go home? Henrietta, you've won again, so I—"

Was he the subject of their wager? Or Caroline? "I didn't know—" Jack stopped, covering his laugh with a snort, deciding he'd rather not know what Henrietta had predicted successfully. "Let's forget it, shall we?"

Henrietta ignored Percy's frown, taking one of each of their arms. "She'll suit you admirably. I expect she's already in love with you."

Jack managed not to cast his gaze to the chandeliers. "I'm touched by your confidence." And in a way, he truly was. Miss Trenholme was beautiful, challenging, exciting to talk with and to hold. But he doubted she'd prove as loyal a friend as

Henrietta. God hadn't made many like her. Just as well. One was more than enough.

Grandmama held back the questions until she and Caroline were alone in the carriage, driving home. "Did you have a nice evening?"

Caroline smiled as the glow of the streetlamps passed over her. No point being coy. "Very."

"Good." Grandmama settled deeper into the velvet upholstery. "I was worried for a moment there. You almost lost him. And he's so nice to look at."

He certainly was, but hearing it from Grandmama...

"It's a pity about his profession, but so long as we're here, he'll make for charming company. Nothing more, though, Caroline. You understand."

Caroline supposed she deserved a warning of some sort. It could have been worse. "I know he's unsuitable, except as a friend. I remember what I owe the family, but surely *you* don't mind if I amuse myself a little."

Grandmama chuckled. "I'm in no position to mind. And since there's no better gentleman to escort you than General Rockwell—"

"Oh, be serious."

"I am. But you are rather a novice at this sort of thing, so I hope you'll forgive me if I offer some advice."

Caroline smiled, unable to resist stopping her. "Your eyes are just the same as they are in the portrait at Coberton," she said. Uncle had moved the picture twice; each time Grandmama pecked at him until it returned to the middle of the gallery.

"Thank you." There was no mistaking the pleased air

with which Grandmama straightened her ruffles. "Romney painted it, you know. Said my eyes were my best feature."

They were clouded around the edges now, and she tinted the lashes, but the mischief was still there. By all accounts, after providing Grandfather with two sons, Grandmama had had her share of adventures. Caroline doubted she knew the half of them.

"Respectability can be so exhausting," Grandmama went on, resting her hands on the handle of her long cane. "Normally you're so prim, but . . . Well, it's a pity you and Sir Wait-Forever put off your wedding so long. If you'd been married, we could forgo this discussion."

Caroline choked on a laugh. There was no escaping. Grandmama was alarmingly plainspoken. "I'm aware of what happens between husbands and wives."

"Only by hearsay, I hope. That fiancé of yours . . ." Grandmama shuddered. "I always wanted to kick him. Worse than your dog! You ought to know most sheet-sport goes on outside of marriage—no, don't interrupt. You young ladies are so namby-pamby. I don't approve of it." Grandmama tapped her forefinger on the silver handle. "If you were that poltroon's widow, I'd say you should take this doctor to bed without delay. You've been so low-spirited. It's unattractive. But since you are still unmarried, you'll have to be more circumspect—unless I'm mistaken and that fiancé of yours did bed you. And if you were that foolish, I'd say you deserved it."

"Grandmama!"

"Doubt he had the gumption though," Grandmama muttered.

"Robert never—"

"Like I said. All that bowing over your hand and eternal delay. I should have kicked him!"

"Grandmama, please!"

"I don't like it, you know. Twenty-five, unmarried. That's why I had to take you in hand. Bring you to Bath."

"I'm twenty-four," Caroline corrected. "And I'm not likely to find a husband here, handsome doctors notwithstanding." Every man who counted was in London.

"No, but an intrigue will be good for you. As for that fiancé, you're well rid of him. Never liked him."

"He was going to be a cabinet minister," Caroline reminded her.

Grandmama snorted. "Recommendation enough for your brother and uncle, but you were the one who'd have to live with him." She flicked her fingers in the air. "He's gone. We needn't quarrel about it."

Recognizing the truth in this, Caroline was silent.

"Does Edwards kiss well?"

The question, flying out at her in the dark, caught Caroline off guard.

"Goodness, child! Learn to keep still. You're too old for these starts and blushes." Grandmama chuckled. "I'll take that as a yes."

"I found him excellent company," Caroline said, her voice even.

"Better," Grandmama drawled. "Mind, there can be nothing more than kisses and gentle pawing for innocents like you." Some involuntary movement of hers must have caught Grandmama's eye. She eyed Caroline closely. "Pawed you already? Best be careful, girl, or he'll think you fast." Chuckling again, she set her stick against the side of the carriage and folded her hands together. "I like his style."

So do I, Caroline thought but didn't say. She didn't know if she was going to snort with laughter or relapse into giggles, but this was almost too much for her. Biting her tongue,

Caroline kept her shoulders steady and held her chin high. She'd drunk only lemonade this evening, but this talk made her uncharacteristically giddy. She hadn't felt like this in . . . certainly years, maybe not ever. Before the thought made her sad, Caroline discarded it.

At the house, the footmen helped Grandmama from the carriage. Caroline took her by one arm, not trusting her steadiness in such tall heels after an uncertain amount of wine.

"Leave me be. Get yourself off to bed." Grandmama's heavily ringed hand patted Caroline's arm. "Sleep well. I hope your dreams are naughty ones."

"You're incorrigible," Caroline told her.

"And I'll die happy," Grandmama said.

Caroline kissed her. "But not yet, please. Good night."

In her own room, Caroline dismissed her maid and stood leaning against the door, fingering her lips, fighting a smile. If she and Jack weren't the worst rascals in Bath, the title surely belonged to her grandmother.

Whatever would Kit say? Not that she was ever planning on telling him.

Jack dressed with care the next morning, ignored Percy's raised eyebrows at his early departure, and walked to the house of the Dowager Countess of Lynher. It was in Camden Place. He'd checked the subscription book.

He was received, to his surprise, by Caroline's grandmother. "Come to call on my granddaughter?" she asked.

"Ormonde," Jack answered. "We fancy each other."

The old lady laughed, a fuller sound than he'd expected from someone of her years. "Then you won't be disappointed. I've heard the beast snuffling about, but I haven't yet seen Caroline."

She offered him a chair and set to work quizzing him about his relations. In several instances, the facts required brazen answers, but Jack knew there was no shrinking. He'd be surprised if the countess hadn't ferreted out all the answers already. She seemed that type. In the middle of their conversation, Ormonde nosed into the room. He took up a post beside Jack, his tail beating eagerly against Jack's boots.

"You weren't jesting," the countess observed as Jack scratched the hollows behind the dog's ears.

"He and I understand each other." Jack smiled.

When Caroline hurried into the room, buttoning her gloves, she was a different girl again, glowing and flustered, as if the kisses he'd pressed on her last night were painted on her skin. Not what he'd expected. She never was—one day prim as a daisy, the next a calculating sophisticate, then a blushing ingenue. He shouldn't stare at her.

"Forgive me," she began.

"Overslept?" Her grandmother's question darkened her blush.

"You look beautiful," Jack said. "Can I persuade you to lend me Ormonde for an hour's walk?"

She stopped in the middle of a nod. "Just Ormonde?" She was dressed for walking, in low-heeled half boots and a green wool pelisse.

"Well, I know I'm a favorite with him." Jack smiled. She was so easy to tease. "I didn't want to presume your willingness. And I worry when the world sees you, it might cause an accident in traffic."

Caroline snorted.

"I have no prejudice against doctors, not when they are as well-mannered as you," Lady Lynher put in.

"If you like, we could walk past the outskirts of town," Jack suggested. "There is a bluebell wood—or so I am told."

"You'll like that, Caroline," Lady Lynher said. "The woods are always pretty this time of year. I'll expect you both for luncheon."

"Dr. Edwards might have other engagements," Caroline said.

"None so important as me," Lady Lynher said.

Jack smiled. "You're quite right, ma'am. Thank you for the invitation. I'm happy to join you." He bowed and was barely upright before Caroline hurried him from the room.

"If you let her have her way this easily, you'll never recover," she warned him. "She'll order you about till the end of her days."

"Oh, I think the invitation was for your sake," Jack said. "She's keeping me respectable." He liked the dowager countess, who looked after Caroline in her own unconventional way.

Caroline pressed the back of her hand to her lips, smothering a laugh. "Grandmama is the least respectable person I know. Including you, and that's saying something."

"Clearly, she's above such mundane concerns herself. I, on the other hand, must abide by the rules."

"Except that you never do."

Not when I'm with you. Jack shifted to his other foot. "I'm not usually— Our first meeting, and last evening... That was uncharacteristic of me."

She bent to fasten a lead to Ormonde's collar, looking up once he was safely tethered. "Do you want to play by the book?"

Jack licked his lips. "I've broken rules already, but I should keep your grandmother's."

"Good. She informed me yesterday that you are permitted to kiss me—" Jack laughed, but she went on, "with occasional pawing."

The Fine Art of Kissing in the Park

He winced. "Was I so clumsy?"

"Her word, not mine." She stood up much too close to him. A large, antlered umbrella stand kept him from taking a step back. "If you just came round to make apology, why stay for luncheon?" Her tone was cool.

"I—" There really was no elegant way to say this. Games were fine, but he wanted her to think well of him. "I want you to know I'm not a fortune hunter."

"You said you didn't have the stature to match me. It's true, though I like your height." She must look straight in the eyes of most men, but he had a few inches' advantage. Just now, he needed them.

"I flirt with you only because you are too lovely to resist. I expect nothing."

"Thank you."

Ormonde butted against his boots. "He's been remarkably patient, but I think it's time we were gone. If we want to go as far as the bluebells," Jack said.

Caroline nodded, and Ormonde took the signal and tore off. They hurried after him, out the door and down the steps to the street. Ormonde strained at the lead, sniffing all over the flagway, keeping them at a brisk pace that brought color to Caroline's face and had Jack puffing.

"At least he'll never get fat like Lady Margaret's pug." Caroline said. "Tired already?"

Jack shook his head. His breath was fast, but it was good for him to be up and about. Kept him from brooding.

"You look a little pale," Caroline told him, tugging Ormonde to heel and slowing her pace.

"I sleep poorly," Jack told her. "Bad habits."

She gave him a sideways look. "But you are here for a holiday," she said, her inflections gently scolding.

Jack shook his head. "A cure. I took sick over the winter.

My family insists on it." In Suffolk, he often saw patients from early morning till long after dark, riding by the light of a lantern if there was no moon. He must take more long walks, so he'd return fit for duty.

"That can't do much good to your reputation," she said. "Doctors aren't supposed to get ill."

"I'll try not to do it again." Nine graves. Jack was silent.

They passed the turn to the park, and Ormonde lunged backward. Caroline's whistle brought him about, but his ears hung sulkily until a carriage rattled by. Ormonde veered away from the wheels, barking indignant protests once they had passed.

"You'd think he'd be used to them by now," Caroline said.

"He'll be happier once we get to the wood," Jack promised, hoping the scenery would be as good as Henrietta's guidebook claimed.

"I spoke with Lady Arundel later at the dance. She told me you saved her son. Is that how you became ill?" Caroline asked.

"Henrietta is a rattle," Jack said.

"But not, I think, a liar," she said quietly.

"If I take credit for the patients who get well, must I blame myself for the ones who don't?"

"Lady Arundel says you do. She says—"

"How much did you talk with her at the ball last night?"

She looked at him, absorbing his reluctant smile to widen her own. "Enough."

"Should I be afraid?"

"No. I'll leave you be." And after that, she didn't press him.

Ormonde's prance quickened as they left the town. "I

should bring him into the country more often," Caroline said, watching him frisk around Jack's feet.

"Have you always lived in London?" It was easy to imagine her there.

She shook her head. "I grew up in Cornwall. After my parents died, we lived with my uncle until Christopher—my brother—was elected to parliament."

"Which riding?"

"Penryn. It was my father's. Christopher is a nominee of my uncle, but the margin was narrower than he'd hoped. He takes the responsibility seriously."

"And you?" he asked, though he knew already.

"In my own small way."

"I never trust you when you pretend modesty. Makes me think you got him elected yourself."

Her eyelashes fell onto her cheeks. "Ladies do not vote, Dr. Edwards."

"I thought between us, it was Jack. You may not vote, but I expect you pay calls on everyone in Penryn who does. Is he married?"

She frowned.

"Your brother."

"No."

"Then you run the household for him?"

"Yes. We've always been a political family. I'd say a good half dozen of our ancestors lost their heads over it. Long ago, thankfully. Not in these times—" She broke off, realizing her mistake. "I mean— I'm sorry. That was incredibly clumsy of me."

Jack looked into the trees, lifting the corners of his mouth. He couldn't manage the rest.

"Was your family . . . ?"

"Yes, but I never saw it." Jack resumed walking, his eyes

on the dirt path. "We were in hiding then, my mother and sister and me." But as they'd escaped their burning home, he'd seen what the mob had done to his grandmother's dog. He'd never forgotten the sight of the pitiful body scattered in pieces on the Turkish carpet. "You said many of your ancestors have been in parliament?"

She accepted the diversion with relief. "Yes. But it was my father and then my uncle who first joined the Tory party. My brother sits with them, which is at least partially why he and Grandmama don't get on. Would you like a turn with Ormonde?" She offered the end of the leash. Jack took it, keeping her hand as well and tucking it in the crook of his free arm. It felt better in moments like these to touch someone. "In case I come over faint," he explained, provoking a smile.

"Were you very ill?" she asked.

"Yes. It's quite embarrassing. I nearly lost Henrietta's baby and her middle boy. Brought him round just as I took ill myself."

"She must be grateful to you for saving them."

"It always frightens me. Treating family." Hoping to distract her, he motioned to Ormonde, who had his nose pressed to the ground. "What do you suppose he's stalking this time?"

She only smiled a response, growing thoughtful. It made him uneasy. He didn't want her thinking overmuch on what he'd said. Some things were best left alone.

Chapter Five

Caroline hadn't walked so far in years, not since Kit had moved to London. At Coberton Park, she'd spent more time outside, every moment that was her own. The countryside and gardens there had been her escape, for Uncle Warren's home was beautiful, but not a comfortable one. She missed her slow hours wandering cliffs in the sunshine or, on days when the sea turned growly, the satisfaction of walking far and fast into a wind.

It told. Her leg muscles were warm, though this path wasn't steep, nothing like the cliffs by Coberton. They'd found bluebells though, thick and brilliant in the wood's shade. Caroline stopped. "It's been too long since I visited Arcadia."

"You like it?" Jack looked back at her, his shoulders splashed by sun.

"It's paradise." She couldn't see or hear the outside world from this little hollow. It was unspoiled, perfect. Once she'd had hopes instead of ambitions—fairy tale dreams to liven the lonely years when Kit left Coberton to go to school. She'd missed him terribly, living for his letters. Then he came back for her, full of plans for their future, eclipsing those foolish fancies she'd lived with for so long.

"Should I let him run?"

Ormonde danced, anticipating freedom.

Caroline smiled, returning to the present. "He'd like to, but I don't know if he'll come back."

From his coat pocket, Jack took a folded napkin. "I brought some ham from breakfast." Ormonde barked, his tail wagging madly. Jack fed him a morsel. "He'll come back."

Caroline nodded, and Jack let go of the lead. Ormonde whined anxiously, but once he saw no ham was forthcoming, he picked his way through the bluebells, circling a tree trunk, then bounding after some sound, stopping with his ears pricked when he lost his direction.

"I'd like to sit awhile," Caroline said. They'd passed a stone wall some yards back, but she chose a bit of sloping ground beneath a tree. Jack took the place beside her, propping his arm on one bent knee. Since waking, she'd hummed with hopes of kissing him, but pride and the remnants of habitual decorum held her back. For now. The wood was beautiful, but she couldn't stop looking at him. "Thank you for bringing me here. It's as good for me as it is for Ormonde. Do you deal this handily with all creatures?"

"Canines are easy to understand. I manage all right with most humans." He smiled at her. "Not very good with horses. Spent too many years in the navy."

"A sailor, a doctor, and a count? How many lives have you had?" There was more to him than what he showed in his easy smile.

"If I were a cat, I'd have used up a few. I started my career in the navy, training as a surgeon. Between voyages I studied medicine. Served on board ship again after that until a few years ago. Now I'm a land animal again." He made it sound ordinary, but it wasn't.

"Where have you been?"

The Fine Art of Kissing in the Park

"Africa, the Caribbean, Gibraltar. Spent some time on the blockade."

"Did it bother you, fighting France?" She studied him for clues, though it would have been easier to stare at her knees. Maybe she shouldn't have asked.

He shrugged. "It might bother me if I ever went back. Perhaps I should feel more loyalty. At the time, I tried not to think of it. To be grateful I had the chance. We were poor, you know. I was lucky." He plucked a blade of grass and rolled it between his fingers. "My brother was much older, but what I remember most of him was his pride in *la patrie*. He was a soldier of the National Convention and wore a blue uniform and the cockade." There was bitterness here, fine as the blade of knife.

"He was the Comte d'Augines?"

"No. That was Father."

Caroline swallowed. "Did they kill him too?"

Jack tossed away the ruined stalk of grass and plucked another. It hurt, watching his forced smile. "They killed everyone," he said. "Anyone. My cousin from the convent. Our priest. Children from the village who spat at *le tricolore*. Of our family, only my mother and sister and I escaped. My mother died four years ago while I was at sea, but Laura is well. She lives with her husband in Suffolk."

Caroline passed him a fresh piece of grass. He tossed it after the others. "Enough. It's my turn now, if you insist on uncomfortable questions. Why aren't you married?"

Caroline shifted on the ground. "Perhaps I choose not to be."

His eyes met hers, compelling her to honesty.

"No, you're right. For nearly three years, I was engaged to marry Sir Robert Symes. He was a member for Truro and a friend of my brother."

"What happened?"

"He died. An accident."

"Do you miss him?"

"No." It sounded heartless, but it was the truth. If anything, she resented his dying, leaving her to start over. "If he hadn't been content with only my promise, we'd have married long before. He might still be alive."

Uncomfortable under his scrutiny, she looked for Ormonde, spotting him far away in the wood.

"Not a love match, then."

"Does that disappoint you?" Caroline asked. She didn't like being judged, especially when her own verdict wasn't commendable. "I don't think he cared much for me," she admitted. "I was useful, but not necessary to him."

"How ungallant."

"It's the way things are."

"But you're hurt all the same."

Caroline shrugged. "It's nothing." Not like the hurts he bore, uncomplaining. "Is it my turn again? How did you come by that scar?"

"Splinter. On my last voyage. I stitched it myself."

Caroline winced. Served her right for asking.

"My turn." He picked a longer blade of grass this time, brushing it across the top of her knees.

"Well?" Caroline prompted.

He laughed. "This is a difficult question."

"Must be, if it's taking you this long." She felt herself tensing under her smile.

"If you believe that's the way things are, why come here with me?"

She wasn't sure what she'd feared, but this was answerable. Her breath loosened. "But I like you. You *are* gallant."

"And that's sufficient to overpower good sense? Because,

The Fine Art of Kissing in the Park

you see, I'm planning to kiss you." He said it as a matter of fact, like some observation on the weather, but the tone didn't match his intent look.

"Jack." Caroline made a show of widening her eyes, but she couldn't maintain the pretense of shock for more than a heartbeat. Lowering her voice to a whisper, she leaned forward. "I'm glad. I thought it over, and I can stand one more."

"Just one?"

"Well, say a few."

He smiled. "Good. Come here, then." He lay back on the grass, and Caroline followed like she was tethered to his coat buttons.

"Kissing's a fine art," he sighed, when she stopped to breathe. "You're much better at it than Ormonde."

Caroline smiled, tracing her finger along the edge of his waistcoat. With her head resting here, she felt his heart thudding, a satisfactory counterpoint to the double-time pulse in her throat. She measured both as they softened and slowed, savoring the tingle left in her cheeks from the friction of his skin.

"Do you miss the sea?" she asked.

"Not often. But when I do, I feel it sharply. The sea is like that."

Caroline nodded. She understood.

Time might have stopped for them both, but it hadn't for Ormonde. He barked, and Caroline raised her head. "Do you suppose he's in trouble?" She opened her mouth to call, but Jack put his hand over her lips.

"Hush. I think he hears someone."

Faintly, they heard voices through the woods. In the

same instant, Jack was on his feet and helping her stand. "You'll have to hide," he whispered. "You look very disreputable."

Caroline glanced down at her rumpled skirts. Bits of bracken clung everywhere.

"Hurry. Over here." Jack took her hand, then her waist, practically forcing her over the wall. "Ormonde!" he called over his shoulder.

"Give me a moment," Caroline whispered, struggling in her tangled dress. "I—Oh!" She toppled off the wall to the grass below. "Jack!"

"Hush! Someone's coming!" She heard footsteps: he was running, calling her dog. "Ormonde! Yes, that's a good boy."

He must have caught hold of the leash. *Only because he keeps bits of breakfast in his pockets.*

"Hello there!" His voice, moving off, was pitched to carry. "I hope my dog didn't startle you."

"Not at all. It's a dear little thing." This was accompanied by a feminine titter. Caroline lifted her head an inch but stopped before she gave herself away. Annoyed, she plucked a fallen leaf from her hair and stared at her shoes.

"I knew I couldn't keep the beauty of these woods all to myself today," Jack said.

"I hope we haven't disturbed you." A different voice this time. Still female.

"You did catch me in the midst of a nap," Jack lied.

"Sorry to wake you."

Caroline waited for them to bid him good afternoon and walk away. They didn't.

"How old is he?"

"Thirty-two," Jack answered. "Oh, you meant the dog."

They laughed. Caroline rolled her eyes. Her knees stiffened as they chatted, the ladies imparting the news that they were just arrived in Bath. From Colchester. Naturally, their proximity to Jack's own home must be discussed. Had he been to St. Edmundsbury Cathedral?

Caroline held in a groan.

Was this Miss Grey and Miss Matthews's first time to Bath? It wasn't? How fortunate. This was his first visit, but he was remarkably pleased. Perhaps they would meet again at one of the assemblies.

"I love dogs," the lower-pitched one said again. Ormonde whined happily. She must be petting him. Traitor.

"You're too kind to him. I warn you, he's flighty in his attentions to ladies."

Flighty, indeed.

"Enjoy the rest of your walk," Jack told them. "I'd offer to accompany you, but I've left a book somewhere—no, I'll soon find it, and in any case I must be heading back. Thank you, it's been a pleasure."

With many goodbyes and protestations of goodwill, they moved off. Caroline peeked over the wall and found Jack smiling guiltily at her. "A pleasure, was it?" she asked.

He leaned over to brush grass from her shoulder. "Weren't they kind? Need a hand over?"

"I don't know. Did you find your book?"

"Think it's lost forever." He held out his hands. Gripping his forearms, Caroline scaled the wall, swung her legs over the top, but held back when Jack tried to lift her down. "I'm surprised you didn't ask to kiss either of *them*."

Jack shook his head. "Two is too many to handle. And if I was to pick one, how would I choose? Very awkward for the other one."

"They'd probably be happy to take it in turns," Caroline said, shaking out her skirts. Ormonde, thinking this was a new game, jumped up, pawing at her flounce.

"Are you going to come down?" Jack spread his hands. "At least they didn't see you. You don't want rumors flying all over Bath."

Caroline sniffed. "Certainly not." But it was lowering, seeing how easily women fell into his lap.

He took her by the waist. Caroline let him lift her off the ledge and, in spite of all her silent admonishing, her heart took off at a run. This close, it was hard to stand properly; the tendency to list against him was so strong.

He cleared his throat, picking a twig from her hair. "You look like some sort of forest creature."

"There's a caterpillar on your sleeve," she told him.

"So there is." Carefully, he coaxed the furry inchling onto his finger and lifted him to the wall. "There's a good fellow. Done being cross?" he asked, flicking a glance at her.

"I'm not cross, I'm jealous." And she lost all claims to dignity when she spoke with that note of pleading.

He kissed her nose and then her lips. "Mmm. I like you. So kind to my vanity."

Caroline nudged him with her hip. "That wasn't my intention."

"I didn't think so. He bent to brush the moss off the back of her skirts. "There. Decent enough to appear in company. Shall we go?"

Caroline accepted Ormonde's leash and took Jack's arm with her free hand. They walked out of the wood, blinking in the bright sunshine. The town spread before them, encroaching on the slopes rising from the river.

Jack bent his head to hers. "I could never think of kissing another lady when my head is full of you."

Caroline squeezed his arm, but all she could say was, "We'd better hurry. Or we'll be late for luncheon."

By the time they returned to Camden Place, Jack was pleased to see that most of the creases had fallen from Caroline's skirts. Only their unconscionable tardiness might draw comment from Lady Lynher.

"I hadn't realized we'd be gone so long," Caroline whispered to him as they climbed the stairs. "Let me make our excuses to Grandmama."

To their surprise, none were required. Their appearance in the sitting room caused barely a pause. The dowager countess was entertaining.

"Caroline. Dr. Edwards. I hope you enjoyed your walk. Come sit down. Or find something to eat if you are hungry." Waving vaguely at the sideboard loaded with cakes, cold meats, fruit, and cheese, she resumed her conversation with Henrietta. There was enough food laid out for a dozen, and if she didn't have quite that many guests, she was close.

From the sofa, Henrietta sent him a triumphant glance. Jack tried quelling her with a look, but she only raised her eyebrows at him. What on earth were she and Percy doing here? The few words he caught told him she was recounting how he'd brought her boys through their influenza.

Too embarrassed to interrupt, he moved to the sideboard.

"Forgive me, Grandmama," Caroline said. "Had I known we were expecting guests, I would have been more prompt. But the woods were lovely and—"

From the corner of his eye, Jack saw an elderly lady in plum taffeta giving Caroline the once-over. He added a pear, some cheese, and cold ham to his plate, glad his efforts restoring her hair and gown would defeat all but the closest scrutiny. But as they'd come into town, Caroline had noticed a bruise on his neck only partially concealed by his neckcloth. He walked to a seat, keeping that side to the wall.

His weight on the sofa startled General Rockwell, who snorted, blinked, and pretended he'd not been sleeping. "I hear your sister's given Rushford an heir?"

"And a daughter," Jack said. Jane was the elder of the two. Lately, it was hard to keep track of all the children: Percy and Henrietta's three boys, little Ollie Bagshot, Laura's Jane and Crispin, Emily Beaumaris, and Lady Fairchild's famously stubborn three-year-old Kate.

"Good for your business," General Rockwell grunted.

"I suppose so," Jack replied, merely to be agreeable. He attended those of the family who lived in Suffolk, but—

"She still a looker?" General Rockwell asked.

"Pardon?" Jack stared.

"Your sister. The actress." He chuckled.

Jack's fingers tightened around the edge of his plate. Rockwell was probably one of many idiots who'd frequented Laura's dressing room back in the day. "Mrs. Rushford is—"

"In excellent health, last we saw her," Percy Arundel put in. "And I believe you had a letter from her just yesterday?"

"She's an excellent correspondent," Jack said, taking his cue.

"We all miss her," Henrietta added. "Lady Lynher, do you attend this Thursday's Fancy Ball?"

The countess shook her head. "I think not. So much fuss and bother. I came to Bath to rest, not wear myself ragged."

"What a pity. I'm sure we'll be there." Henrietta smiled at Jack and her husband. "Perhaps your granddaughter?"

Caroline glanced at Jack. "I couldn't go without my grandmother. But it's kind of you to think of me." She took a place beside the lady in plum taffeta and didn't look at him again. Jack cleared his plate, waiting for a chance to speak with her. It didn't come. When at last Henrietta and Percy rose to take their leave, Jack stood with them, giving formal thanks to the dowager countess and to Caroline for giving him her company. All he got in return was a smile and a nod.

Jack pressed his lips together. So he was good enough on his own, but not in company?

"That general. What a rudesby!" Henrietta grumbled on the walk home. "Chortling over Laura to your face. I could have dumped my tea all over him."

"It's nothing new," Jack reminded her. It was good for him to remember that no matter what Caroline permitted in private, he was not an acceptable match for her. He worked for a living, and his sister had spent years on the London stage. Caroline had made her opinions clear. If she couldn't have someone rich and political, like Sir Robert, she'd stay a spinster.

Jack remembered *that* story. Fellow had broken his neck trying to ride a horse up a flight of stairs. Well, if she wanted a fool, she could have one anytime she pleased. He wasn't a pet to come when called—not that she often succeeded with Ormonde. He might be sunk up to his ears he was so infatuated with her, but he couldn't respect a lady foolish enough to prefer a man like that. It hurt, mostly because he'd thought better of her. Though Jack knew in society's eyes he was no catch, pride and his own sense of competence wouldn't let him rate himself below the blockheaded Sir Robert Symes.

He liked what he'd made of himself. It was time to stop wallowing. He would write Dr. Fielding tomorrow. His patients needed him.

"Let's go out for a drive tomorrow," Percy suggested, breaking the silence.

"Excellent idea," Jack said. He'd still have time for his letters. "It will be a fine thing for the boys."

Caroline was uneasy after Jack left. They'd hardly spoken—but they couldn't, not after arriving together in front of so many. She wasn't ready for stares, for whispers linking them together. Still, his stiff manner as he left and the irksome comments of General Rockwell were by no means reassuring. Next morning, she set out to call in the Royal Crescent with Ormonde. Jack and the Arundels were not at home. By dinner, she was growing anxious.

"Missing your beau?" Grandmama asked between spoonfuls of soup.

"A little."

Grandmama pursed her lips. "You spent all morning with him yesterday. Doesn't do to seem too eager. That's why I said we'd miss the ball."

"But you invited him and the Arundels for luncheon," Caroline said. "If you keep blowing hot and cold at him—"

"That's what you're supposed to do. That's what flirting is. Your mother was never any good at it, but you'd have thought she'd make some effort to teach you."

"When I was six?"

Grandmama set down her spoon. "I suppose not. But you may wish to examine how much you like him."

She didn't know. Even still, she shouldn't have been scared into snubbing him like that.

"Please excuse me. I'm not hungry." Caroline rose from the table, leaving in a fanfare of clinking china.

She called again in the Royal Crescent, but only visited briefly with Lady Arundel, who was stiffly polite at the start of the visit but eventually warmed. She told Caroline that Jack and Percy had gone riding, then introduced her sons. "They are pretty stout now," she said, "but we had quite a time of it."

The next day Caroline spent at home. She had letters from Uncle Warren asking after Grandmama and one from Kit, suggesting that now Grandmama was settled Caroline may wish to return to London. He'd made a new acquaintance, the MP Richard Snaring, who'd expressed a wish to meet her. Caroline penned a pungent reply—she was no horse to be looked over!—and sent it with the post. By dinner, she was despondent, regretting her harsh letter to Kit and her coldness to Jack, who'd probably renewed his acquaintance with the ladies he'd met in the wood.

She didn't know how to flirt, not well. Not like Grandmama.

"He's touchier than I expected," Grandmama admitted that evening. "You may have lost him. Pity."

Caroline rose without a word and left to walk Ormonde. He answered her calls much better with the inducements of bits of cheese she carried in her reticule. They raced about the park and saw acquaintances aplenty, but not Jack.

Two days later, having given up, Caroline was morosely reacquainting herself with Kit's letters. He was making progress with Miss Clarkwell and her fortune, but Caroline couldn't muster any enthusiasm for the news. Once Kit married, he'd have no need of her at all.

Caroline was finishing her written apology when she heard Lady Arundel in the hall. Her pen arrested mid-stroke.

The butler, instructed that Caroline was not at home to visitors, was turning Lady Arundel away. Caroline rushed into the hall.

"Wait! Lady Arundel!"

"Miss Trenholme!" It was Jack.

"They said you weren't at home," Lady Arundel said.

"I was just about to go out . . . to walk Ormonde," Caroline lied.

"If we could detain you just a moment. We bear an invitation," Lady Arundel said.

"A dinner," Jack said. "Nothing formal. Just you and Lady Lynher and ourselves. I'm sorry I missed your call the other day." His face was solemn, but he looked at, not around her. "Perhaps afterward, we could attend the concert. Are you free next Wednesday?"

"I'd like that. We have no plans that evening."

Then, because she'd said she was leaving, she had to wish them good day. But she couldn't help smiling like an idiot or the fluttering that took hold of her when Jack's face softened and did the same.

"Come walking again with me?" she whispered.

"Where?"

"Anywhere. The woods, the Pump Room, the park . . ."

The etching between his eyes dissolved. She'd done something right.

"Tomorrow." He collected Henrietta, who was humming beside the front door, but he looked back once more as he left. The moment the door shut, Caroline mounted the stairs, flying into her grandmother's sitting room.

"We're invited for dinner. Before the concert. I hope you are in the mood for music," Caroline said.

Grandmama took off her spectacles and closed her book, studying Caroline for an uncomfortable minute, her withered lips finally spreading in a smile. "This is with Dr. Edwards."

Caroline drew in a breath. "Yes."

Her grandmother patted the seat beside her. Caroline took it, letting Grandmama brush back a strand of her hair, rubbing her knuckles over Caroline's cheek. "I'm glad, darling."

That week, she and Jack walked—with Ormonde, with Lord Arundel, with two of the three young boys, with Lady Arundel, who informed Caroline it was thanks to her persuasion that Jack had called again.

"Henrietta! You must keep some of my secrets!" Jack groaned.

They walked in the wood. Caroline asked him about his work and learned he'd put off his return another fortnight. "I'm busy enough I could take Dr. Fielding into partnership. He's considering the idea, so I'll let him alone a little longer."

They walked the circuit in the Pump Room, snickering together as young ladies fled from General Rockwell. The Bath tabbies swallowed their words when Caroline and Jack walked by arm in arm, but Caroline was too happy to mind.

Grandmama played cards in the evening with Jack, sent him and Caroline on spurious errands, reminisced with him of the France she had known in her youth—with her, he spoke freely of the gilded world he had known. Again and again, Caroline's heart broke for him.

"I like your Dr. Edwards," Grandmama said one evening as Caroline helped her to bed. She was overtired but talking excitedly. "We must decide what dress you'll wear to Lady Arundel's dinner. Do you have anything pink?" Quieter, almost to herself, she mumbled, "It always looks well on young girls in love."

Caroline could have contradicted her. But she didn't.

Chapter Six

Caroline must have tried on every one of her gowns twice before choosing, on the very eve of the concert, a dress of warm-toned red net. It had a wide band of flowers worked in paisley at the hem and a fringe the color of old gold.

"Very handsome," her grandmother agreed, surveying Caroline in the long mirror.

"I'm not eighteen," Caroline said, feeling some justification was needed.

"True. Come with me." Picking up her stick, Grandmama led Caroline into her own dressing room. "Bring out my box," she ordered her maid. Motioning Caroline onto the low velvet bench beside her, she patted her knee. "You take after your father, you know. He was the handsomest of my children, but so stuffy." Caroline looked at her grandmother through the mirror, wiry and tough, but not as baffling as before. Grandmama cared for her much more than she'd known or previously cared to discover.

"Thank you for agreeing to this dinner," Caroline said.

Grandmama dismissed this with a sniff. "I've always loved a good party. Say what you will about Lady Arundel and her connections, they know how to have fun. Edwards is . . .

Well, I like him." She straightened, giving her shoulders a shake as her maid set down the jewelry box in front of her. "I must have something here that will go with that dress."

She held up a brooch, and Caroline flinched. "Ugh! Where did you get that?" It looked just like an eye.

"Macabre, I know. I used to wear it to fasten a burgundy velvet cloak." Grandmama set it aside. "This might do—the color is the exact shade of your gown."

It was a pretty piece, but— "I'd feel I was shamming it, wearing a cross," Caroline said. She seldom went to church.

"I see your point," Grandmama said. "What about this?" She held out a heavy bracelet of antique cameos. "I always liked this one."

It was a curious piece. Caroline turned it over in her hand, studying the faces.

"Try it on." Grandmama clasped it around her wrist.

"I like it," Caroline said, testing the weight.

"You must have it."

Caroline looked up. Grandmama's eyes were bright. Buried in the lined cheeks, Caroline thought she detected the infamous dimple Reynolds had preserved in his portrait of her. "Just lend it to me. I—"

"It's yours. Come. This isn't any old party." She smiled. For her age, Grandmama had excellent teeth. "Whatever comes, you'll want to remember this evening." She gestured to her untidy box. "Sometimes it's nice to tie a recollection to something you can hold."

"But what if this is a memory of yours?"

"Take it and give it a better one. It will bring you good luck.'

Caroline felt her resolve weakening. The bracelet was peculiarly attractive. "With my gold earrings and a plain circlet of pearls—"

The Fine Art of Kissing in the Park

"And a shawl. I have just the one." Springing up, Grandmama went for the chest of drawers, reaching for the drawer on top.

"No, let me—!" Too late. Caroline lunged but couldn't reach her. Grandmama toppled to the floor, landing with a heavy crash. Caroline ran to her. "Are you hurt?"

"I'm fine, I'm fine. Give me room to breathe." Waving Caroline and her maid back, Grandmama continued to wheeze, a disjointed heap on the floor. She tried to push herself up and fell back with a moan.

"Grandmama." Kneeling, Caroline bent closer. "God! Your arm." She shut her eyes, feeling faint. Grandmama's reedy arm was bent at a grotesque angle.

"Oh, my lady!" the maid cried.

"Bring Walters," Caroline said, closing her throat and forcing control on her shaking hands and heaving stomach. "We must get you to the bed," she told her grandmother.

"It's that damned stick of mine," Grandmama said. "Tripped me! Why was it there?" She turned on the maid. "You're supposed to put these things away!"

"Be still. I don't want you to hurt yourself further," Caroline said. "Rawlings, send someone for Dr. Edwards. Ask him to come at once."

Jack, not yet in his evening clothes, was blindfolded and playing hide-and-seek, his half-finished letter to his sister forgotten on the desk by the window. Since he couldn't untangle his thoughts, it was no good putting them to paper. He might as well stagger about the parlor, eliciting whoops from Percy, Henrietta, and their half-dressed boys, who'd gotten no farther than their nightshirts after the evening bath.

"Warm . . . warmer . . . watch out, you'll get burned!"

Laurie, the eldest boy, shrieked as Jack groped his way past the window. "Nope. Gone cold again," he said as Jack stumbled into the curtains.

Perhaps he'd find William in the cupboard below the window seat. For a stocky child, he was alarmingly flexible.

"Hot! Hot! Scorching!" Behind him, Henrietta laughed. Jack opened the cupboard, found William, and lifted him out, tickling his ribs.

"May I lose the blindfold now?"

William slid it off. "My turn!"

"We should probably dress. It's nearly time for dinner. Yes, what is it?" Percy said, noticing the footman clearing his throat on the threshold. He carried a note in his hand.

"A message. For Dr. Edwards."

It was from Caroline. *Please come at once. It's my grandmother.*

He was half a second later to comprehension than usual. She needed a doctor. "Fetch my coat and my bag. Lady Lynher requires me," he explained to Henrietta.

She nodded, moistening her lips. "Shall I cancel dinner? Send at once if there's anything we can do."

Jack nodded. Until he knew why he was needed, there was nothing to say. He went out, shoulders set, his fingers clenched around the handle of his bag. Dusk had fallen. He walked quickly, his shadow swinging in broad arcs as he passed from one lamp's glow to the next. It was always impossible not to speculate. Had he missed some symptom at their last meeting? What would he find? She must be nearly seventy, perhaps even beyond. Would he be able to help? Shades of his failures hovered about him, making him forget he'd ever had any success.

Caroline cared deeply for her grandmother. Among her family, the dowager countess seemed the best of the lot. Jack hadn't met the others but was forming no great opinion of her brother or Uncle Warren.

The front door opened before he reached the top step. "Thank you for coming, Doctor." The butler relieved him of his coat and hat and brought him upstairs to a bedchamber encrusted in ornamentation of the former French style. Lady Lynher, dwindling to a scrap beneath the massive bed hangings, lay pallid and sweating.

"It's this stick! Had no business being where I'd trip over it!" She spoke petulantly, her lips tight with pain.

Caroline came to him. "I should have stopped her or talked her out of those ridiculous heels."

"She fell?" Jack whispered.

A nod. "And—"

"Her arm is broken." It rested, bent and swollen, on a broad damask pillow.

"I wish she'd fainted. When we moved her, she went all gray and trembling. Such groans!" Caroline bit her lip.

She looked gray herself. Jack steered her to a chair. "Have something to drink. Sweet tea?" He caught the eye of the maid, and she vanished. "Sit right here. I'll examine your grandmother."

He advanced to the bed.

"If these fools would just put things away—" the countess began.

"Lady Lynher, you may snap at your servants as much as you please, but don't try to fool me. I expect you were in too much of a hurry, which in my medical opinion ill-accords with your years and your dignity."

The lecture made her smile. "Yes, but can you fix me?'

"I shall certainly try, but first, we must make you more comfortable. You won't like me at all if I try prodding you now." It might be a simple break judging from the shape of the deformity, but he didn't want to raise false hope. From his bag, he took out a vial of strong laudanum.

The countess made a face. "Can't stand that stuff."

"Yes, it is wretched, but you feel that way already."

Caroline appeared at his elbow with water and a glass. Jack kept up a light patter as he measured and mixed the dose, saying how desolated Lady Arundel was, and how they were missing a rare dinner—only three removes, but all excellent dishes. There was to be a haunch of venison, a turtle soup, and an excellent selection of jellies. "I expect she'll send some of those to you once I tell her I'm keeping you on invalid's food. After a few days, if you are doing well, you may have your French creams and port wine again."

She looked mollified, but only slightly.

"Caroline, will you help the countess with her medicine? Please drink it all."

Lady Lynher took two swallows, then pulled away from the glass, a bead of water rolling down her chin. Jack didn't like that she was still trembling.

"'Caroline,' is it?" the countess asked. "What does she call you?"

"A scallywag," Jack said evenly. "Finish up."

Obediently, Lady Lynher drained the glass.

"Now we wait," Jack said, answering the question in both their eyes. "I'd rather set the bones once you're asleep."

"What I don't know won't hurt me?" Lady Lynher asked skeptically.

"You will be quite uncomfortable when you wake," Jack told her. "But I'll have another dose ready. Caroline, you didn't drink your tea."

She retreated to the enamel-topped table holding a tray with a steaming cup. While she sipped, Jack watched her fingers—a trifle clumsy, but better than before.

The Fine Art of Kissing in the Park

"Doesn't she look fine?" Lady Lynher asked.

Jack nodded.

"Such a pity. I'm sorry for spoiling the evening," Lady Lynher said.

"It's of no consequence," Jack said. "So long as you haven't spoiled your arm. We'll get you back in good order before too long, but I wish you could be spared this."

She gave a wan smile. In another minute, Caroline returned her empty cup to the saucer and was back at his side.

"Rest now," Jack urged the countess. "Tomorrow, you may complain to me all you please, including how that stick of yours plotted against you."

"I'm not tired in the least." But she closed her eyes. Jack consulted his watch. It shouldn't take long.

"You're wonderfully calm," Caroline whispered. "Thank you."

It was forward, but—let him presume. Jack covered her hand with his and held it. A broken arm, even one belonging to Lady Lynher, wasn't enough to worry him. Tying off arteries in a rolling ship's surgery beneath the gun decks as cannons blasted and timbers shuddered—that experience wouldn't leave him. That, and waking some weeks ago, too weak to leave his bed, and quarreling with Percy until he admitted how many of Jack's patients had died. Too many.

But he was ready to go back, to start again. He'd written the families of the patients who had died, and would have returned already, if not for Caroline. Her hand turned, palm to palm with his. Perhaps she knew he also took comfort from the touch. He was glad she felt no need to talk.

Lady Lynher was deeply asleep when the maid returned. Jack rose, telling her the supplies he needed. Splints and bandages he had, but ice would reduce the swelling and make the countess more comfortable.

"Should I leave?" Caroline asked. Clearly, she didn't wish to.

"It can be a bit rough, bone setting," Jack warned her. "You might rather lend me one of your footmen."

"No, let me. Unless you think I'm too clumsy."

Jack shook his head. "I worry more that it will be painful for you to see. And you are wearing your evening gown."

"That can be remedied." She unfastened the heavy bracelet from her wrist and set it on the bedside table. "I won't be a moment."

She returned minutes later in a plain blue gown. "I've sent messengers to Kit and my uncle. I'm ready, if you still wish me to help." Though she turned white when he insisted she brace her grandmother's shoulder and pull the elbow harder to provide sufficient traction, her hands were steady and her actions sure.

"Hand me the splint now," Jack ordered. "Good. And another. A rolled bandage . . . Now, keep these still for me." With practiced speed, he wound the length of linen around Lady Lynher's arm.

"That was quick." She sounded breathless.

Jack looked up, surprised. He thought he'd been taking his time. "You did very well for a first endeavor."

She rubbed her hands together. "I'll see if Rawlings has found any ice."

When this was applied, they stood together, watching the countess. "This is selfish of me, but I don't want you to go," Caroline said, taking hold of his hand.

"Perhaps it is ill-mannered of me, but I wasn't going to," Jack told her. "She's fine for the present. I'm staying to keep watch on you."

The tension left her shoulders. She turned down the lamp. "We may as well sit down."

There were chairs on either side of the bed, gilded wood and brocade, wide and comfortable. Instead, they went to the matching, round-backed sofa—a small seat for the two of them. Caroline tucked up her feet and put her head on his shoulder.

Around midnight, Lady Lynher woke briefly to swallow her next dose. At two, Caroline also slept. At four, Jack moved his numb arm and accidentally woke her. She sighed, her breath brushing his cheek, their heads were so close.

Perhaps he was tired, too worn to edit his thoughts or guard his tongue. He spoke without thinking. "Caroline, I think you should marry me."

Chapter Seven

Caroline stretched her shoulders, smiling sleepily. "Wouldn't that be wonderful?" The world would never dismay, oppress, or frighten her, not when she held him close. This felt too good, this snuggling way of sleeping.

Beneath her head, he'd gone very still. She couldn't feel him breathing. Caroline looked up. It was dark, but she sensed hurt, and also that he was smiling.

"I should probably stop while I'm ahead. Do you mean that, Caroline? Because I did."

Involuntarily, two of her fingers twitched, curling into his waistcoat. The coat had been discarded while they were setting Grandmama's arm. "It *would* be wonderful, being married to you."

Her heart wrung as she said it, for she could see it in her mind's eye: laughter and eagerness and exquisite courtesy the first time he took her to bed. A short honeymoon in a moderately priced hotel where they barely left their rooms. Then home to a pretty house in the country, but with her about, he shouldn't be allowed to work himself into exhaustion. They'd curl up together like this when he came home late at nights, cold and tired from tending his patients.

She'd manage the kitchen so there was always something warm and wonderful for him to eat. She'd tend to his letters and correspondence, and read over the cases he wrote up for medical journals. She'd insist he take time for his researches, and when his shoulders hitched up and his brow furrowed, as talk of his responsibilities made them do, she'd knead his shoulders until they hung loose the way they ought. Then, when they had children—how fortunate those babies would be to have such a father.

Caroline swallowed. "But of course I could not."

His thumb drifted over her cheek, gliding down to the point of her chin. "I expect I know why, but it might be easier to believe if you said it. Will you do that for me, Caroline?"

Not if he kept saying her name like that. Thankfully, he was silent. "I hardly know you," she said.

"Do you truly think so? And what of this thing we feel?"

How could she answer that? Her fingers, those awful betrayers, held him tighter. It was impossible to deny she loved him, with her head resting on his shoulder.

"I've never experienced this before. I hardly know what to do with it."

"Don't you?"

He wasn't going to let her lie. "Very well. I know, but I can't. You understand. I know you do, because you said right from the start this was hopeless. I'm meant to be a politician's wife. It's what I am bred for." Rather wistfully, she toyed with one of his buttons. "Perhaps if *you* became a member of the cabinet."

"That, my love, is quite impossible."

Caroline sighed.

He bent his head to look at her. "Should I leave you now?"

"Must you?" If all they had was this time in Bath... "We only get such a little while."

"Then I will stay."

"And Grandmama? Will you still attend her? Or—am I being unkind to you?" Perhaps she should let him go.

He picked up her hand and kissed her fingers. "My dear love. Keeping you forever would honor me beyond measure, but I'm not such a fool I can't enjoy what you give me today."

"And tomorrow. For as long as we are in Bath." Caroline laced their fingers together, glad their talk hadn't stirred Grandmama's sleeping. "I love you, Jack."

Caroline didn't sleep, but she left the sofa before the servants began stirring and went to her room to wash and change. Grandmama was bleary but awake when she returned. Jack examined her, and the tartness of her replies was immensely reassuring.

"A short convalescence and you'll be as magnificent and ornery as ever," Jack assured her.

"Huh! Better to be magnificent and ornery than magnificently ordinary," she huffed.

"Quite." He kissed Grandmama's hand, which surprised Caroline, but Grandmama took it as no more than her due.

"Feed him breakfast!" she said, ordering them from the room.

"You're good at fixing people," Caroline said as they took chairs in the breakfast parlor.

"Sometimes." Jack reached for the coffee. "She'll mend. There's no reason to worry, but I can come round this afternoon to see you both."

"Please do."

They ate, and while much of their unspoken conversation was tinged bittersweet, they had no lack of things to talk about.

He kissed her in the empty hallway before he left, solidly, pressing her against the console table. Over almost as soon as it begun, it still left her breathless. Caroline stood at the door after he tipped his hat to her, watching him stride down the street.

She had scarcely made her way upstairs again when there was noise at the door. "Jack? Did you forget something?" She glanced about the room, but all paraphernalia had returned to his black bag. Perhaps he'd forgotten to tell her something about Grandmama's dose?

Caroline hurried to the top of the stairs. "Kit! I'd no hope of seeing you this quickly." He must have left the instant her messenger arrived and traveled all night, explaining his frown and the rumples. "Grandmama will be so pleased to see you. She says she hates fussing, but it will mean a great deal that you've come. The doctor has just left, but he says—"

"Doctor? What's the matter with Grandmama?"

Caroline frowned. "Isn't that why you've come?"

"I came to bring you to London. I told you I needed you."

"What for?" If it had been so urgent, why stand against her when she'd protested coming to Bath in the first place?

"Well, I didn't like putting it in a letter, and I want you for Saturday, but if something's the matter with our grandmother—dash it, we'll have to figure out something. Hire a nurse?"

"I'm not leaving her. She broke her arm!" Caroline frowned at him, unwilling to believe he spoke in earnest. "If you think for half a minute, you'll realize she needs me. She's in pain, rattled by the fall, and I'm not leaving her with only servants, most of whom were hired with the house!"

"Yes, but—" He turned his hat in his hands. "Listen, Caroline. I've been getting to know Mr. Snaring—"

"Him? Or his niece, the heiress you've been going on about?"

"Both. I hadn't heard, and he was late coming up to town, but he lost his wife over the winter."

He couldn't be suggesting . . .

"He's a prominent speaker in the House of Lords, has a financial stake in a newspaper—"

"I see." Her pulse throbbed in her temples. "You recommended me, sight unseen, and he was willing?" It was utterly insulting.

"It wasn't quite like that. He's simply anxious to pursue your acquaintance."

"Then he should come to Bath."

"He's got small children," Kit said. "Surely you understand he can't do that. Not while the House is sitting. It's the wrong time of year."

"Have you any luggage?" Caroline asked.

"Just my cloak bag. I didn't think—"

"Clearly. I'll see it's taken upstairs. We'll find you a room. I suggest you freshen yourself up before you see Grandmama."

Kit followed her up the stairs. Outside her chamber, he caught her arm. "I thought you'd be pleased. You said you were missing London."

"I was, then." Caroline shook him off. If she didn't find some privacy to recover her temper, they'd soon alert more than the housemaid who'd ducked out of sight coming upon this nasty scene. Caroline quivered with accusations.

"Don't pretend, Caroline. This is more than Grandmama," Kit said. "Who's Jack? You called for him."

"A friend. Grandmama and I made his acquaintance here in Bath."

Kit's eyes narrowed. "French? A doctor?"

Surprised betrayed her. "You know him?"

"Dash it, Caroline." Kit stretched his tired shoulders and took a short circuit around the hall. "It's true, then?"

"I don't know what you mean." But she was unexpectedly nervous.

"I heard reports—"

"From whom?" Caroline demanded. Once she knew who dared—and what was Kit about, listening to reports?

"Rawlings." Kit scratched beneath the edge of his shirt collar.

"Grandmama's maid?"

"She—she keeps watch on her for Uncle Warren. And me," he admitted.

"You have spies on us?" Unbelievable. At least of Kit. Uncle Warren was another matter.

"Not you!" Kit hastened to explain. "Just Grandmama! We never thought you would give any trouble—"

"Which is why you let Grandmama carry me here to Bath," Caroline finished.

"She is difficult. You must admit that."

"But she's not a dirty spy!" Caroline retorted. She licked her lips and let out a breath. "You'll have to excuse me, Kit. It's time for me to take Ormonde for a walk."

Her dog bridled when Kit insisted on following them to the door. Caroline silenced Ormonde's growling with a single command, but Kit wasn't so easy. All the way he argued with her, saying she couldn't object—they were family!

"That's what disgusts me." Yielding to her temper, Caroline slammed the door. On the pavement, a lady with a parasol stared.

The Fine Art of Kissing in the Park

"Come, Ormonde!" Caroline sniffed as she walked past.

All morning, through lunch, and into the afternoon, Jack held imaginary discussions with Caroline. A wasted exercise. If it weren't that she loved him, he'd stop their acquaintance, leave Bath, and find somewhere to nurse his wounds. The trouble was, she did. Love just wasn't the star to guide her.

Duty to her name and her brother would chart her through life, and because this was an honorable choice, he couldn't argue with her. She loved him; he loved her, and if this was all there was to be, he must not spoil the time they had with each other.

You knew from the start this was how it would be. They had only a few weeks left, and due to her grandmother's misfortune, he had an excellent excuse to frequent her company. Perhaps in time . . . No. She'd been engaged to Sir Robert more than two years. She hadn't known him nearly long enough.

Eluding Henrietta's more probing questions, he restocked his bag and went out. The half-mile walk to Camden Place put him in better frame. He was glad the Arundels had insisted on bringing him to Bath, glad even Henrietta had exposed his unlikely background, since it had given him the chance to know Caroline—and to love her.

Unexpected news greeted his arrival. "Mr. Trenholme asks first to speak with you," the butler reported.

Mr. Trenholme? "Caroline's brother?" Jack asked.

Nodding, the butler showed him into the library. The Honorable Member for Penryn sat at his desk, writing. He didn't look up or invite Jack to take a chair. Faintly, from the drawing room, came the sound of a hasty, mercilessly executed Bach concerto. Jack waited until Caroline's brother put down his pen. This was the end, then.

"I'd like you to refer another physician to my grandmother," Mr. Trenholme said.

"She's unhappy with my care?"

"No. But I'm aware of the *tendre* developing between you and my sister. I must ask you to put a stop to it."

"Caroline has told you this?" He thought she'd be braver than that.

"No. She admits nothing, but I've heard tales from a person within this household. Caroline travels with me to London tomorrow, and I must ask you not to interfere with her departure."

"I would never presume to interfere with Miss Trenholme's decisions," Jack said.

"That's not what I am asking. I want you to encourage her to go."

The cold creeping over him eased a little. Jack caught his breath. "She doesn't wish to leave?"

"She refuses to. I—"

"Thank you, Mr. Trenholme." Jack bowed. Ignoring Caroline's sputtering brother, he went to find Caroline. She stopped playing when he entered the room, her fingers suspended over the keys.

Jack shut the door and leaned his shoulder against it. "I had my suspicions, but he's worse than I thought. You have a perfect ass for a brother."

Behind Jack, someone rattled the door. "Edwards! Caroline!"

"You see? He proves my point. Just a moment, Mr. Trenholme," Jack called.

At the piano bench, Caroline clenched her hands

together until the knuckles blanched. "It's utterly humiliating."

He hadn't meant to do this, but in light of the circumstances . . . "Will you reconsider my offer?"

"I think of it all the time. But I can't marry you to spite my brother. We still hardly know each other, Jack."

"And what we feel isn't enough?"

"Marriage is for a lifetime. I—"

"I know." So her brother's arrival didn't change anything. Jack smiled. "You aren't meant to share mine. Should we see your grandmother?"

"I think so." Caroline got up and smoothed her skirts. "Kit, go back to your hotel," she called through the door. "I'm not having you upset Grandmama."

"Caroline, I'm warning you—!"

"Unless you intend to remain in Bath to support our grandmother in her distress, I recommend you return to London. I have no wish to speak to you nor meet any of your friends. And you may tell the same to Uncle Warren!" Her voice rose at the last, and she bit her lip. "I'm sorry, Jack. I never meant to drag you into this."

Jack opened the door. Kit stumbled into the room, righted himself, and went on as before, in a smoldering temper. Caroline ignored him, leading Jack up the stairs. Kit remained below.

"Has he gone?" Lady Lynher asked.

"Not yet," Caroline sighed. "I'm glad you have reason to need me, because I expect I'll be sharing your roof for some time."

"Don't say it like it's a penance!" Lady Lynher retorted.

"Forgive me." Caroline smiled. "Will you let Dr. Edwards look at you?"

The countess showed dark and quite remarkable bruises,

but otherwise nothing to concern him. When she conspicuously motioned them away and shut her eyes, Jack allowed Caroline to detain him in the far corner of the room.

"I'm so sorry," she began.

"You have nothing to apologize for," Jack told her. Though he'd happily thrash her brother.

"Will you come again tomorrow? Kit won't be here, not if I must have him thrown out the door."

Jack glanced over Caroline's shoulder. Lady Lynher might be peeking, but he kissed her once and pushed back a few falling strands of hair. "Caroline, I'm leaving tomorrow." He hadn't made the decision, but he accepted it, from the moment her brother refused to offer him a chair.

"Leaving? Why?"

Because it was the only thing he could do. He smiled. "I found my cure, so I must get back. I can't leave my patients forever."

"But—"

He stopped her with his lips. This one would be the last. "Until one of us left Bath, is all. We never said how long that would be."

She swallowed. "I'm sorry you must go."

Not as sorry as he. "Take care of your grandmother. You're a good physic for her. You've been a good one for me."

"You—you won't be unhappy?"

"From time to time." *Liar.* "I *am* quite attached to Ormonde."

Her lips trembled. "Jack."

"Shh." He nodded in the direction of her grandmother, who could not possibly be sleeping. Now was the time to leave, before the joke faded away. It wouldn't take long. "You'll give my best wishes to the countess?"

"She'll be furious with you," Caroline said. "But she'll understand."

"Goodbye, then."

"Goodbye."

Perhaps she sensed the limits of his resolve because she remained in the room as he left. He hurried from the house, ignoring Caroline's scowling brother, wishing he wasn't lashed by memories of kissing Caroline in the hall or on the third stair. It wouldn't always hurt this badly. It couldn't.

Staring at the door by which he'd gone was excessively tragic, especially with Grandmama pretending she wasn't watching. Caroline composed her face into something less stricken and returned to the bedside, taking one of the chairs.

Crocodile-like, Grandmama opened an eye at her. "Don't blame me."

"I don't." Caroline wanted to, but she couldn't even blame Kit. His interference certainly sped Jack's departure, but Jack would have left eventually. "Better this way," Caroline murmured.

Grandmama snorted from her pillows.

"Would you like me to read to you?" Caroline asked. Grandmama's refusal was as much disheartening as it was a relief. The effort of pretending all was well was beyond her, but without distractions, she would have nothing to do but think.

Kit took his starchy, formal leave an hour later. Caroline was too angry to do more than nod at him.

Word of Grandmama's accident spread. By the following afternoon, they were set upon with callers who brought flowers, cordials, and offers of company. Fearing the parade would tire her grandmother, Caroline attempted to divert most of them until she saw how Grandmama reveled in it. Arrayed in her prettiest wrapper and a dainty lace cap, she accepted the sympathy of her acquaintances like a queen receiving offers of fealty. In spite of the pain in her arm and the attentions of a new, less-liked physician, she was in high spirits and spent all of an hour closeted with one friend, a middle-aged bishop, son of one of her oldest friends.

Caroline, who couldn't sleep, was glad of it. With Grandmama happily occupied, there was no one to peck at her or notice how badly she performed for company. Except Ormonde. Tired with her inattentiveness, he chewed her newest pair of slippers to shreds. Instead of scolding, Caroline took him out for a walk, reminding herself all the reasons why marrying Jack was impossible. They'd barely met. Tying herself to a man she scarcely knew was the height of foolishness. She'd liked and respected Robert—known him for years—and yet she'd never suspected him capable of that final drunken folly. In the end, she had known less of him than she'd thought.

More certain, though, was her position and that of her family—though she was entirely fed up with Kit and her uncle. If only Kit would treat her as an ally, instead of a pawn! To Uncle Warren, she might as well be a piece of furniture. Just now, the only one she liked was Grandmama, who wouldn't hold with such a marriage, for all she'd encouraged the flirting.

"There's a long face," Grandmama observed when Caroline returned, finding her, for once, alone. "Missing that doctor of yours?"

"Yes." But it would pass. Caroline deflected scrutiny with a question whose answer meant nothing to her. "How long did you listen to Lady Margaret?" The only thing she truly wanted

The Fine Art of Kissing in the Park

to know was if Jack was home yet. Or, more honestly, was he as miserable as she?

That evening, Caroline passed Lady Arundel in the park. Mustering a smile, she received a curt nod in return. Not undeserved, Caroline admitted to herself, hurrying away with Ormonde. She went out the next morning to the bluebell wood. It was every bit as lovely as before and utterly desolate. Caroline found their patch of ground and sat hugging her knees. She allowed herself to cry, but the tears didn't spark any healing of her heart, and her list of reasons for refusing his proposal felt more threadbare than ever.

Heiresses of excellent family married titled and important men, and she was trained to be a political hostess. Jack, gentleman that he was, had refrained from pressing her. Yet he could have. How stupid, to make such an argument to a man who'd been born a count. Her own ambitions and sense of importance seemed foolish. Jack wasn't the man birth decreed him to be—and he didn't complain of it. He was remade, and his pride made it clear he wasn't ashamed of any of it. Why had she been too small-minded to see?

It was coming on dark by the time she got home.

"You're back." Grandmama looked up from the letter in her lace-mittened hands.

"I'm sorry I was away so long." Caroline kissed her.

"I'd started to wonder where you could be."

"I hope you didn't send out a search party." Caroline set to work tidying the bedside tray, wishing it were possible to right her course so easily.

"I shouldn't do that," Grandmama protested. "I thought perhaps now that your brother has taken himself away . . . Well, if you had eloped, I'd be the last one to—"

"Grandmama!" Caroline looked at her, unable to keep her hands from trembling. "Do you think I would ever—"

"I hoped."

Caroline was still. "You can't be serious." An elopement? Well, in the face of Kit's opposition, they could hardly wed otherwise. She felt sick.

"Sit down, Caroline."

Dropping numbly into the chair, she scarcely noticed when Grandmama picked up her hand.

"Why won't you marry him?"

Caroline brushed a hand across her eye.

"I have all sorts of excellent reasons."

"Understandably. Forgive me, but they don't seem enough. You're wilting without him."

"I daresay I'll recover."

Grandmama nodded. "One does, eventually. But why should you have to, my dear?"

Caroline gave a watery smile. "I already refused him. I could hardly—"

Grandmama tsked at her. "Goodness, everyone knows a lady can change her mind."

"He may have changed his."

"I don't think so." Grandmama patted her hand.

"Even so, I can't imagine you'd like us bolting to Gretna Green!"

Grandmama shuddered. "When I thought you might have gone with him today, it was my one complaint. So unnecessary. You are of age. That doctor of yours might lack the ready, but—"

Caroline groaned, looking up at the ceiling. "You think we should marry by special license?"

"It certainly has more style."

Caroline hiccupped once and dissolved. After all the tears she shed in the wood, she couldn't tell if she was laughing or crying. She missed Jack, missed him with her kidneys and her littlest fingernail. "I suppose you'll flatten me now by telling me to trust you with the arrangements."

Grandmama huffed. "Well, you're wrong there. You'll have to speak with him. But I thought it prudent to acquire a license." Caroline stared, long enough that Grandmama flustered, plucking at her lace mittens. "Always useful, knowing a bishop."

"Enough!" Caroline pleaded, wiping her eyes. "Grandmama, I can't!"

"You're a fool if you don't! I'm amazed you've done nothing all this time. Every day, I expected him to come back for you."

Caroline shook her head. "He wouldn't. Not after I refused him a second time, and not after Kit—"

"I'll never understand why you coddle your brother so much. He's quite insufferable."

"Just now, I'm inclined to agree, but—"

"You *should* abandon him. Kit will never make anything of himself if you don't. A good setback will be just the thing."

Caroline didn't feel up to arguing, no matter how absurd Grandmama's reasoning. "I can't abandon you to chase after Jack!"

"Pride is a terrible thing, Caroline. Don't trouble about me. I'll be quite all right if you're back within a week. You won't get a honeymoon, but—"

Caroline's eyes narrowed. "Is this a ploy so you can get back your doctor?"

Grandmama shook her curls. "It's true I haven't much confidence in this new fellow, but that's hardly the point. You, my dear, need to decide what to make of your life. It's not what you've planned, but I think you could do very good things for that man's career."

Perhaps that was true—if Jack let her. She wouldn't know unless she asked him. "All right, then."

The next morning, Caroline set out in a post chaise with Ormonde on her lap, thinking there was nothing like a journey of two hundred miles to play with one's resolve. For two days, she alternated between longing and dread as the coach rattled and bounced across England. She'd never been to Suffolk, which couldn't compare to the west counties, though she had to admit the scenery here was pleasing.

The village smith gave her directions. Jack's house wasn't far, set only a small way off the road, hiding behind overgrown trees. It was small, sixteenth-century, with a miniature moat that probably made the rooms damp. Surrounded by a neglected garden, it looked impossibly romantic. Caroline, her preference for Mayfair elegance and new water closets forgotten, ordered her maid to remain in the coach with Ormonde.

Waiting on the step for someone to answer her knock, she rehearsed a matter-of-fact request to see Dr. Edwards, when the man himself answered the door.

"Jack!" Caroline said, startled at the sight of him. Had he no servants?

"Caroline?" He looked at her a long moment. "Will you come in?" His face was inscrutable.

"I'd rather walk with you outside," she said, her nerve failing.

"Allow me to fetch my coat."

Ormonde barked. "He's tired of being in the carriage," Caroline said.

Jack nodded. "Fetch him out. I'll be back in a moment."

Ormonde gave up prancing around Caroline's skirts the

The Fine Art of Kissing in the Park

moment Jack reappeared, groveling ecstatically at his boots. Jack bent and rubbed his ears. "I've been racking my brains trying to think why, but I'm afraid to guess, Caroline. Why are you here?"

She swallowed, her fingers tangling in Ormonde's lead. "I was wrong. You hadn't been gone a day before I realized what I felt for you was more important than the reasons for my refusal."

"But now it's been ten."

"It took some time coming all this way," Caroline said. "And I had to think it out in my mind. What I wanted was—has always been clear, but convincing myself I could choose to please myself and to make you happy took longer. If I still can? Make you happy, I mean." She was no longer sure.

"Yes, but we can leave that matter aside."

Why? His impassive face frightened her. "I must have disappointed you, but I came hoping it was not too late to prove I'd grown wiser. I want to marry you, if you'll still have me."

"And your brother?" He was looking, from what she could tell, at a fence post.

"Kit won't like it, but that's not important."

"It's not nothing, though. I thought about it all the way home," Jack said. "You're right. We hardly know each other."

She hadn't expected her own words turned on her, not like this. She looked down at her empty hands, realizing she'd dropped the lead and that Ormonde was now happily digging at the end of the garden. "I spent years engaged to a man I merely liked," Caroline said. "When he died, I discovered I knew him less well than I supposed. But there were signs—I should have known his character better, that his feelings for me were weak. Yours aren't. Or they weren't, ten days ago. Mine—mine are too strong to ignore. They have overpowered everything else. I may not have known you long, but I'm willing to stake my hand on you."

"You didn't give me bad reasons, Caroline."

"But they weren't good enough."

He picked up her hand, turning it over in his own. "So you say. Plenty of people would claim otherwise. I've been thinking these last days, too."

Her heart plummeted, a heavy stone in ice-cold water. "You know I was wrong—or you did. Come away with me."

His eyebrows jumped. "Are you suggesting—"

Caroline nodded. This was no time for pride. "I have a special license. Grandmama got it for me. We can marry today if you like."

"If I like?" Jack took a step back, laughing and running a hand through his hair. "Caroline, you can't be serious."

"I *am* serious. Besides, I can't leave Grandmama for long. She wants me back in a week." Her frantic pulse made it possible to pretend this wasn't ridiculous. "Say yes, or I'll have to abduct you."

"Turned rogue, have you?"

Before she could reply, he took hold of her. Gratifying, yes, but she couldn't see his eyes. Until she was sure—

"You weren't all wrong." Jack's voice was thick. "I want you to know me well. Not to feel like you're staking your life and your fortune on a desperate gamble."

"Desperate?" Caroline protested, breaking off when he raised an eyebrow at her.

"I should have come back to Bath," he said. "Because I have another proposal for you."

Caroline waited, scarcely daring to breathe.

"A rascally female is no fit match for a diligent country doctor, but—"

Caroline nudged him with her hip. "Come to the point."

"It seems a pity, when you have the license, but I think we should wait for banns."

Her heart swung wildly. Perhaps from now on it would live in her throat. Caroline looked at him, afraid she couldn't have heard right.

His smile teased her. "I'm a country physician. I've a reputation to consider."

"Jack—"

"I'll look mighty shabby, eloping with an heiress. And I must admit I've no wish to pack you off so soon after our wedding to your Grandmama. Marriage is for keeps. I don't suggest a long engagement, but two or three months? That's not a long time when you're betting your life on me."

Two or three months? She was deliriously happy, yet because she'd been prepared to race to church now, a respectable engagement seemed anticlimactic.

"Lady Lynher will be well by then," Jack went on. "I think she'd like to attend the wedding."

True, but—

"If she's willing to leave Bath, I'll arrange for her to travel to Chippenstone this week. Percy and Henrietta will bring her. The journey can be accomplished in comfort, and she will be well tended. Chippenstone is little more than a mile from here, the house of my friends. In three month's time, you'll have gotten to know me and the county. I'll show you the surgery and the village, and you can decide what to do with the house. You'll meet my friends the Bagshots and my sister and—"

"Yes, but is there a wood we can get lost in?" Caroline asked.

His hands tightened on her shoulders. "Can you doubt it?"

"I accept," Caroline said, but before she was done, he had kissed her. It might have lasted forever, if not for Ormonde. Giving up on his rabbit hole, he bounded up to them.

"Does he have a basket?" Jack asked.

"With my maid. In the coach—" Caroline broke off, blushing. She didn't dare look over her shoulder.

"Hmm." Jack had no such qualms. "Didn't you tell them what you were about? They look scandalized."

"Let them." Eventually, she'd have to face them, but they could wait. After all, her personal concerns were no one's business but her own. "My only quarrel with your plan is it seems very tame, compared to an elopement. And a sad waste of the license."

"Tame?" He frowned at her. "I shouldn't think so. Three months of romance? And then a lifetime ever after?"

"I'm convinced." This was perfect.

"Come inside," he urged her. "And bring your servants, before they fall over from curiosity. My man can get them some supper. I'll take you to Chippenstone tonight, but first I must see how you light up the rooms. I've hated being here without you."

Caroline took his hand. "Yes, and I'll teach you my family motto: *Quod autem habeo, hoc tenete*," she quoted.

Jack puzzled it out, then he laughed. "I should have known."

"What I hold, I keep fast," Caroline said. "Don't say I haven't warned you."

About Jaima Fixsen

Jaima Fixsen is the author of the popular Fairchild regency romance series. She would rather read than sleep, and though all her novels take place in the past, she couldn't live without indoor plumbing or smart phones. When she isn't writing or child wrangling, she's a snow enthusiast. She lives with her family in Alberta, Canada, and most of all just tries to keep up.

Visit Jaima online:
Website: JaimaFixsen.com
Facebook: https://www.facebook.com/jkfixsen

Dear Reader,

Thank you for reading *A Holiday in Bath.* We hope you loved the sweet romance novellas! Each collection in the Timeless Regency Collection contains three novellas. **Sign up for our Timeless Anthology newsletter and receive a free book!** Your email will not be shared and you may unsubscribe at any time. We always appreciate reviews but there is no obligation. Reviews and word-of-mouth are what helps us continue this fun project.

Also, if you're interested in becoming a regular reviewer of these collections and would like access to advance copies, please email Heather Moore: heather@hbmoore.com

We also have a blog where we post announcements as well as a Facebook page.

Thank you!
The Timeless Romance Authors

More Timeless Regency Collections:

DON'T MISS OUR TIMELESS ROMANCE ANTHOLOGIES:

www.ingramcontent.com/pod-product-compliance
Lightning Source LLC
LaVergne TN
LVHW021235080526
838199LV00088B/4353